Praise for

MS. BIXBY'S LAST DAY

A Junior Library Guild selection

New York Public Library Best Books for Kids List

School Library Journal Best of 2016 selection

Publishers Weekly Best Books of 2016 selection

New York Times Notable Children's Books of 2016 selection

Chicago Public Library Best Fiction for Older Readers of 2016 selection

Charlotte Huck Award Honor Book

"What a beautiful book—a full-hearted and emotional exploration of friendship, grief, imagination, and the inner life of boys. But most of all, it reminds us about the power of the 'Good Ones': those once-in-a-lifetime teachers who not only saved us but also became a part of us, long after they're gone. Kids won't just love this book. They need it."
—**SOMAN CHAINANI**, *New York Times* bestselling author of *The School for Good and Evil*

"Certainly it would not be difficult to amass a longish list of books for young readers with wise, feisty, and beloved teachers. Ms. Bixby is in this glorious line, but this is not a book about her precisely; it is a book about three hurt and damaged sixth-grade boys who have been given a tremendous gift by Ms. Bixby's teaching and life."
—**NEW YORK TIMES BOOK REVIEW**

"Anderson skillfully balances realism and comic exaggeration in an emotionally rich tale that holds no miracles, other than the small human kind."
—**PUBLISHERS WEEKLY** (starred review)

"Anderson's dialogue is realistic, and his choice of first-person narration gradually reveals each boy's history and personal growth. His characters are believable twelve-year-old boys. The urban setting is appropriately diverse and gritty, and humor and pathos are nicely balanced. Sad and satisfying in just the right amounts."
—*KIRKUS REVIEWS* (starred review)

"Brand, Steve, and Topher are a comic, lovable crew, and wise, pink-haired Ms. Bixby is the teacher every child deserves. This is a touching, often hilarious story of endings, beginnings, and self-discovery. As Brand would say, *frawesome!*"
—**TRICIA SPRINGSTUBB**, author of *Moonpenny Island*

"Through their individual, interwoven narratives, these well-developed characters become the most intriguing elements of the story. A smart, funny, ultimately moving novel."
—**ALA** *BOOKLIST* (starred review)

"This story provides a full-spectrum, emotionally satisfying experience that will have readers laughing, crying, and everything in between. As Topher would say, this is one frawesome (freaking awesome) book."
—*SCHOOL LIBRARY JOURNAL* (starred review)

"This is a bittersweet story, one without a simple or easy resolution—which makes it all the more relatable and compelling."
—*AUSTIN-AMERICAN STATESMAN*

MS. BIXBY'S
LAST DAY

MS. BIXBY'S LAST DAY

Middle School of Plainville
Plainville, CT 06062

JOHN DAVID ANDERSON

WALDEN POND PRESS

An Imprint of HarperCollins*Publishers*

Walden Pond Press and the skipping stone logo
are trademarks and registered trademarks of Walden Media, LLC.

Ms. Bixby's Last Day
Text copyright © 2016 by John David Anderson
Illustrations copyright © 2016 by Emma Yarlett
All rights reserved. Printed in the United States of America.
No part of this book may be used or reproduced in any manner whatsoever without
written permission except in the case of brief quotations embodied in critical articles
and reviews. For information address HarperCollins Children's Books, a division of
HarperCollins Publishers, 195 Broadway, New York, NY 10007.

www.harpercollinschildrens.com

Library of Congress Control Number: 2015947628
ISBN 978-0-06-233818-1

Typography by Carla Weise
17 18 19 20 21   CG/OPM   10 9 8 7 6 5 4 3 2
❖
First paperback edition, 2017

TO ALL THE MS. BIXBYS.

*And everyone else who sees
it through, no matter what.*

"There is a long road yet," said Gandalf.

"But it is the last road," said Bilbo.

—J.R.R. Tolkien, *The Hobbit*

Topher

REBECCA ROUDABUSH HAS COOTIES.

I'm not making this up. We've run tests. She came up positive on the cootometer, all red, off the charts. Steve and Brand and I are in full quarantine mode. Steve has his ski gloves on to minimize exposure even though it's seventy degrees outside; he looks like Darth Vader from the elbow down. He says this is the sixth case of cooties in room 213 already this year. I don't ever doubt him. Of course, Rebecca insists she's clean, tells us that there is no such thing as cooties.

They all say that. They stick their tongues out at us and call us morons, but we know better. Rebecca's in denial. She needs a support group. We tell her we can give her the names of several kids who have been through this already.

"You guys are so idiotic," she says.

"We're not the ones who got saddled with a case of the coods."

That's Brand. He likes to make up words or abbreviate them or change them somehow, mashing them together to make new ones. He made up the word *tunk*, which means to bomb a test so bad it's funny, like tanking and flunking all at once. And *flip-wad*, which is what we call the older kids who give us a hard time or anyone else we don't like, which isn't a lot of people, though we do have a typed-up list.

"So I have cooties, then?"

"The numbers don't lie," I tell her. "We ran several tests. You came up positive on all of them."

I show her the printout. Actually, it's not a printout, it's a piece of scrap paper that we dug out of recycling and scrawled a bunch of random numbers on in red marker. But it's got her name at the top, and on the bottom in big bleeding letters it says *POSITIVE*. There's also a drawing of a dinosaur I made in the margin, but I cover that with my hand. Not because I'm embarrassed. Just because it's not relevant.

"So that stupid scrap of paper means I'm contagious?"

"Highly," says Steve, Vader arms crossed in front of him.

"And these cooties . . . they're, what, fatal?"

Rebecca has been in school for over half her life. You would think this would be common knowledge. "Only to some," I say.

"There are some who can carry the infection for years and never present symptoms. But awesome people are highly susceptible."

Rebecca nods way too thoughtfully for someone with a debilitating imaginary disease. I've known her since second grade and I can tell she's planning something. She's all narrow eyes and tapping feet. My mom once said she thought Rebecca was cute. That was the last time I ever talked to my mother about girls.

"And they are transmitted how, exactly?" Rebecca asks.

"Physical contact, primarily," Steve says, looking at his shoes, which is what he does when he's about to tell you a bunch of stuff you don't know and probably never cared to. "The cootie virus is transmitted by touch, though it's even more highly concentrated in saliva. Just one milliliter of spit from someone with the virus is enough to infect the entire population of New York City—roughly eight point four million people."

I don't know if that's true or not, but I nod along. Steve is full of facts and figures. Sometimes I write down the things he says and Google them when I get home—things like the fact that hornets can sting multiple times because they have smooth stingers, and that the number one cause of death in Guatemala is the flu. He's never wrong about stuff like that. After so many years of best-friendship, I've pretty much learned to stop doubting him. Steve pushes his glasses up, all scholarly-scientist-like. It's not part of the act. He really has trouble keeping them in place.

3

Rebecca stares at each of us in turn, contemplating her next move.

"Saliva, huh?"

"Yup," says Brand.

"Okay . . . then it would be really horrible if I did *this*."

Rebecca Roudabush licks her hand, tongue pressed flat against her palm from wrist to fingertips. Then, before any of us can react, she rubs that same cootie-infested hand all over Steve's face.

This is exactly how epidemics start.

Steve screams, burying his face into his own oversize mitts, smearing Rebecca's infection around and making it worse. Brand tries to pull him away, but Rebecca's too quick. She reaches out and grabs Brand by the arm, pushing his sleeve back and planting a zerbert right below his elbow, just like when we have fart-sound contests before school. *Flrrrrbbbbttt.* He instantly buckles at the knees, just staring at the ring of Rebecca's wet, cootie-infested spit in horror. Steve is floundering, wiping his face with his shirt, as if that will help. As if he isn't a dead man already.

Rebecca turns to me. "You're next, Christopher," she says, using my full name like a four-letter word. I look at Steve and Brand convulsing on the ground, faces scrunched in disgust. There's a code, I know. Unspoken rules about not leaving your comrades behind when they're paralyzed in the mulch, victims of a biological terrorist with a wavy red ponytail. But Rebecca is malicious. Plus she has freckles, which I take as a sign that her particular cooties are somehow advanced in nature. Incurable. There is nothing I can do for my friends now.

So I run.

With Rebecca trailing, I take off across the playground, dodging in and around the swings and beneath the monkey bars, RR right on my tail, determined to tackle me, pin me to the ground, and probably cough all over my face—or something even worse. But she won't catch me. I'm Usain Bolt. I am Cheetah Boy. Faster than a lightning strike. Mulch chips burst into flames at my heels. Yet somehow, she is gaining on me. I make a full circuit of the playground and find Brand and Steve standing again, miraculously cured, or perhaps just incubating, ready to collapse to their deaths at any moment. They see me coming, trailing Rebecca behind me, and take off as well, all three of us charging blindly through the middle of a pickup kickball game. Turning a sharp corner around the redbrick facade of the school.

And running straight into Ms. Bixby.

There are six kinds of teachers in the world. I know because we classified them once during indoor recess. First you have your Zombies: those are the ones who have been doing it for a few centuries, since Roosevelt was president—the first Roosevelt, with the broomy mustache from those museum movies. The Zombs speak in a mumbled monotone and come equipped with an armory of worksheets all designed to suck any fun out of the learning process, which doesn't take long, considering how little fun comes included at the start. They may not eat your brains, but the Zombies won't do much to nurture them either.

Then there are the Caff-Adds. Brand calls them Zuzzers. You can spot them by their jittery hands and bloodshot eyes and the insulated NPR travel mugs they carry around with them. Unlike the Zombs, the Caff-Adds are like little bouncy balls, but you can't really stand to listen to them either because they talk so fast, *zuzzuzzuzz*, like sticking your head in a beehive. Unfortunately, our Spanish teacher is one of those, so not only can't I understand her, but even if I could, I couldn't.

Then you have your Dungeon Masters. The red-pass-wielding ogres who wish paddling was still allowed in schools. The kind who insist on no talking, whether it's reading time, work time, sharing time, lunchtime, after school, before school, the weekend, whatever. You are supposed to just sit still and shut up. Mr. Mattison, the art teacher, is one of those. We draw in absolute silence during art. Graveyard quiet, which is actually fine by me, because it's the one specials class worth concentrating in, though while I'm there I mostly draw pictures of Mr. Matt carrying a club and picking the meat off the bones of the latest student to whisper a word.

Then you've got your Spielbergs. They're not nearly as cool as Steven Spielberg. We just call them that because they show movies all the time. Some of them are Zombie Spielbergs. Mrs. Gredenza falls into this category. She once showed us a film on the life cycle of fruit flies that was pretty gross but also didn't make much sense, seeing as how she was supposed to be teaching us geometry. At least with Spielbergs you often get a chance to doodle or nap or text—that is, if one of the Dungeon Masters hasn't captured your phone yet and fed it to his goblins.

My personal favorites are the Noobs. The overachievers. Fresh picked from the teacher farm. With their bright eyes and their colorful posters recently purchased from a catalog and the way they clap like circus seals when you get the right answer. They don't stay Noobs for long. They get burned out pretty quick. A year. Maybe two. I don't think it's the students' fault, though. I blame the system.

The last kind we simply call the Good Ones. The ones who make the torture otherwise known as school somewhat bearable. You know when you have one of the Good One because you find yourself actually paying attention in class, even if it's not art class. They're the teachers you actually want to go back and say hi to the next year. The ones you don't want to disappoint.

Like Ms. B.

I remember the first time I met Ms. Bixby. It wasn't day one of class or even Meet the Teacher Night. It was actually three years ago. At the circus.

We were in the concession area, my parents and my little sister and me, buying six-dollar snow cones and swirly suckers. My parents are firm believers in "maximizing invested family time," meaning that on the few occasions we all go somewhere together, they bribe my sister and me with sweets so we won't whine. It usually works.

The circus was the latest monthly-mandated-whole-family-outing, and we were making the most of it, turning our tongues blue and taking in the preshow show—mostly clowns flopping around in giant red galoshes and mongo honkable schnozzes. We stopped in front of a juggler, a woman with short blond hair streaked with pink, dressed in a tuxedo, expertly weaving three bowling pins in the air. Her cheeks were blushed red, one painted lip tucked under the other in concentration. Then she saw my mother and stopped, stuck one pin under her arm. She looked familiar. "Linda?" she called.

"Maggie?" my mother squeaked. Hugs followed.

"You actually did it? You quit your job to join the circus?"

"Pays better than teaching," said the juggler, and she and my mother laughed. The woman explained she was just an amateur, but when the circus came in, they sometimes hired local talent to act as lobby entertainers. My father coughed and smiled politely.

"Saul, this is Maggie Bixby. She teaches at Fox Ridge," my mother said. "Sixth grade, right?"

The teacher masquerading as a part-time circus performer nodded. "The last one before we ship them off." She had bright-green eyes, the color of new grass.

"Sixth grade," my father echoed. That at least explained where I had seen her before. Probably in the halls. Or making a mad dash for the parking lot when the last bell rang. She looked like a Noob, or maybe a Zuzzer with her wide eyes and cockeyed smile, though at the time we hadn't classified them yet.

"Linda is one of our best PTA members," Maggie Bixby said, putting a hand on my mother's shoulder. "I don't know what I would do without those Friday-morning bagels." Then she looked at me. "How are you, Christopher? You ready for the circus?"

I wasn't sure if she meant the actual circus or the next year of school, but I remember being impressed that she knew my name. It made me feel famous or something.

"It's just Topher," I told her. "Nobody really calls me Christopher." At least nobody I like.

"I'll remember that," she said.

Then she put on a little show for the four of us, right there, juggling five multicolored balls and then pulling a quarter from behind my sister's ear, which she was even allowed to keep. As we left to go see the real show, I asked her if she could teach me how to juggle.

She said to wait a couple of years.

She'd probably teach me something.

We topple into Ms. Bixby like dominoes, the three of us. We obviously startle her; she takes a step back, a hand over her heart like she's ready for the Pledge, and fixes us with a look that is disapproving, but not out-and-out angry, as if she isn't sure whether to lecture us or laugh at us.

"What are *you* doing?" With anyone else, she would have emphasized the *doing*. But with us it was always the *you*. As in, you three . . . *again?* Before I can answer, Rebecca turns the corner and runs into us, causing us to catapult forward, nearly bowling Ms. Bixby over again.

"Sorry," Rebecca exclaims, breathless. "I was . . . we were . . ."

"Playing tag," I say, turning and giving Rebecca an imploring look, begging her to go along. But she must still be infected: the coots have gone to her brain and made her too honest for her own good.

"You little liar!" she shouts back. "You said I was *diseased*! I was chasing you!"

"That's sort of like tag," I mumble.

Ms. Bixby pins me with cat eyes. She has a way of asking you questions without speaking a word. I try to explain as calmly as possible.

"She tried to kiss me."

"I absolutely did *not*!" Rebecca shouts.

"You sucked on my arm!" Brand seconds.

"I gave you a zerbert!"

"And licked my face!" Steve adds.

Now it's Ms. Bixby's turn to grimace. She looks at me for confirmation. "Technically she licked her hand and then *touched* his face, but by the transitive property of equality, it's pretty much the same thing."

Ms. Bixby taught me the transitive property of equality this year. This is what teachers call "applied knowledge." I secretly suspect Ms. Bixby is impressed, but she doesn't want to show it. She's good at hiding what she's really up to, I've noticed. She puts a grumpy face on instead.

"You said I had cooties!" Rebecca implores, stomping her feet.

Ms. Bixby sighs the Teacher Sigh. The one they must give you as you walk out the door with your teaching degree. Equal parts exasperation, disappointment, and longing for summer vacation. "Did you tell Rebecca she had cooties?"

It's a question for all three of us, but Steve, thankfully, answers. He has all the answers.

"We informed her of her positive diagnosis, yes. But only in the interest of keeping the rest of the population safe. It was for the greater good." I hand over the sheet of paper with the doodled dinosaur and Rebecca's made-up lab results.

"I see," Ms. Bixby says. I still think she's trying not to smile. "And did you zerbert Steve's arm?"

Rebecca drops her head, red ringlets curtaining her eyes.

"Right. Okay. Listen up. All four of you. I'm going to tell you something your parents should have told you a long time ago."

I look up at Ms. Bixby, afraid of what's coming next. No doubt something about spit and kissing and germs and zerberts. I think back to that video about fruit flies. I hope this isn't one of *those* conversations.

"Cooties don't exist," she says, her voice tinged with fake relief. Steve looks sort of surprised, and I wonder if this is actual news to him. "They did, once," Ms. Bixby says, "but scientists eradicated them back in 1994, thanks to a vaccine discovered by three smart girls who were hoping it might help keep boys from acting like total doofs all the time."

She looks at me as if she's waiting for something. The *aha* moment.

12

"It didn't work, did it?" I ask.

"Apparently not," she says. "Now I want you three to apologize to Rebecca."

"Apologize to *her*? She chased me around the playground!"

"Yes, and in a few more years you'll *want* to be caught. But for now, apologize. And no more talk of cooties or any other imaginary diseases."

There's nothing to it. Sorry is the only way out of this.

"Mrmfwrmrmm."

Rebecca glares at me.

Ms. Bixby glares at me.

I want to glare at somebody, but Steve and Brand are looking down at their feet. So I glare at Rebecca, who glares back at me harder, if that's even possible.

"I'm sorry," I say a little more clearly.

"Me too," says Steve.

"Yeah," adds Brand.

Then Ms. Bixby whispers something in Rebecca's ear, and she smiles. It kind of makes me jealous. Then Rebecca gives us each a warning look, one eyebrow raised, and runs back off to the playground. We turn to follow her when an "ahem" from Ms. Bixby stops us. Apparently we aren't finished yet.

We all three turn around, tensing for whatever is about to come. Ms. Bixby doesn't look happy. She doesn't look ticked off either. She actually looks *sad*. Lost. Like she's forgotten that we are even there. But she takes a deep breath and the clouds seem to pass.

"I've always said the greatest gift you are ever given is your imagination. But you have to stop and think about how your words and your actions impact those around you, right?"

We nod dutifully. Even the Good Ones go into lecture mode every once in a while. They're entitled to. It's the slack we cut them for not boring us to death.

"We are what we pretend to be, so we must be careful about what we pretend to be," she adds.

That was another thing about Ms. Bixby: She was always saying little quotes like that. She called them "affirmations." They were basically sayings she had collected. A few of them were hers, but most of them were borrowed. Except she hardly ever said where she'd borrowed them from. She spoke them like they were universally true, written in the wind for everyone to hear. We called them Bixbyisms. Another Brand word.

"Now go wash your hands and faces. Because even though I'm certain Miss Roudabush doesn't have cooties, I can't speak for any other germs."

We all wait one more second to make sure the lecture is over; then we nod in unison and I follow Steve and Brand toward the door. As I slink inside, I turn and spy on Ms. Bixby through the window. I do that sometimes, when she's not looking.

Ms. B. is huddled against the wall, arms wrapped around in her cable-knit sweater. Rebecca's positive diagnosis sits crumpled in her hand. She isn't watching the other students on the playground. She is staring out over the slides and swings to the stretch of fields and the sky beyond and the three clouds reaching out for each other with wispy fingers but not quite there yet.

Three weeks later she gives us the news.

STEVE

WE FOUND OUT ON A TUESDAY. I WAS WEARING a red sweater. Not bright red. More of a maroon, like the color of cherries—real cherries, not the ones you find in canned fruit that taste a little like medicine. I remember it was raining that day, spattering against the windows. I don't like the rain because the water sloshes up and soaks the cuffs of your socks when you run through the grass, and then your ankles are red and itchy the rest of the day. Ms. Bixby and I don't agree on this. She thinks rain is fantastic, but maybe that's because she wears sandals all the time and doesn't have to worry about the sock issue.

She waited until the end of the day to deliver the news, but I could tell it was coming. She had been acting differently for a while. For instance, the week before, I was informing her about the world's deadliest snake based on venom toxicity, and she completely zoned out and didn't hear a word I said, as if the world's deadliest snake didn't matter. Normal Ms. Bixby would care about that sort of thing. She would find it interesting. She would ask me questions. But she just nodded and told me to go back to my seat. That's when I knew something was wrong.

That whole Tuesday was wrong, in fact. It wasn't just that we were stuck inside because of the weather. That was also the day Tyler Fisk slipped a ketchup packet onto my chair before I sat down at lunch. It was also the same day my mother forgot to cut my sandwich diagonally, instead hacking it straight down the middle, which, as anyone can tell you, makes it harder to avoid the crust. I took four bites and left the rest.

Then, twenty minutes before pack-up, Ms. Bixby sat us in a circle and told us about her diagnosis. I remember writing the words down in my notebook, asking her to spell them: ductal adenocarcinoma. I wanted to make certain I looked up the right thing when I got home. We all sat quietly while she explained. It's a type of cancer that attacks the pancreas. They ran tests, she said. They took pictures. There was no question. She had a tough battle ahead of her, but she was going to "beat this thing."

It did mean that she wouldn't be able to finish out the school year, however. In fact, she had already arranged for her last day—the Friday of the next week. In the meantime, they would find a sub to take over the class for the last month of school. I sat and stared out the window at the rain forming ankle-deep puddles on the sidewalk.

I remember Grace Tanner crying and Ms. Bixby giving her a hug and telling her to be brave. I remember Topher giving me a confused look, as if he needed me to explain what a carcinoma was, and me scooting closer to him. I remember the quote she had on the board that day. "Things are never as bad as they seem." I'm sure she put it there just to make us feel better, though Ms. Bixby was so calm that the news didn't seem as terrible as it should. Brand sat at the very back of the room and didn't say a word. He looked angry, but I think he looks angry a lot of the time.

I shifted uncomfortably on the floor. My pants were still wet from where I tried to rinse the ketchup stain out. I didn't cry, because I knew that if Ms. Bixby put her mind to it, she could "beat this thing," just like she said. She's one of the smartest people I ever met.

The deadliest snake in the world is the inland taipan, by the way. A single drop of its venom is enough to kill a hundred men. And yet, in the recorded history of snakebites, this species of snake has only ever killed one person. I told that to Ms. Bixby at the end of that day, the day she broke the news. She asked me what the moral was. She's always asking me what I think the moral is, because she knows I sometimes don't get that part. But the moral of the inland taipan was easy:

Just because it can doesn't mean it will. Things are never as bad as they seem.

She said I was brilliant and gave me a high five and I smiled. She has a way of making even minor victories seem big. Then she turned away from me and blew her nose. She's very polite that way.

It's important to be recognized for one's accomplishments. That's what my dad says. *Accomplishment* and *recognition* are two of my parents' favorite words.

I won an award once for being able to name every country in the world, along with their capitals, populations, and official languages, a total of 194, though the number has changed since then. Believe it or not, they are still making new countries. I should think 194 would be plenty.

I memorized them in alphabetical order, from Afghanistan to Zimbabwe. The capital of Zimbabwe is Harare, but if you're like most people, you don't care. Every two years, during the Parade of Nations at the opening ceremonies of the Olympics, I can tell you exactly who is going to come next. Hungary, Iceland, India, Indonesia, Iran, Iraq, Ireland, and so on. I could go on, but as Topher often tells me, I probably shouldn't.

The award was a red ribbon with gold embossed letters that said *Holy Cross Christian Fellowship 13th Annual Talent Show. Honorable Mention.* Honorable mention because I wasn't one of the three most talented kids to take the stage that night, though it wasn't actually a stage, just the pulpit decorated with tufts of white flowers. I didn't get the fancy blue ribbon or the twenty-dollar iTunes gift card. The most talented participant was Christina Sakata, who played Beethoven to a standing ovation, curtsying in a puffy black dress that cost way more than twenty dollars. In my defense, Christina Sakata had been playing the piano since she was four, and I only started memorizing countries three weeks before the show. Also in my defense, Christina Sakata is better than me at just about everything. She is better than me at reading and roller-skating and cooking and basketball (though I haven't met anyone who is *not* better than me at basketball). She has perfect skin and 20/20 vision. I think she's convinced the entire world that she is perfect. I know she's convinced my parents. I'm always hearing about how great she is. Talented pianist. Natural gymnast. Straight-A student. A model child.

Very few things in life are perfect. Snowflakes are perfect. The way Lego bricks fit together is perfect. My sister is not perfect. But try as hard as I could, I couldn't point out a single mistake in her playing that night, even though she has no problem pointing out mine. After the standing ovation, my mother turned and told me I did a nice job too.

I still took my honorable mention ribbon to school the next day and showed it to Ms. Bixby, who let me tell the class about it and recite the countries all over again, even though I didn't even make the top three. The only person who laughed was Trevor Cowly, who apparently found something amusing about the nation of Djibouti. "Ja-booty," he said, and collapsed in a snorting fit. Ms. Bixby fixed him with a look and he instantly shut up. Most of the class clapped at the end. Topher let out a whistle because he's Topher. When I finished, though, I saw Trevor turn to Brian Frey and whisper, "What a weirdo." I couldn't hear him, but I'm a better-than-average lip reader. It comes from having people talk about you out of earshot all the time.

It didn't bother me much—being called a weirdo. I know I'm the only person in room 213 who has ever heard of Lesotho or cares that it is a country completely surrounded by another country. I know that the other kids have names for me. The nice ones call me C-3PO, or Data, which is either a *Star Trek* reference or a *Goonies* reference or both. And I know what the not-so-nice ones call me too.

I was just going to let Trevor Cowly's comment slide, but Ms.

Bixby had heard it too. She cleared her throat to get everyone's attention and thanked me for sharing. Then she said, "'To be yourself in a world that is constantly trying to make you something else is the greatest accomplishment.'" And she looked right at me and smiled, and I smiled back, because I like her quotes. I have most of them memorized too.

Then Ms. Bixby asked if she could display the ribbon on the chalkboard for the day, and I let her, because I knew when I got home I would just take it up to my room and tuck it away in my sock drawer and probably not look at it again, mostly because it was only an honorable mention, but also because it would only remind me of who actually won, and I didn't need another reminder.

Christina has so many trophies and ribbons that my parents had to build an additional shelving unit in her room to display them all, but for an hour at school at least, in room 213, my sister's trophy case didn't matter, and I would steal glances at the chalkboard and my red-and-gold ribbon hanging proudly from Ms. Bixby's smiley-face magnet.

It takes time to memorize every country and its capital and population. Ms. Bixby can appreciate the effort. She knows the state capitals. Of course, teachers are always making their students memorize state capitals, but most of them cheat and use an answer sheet to grade you. Ms. Bixby actually *knows* them.

I quizzed her on it. She knows all the presidents, too, though her understanding of the planets of our solar system is less than thorough. She didn't know, for example, that Venus is actually warmer on the surface than Mercury. When I suggested she brush up on her astronomy, she seemed offended, saying that she probably knew things that I didn't.

I told her that was highly unlikely.

Then she asked me who the lead singer of Led Zeppelin was. I told her zeppelins could not be made of lead due to the obvious weight issues. She said, "Case closed."

Led Zeppelin is a band. I know that now. I looked it up. The lead singer was a guy named Robert Plant. Their best-selling song was about a woman who purchases a stairway to heaven so she can go shopping. It's eight minutes long, the song, which is too long to pay attention to any one thing, even Ms. Bixby, and it doesn't make much sense. Still, I guess she proved her point. There are probably a few things she knows more about than me.

That same afternoon that Ms. Bixby put my ribbon on the board, Trevor Cowly missed ten minutes of recess for his "weirdo" remark. Even though the comment didn't bother me, it wasn't so bad to see him standing against the wall. It's important to have your accomplishments recognized.

✦ ✦ ✦

The day Ms. Bixby told us she wouldn't be able to finish out the school year, I came home and found my honorable mention ribbon right where I'd left it: tucked beneath several carefully folded pairs of socks. It had a crease across the middle, and the yarn tied to the top was frayed, but it felt smooth and slick in my hand. I could hear my sister practicing some new, complicated piece on the piano downstairs.

I sat on my bed and stared at the ribbon in my hand. Just stared and thought about Topher and Ms. Bixby and songs and ductal adenocarcinoma and all the things I still didn't know about, and maybe didn't want to. And then I heard my sister growl in frustration and bang on the keys, which normally makes me smile.

Brand

YOU CAN PICK YOUR FRIENDS, AND YOU CAN pick your nose, but you can't pick your friend's nose. That's something my dad told me. Turns out . . . not entirely true. I mean, the middle part is obviously true. But the last part isn't true at all.

Steve once had a booger, just, you know, kind of stuck there, on the rim, all crusty and stuff. It was reading time, and everybody was planted in their books, but I couldn't concentrate. I just kept staring across the table at that booger. And I whispered to him, told him about it, like, *Dude, you've got a little something, right . . . there . . . on the end.* And he brushed his finger across his nose, or gave it a little flick, but it was, like, glued there. And he didn't seem to care. He sniffed and shrugged and went back to his book. And I went back to my book. But every other word I'd look up and see it there. Greenish gray, and rock solid, like snot lava that had erupted and then hardened over time. And I whispered and hissed and pointed, and he brushed and blew and shrugged, and it stayed. And I don't know why, but it was totally driving me crazy, like when the roof of your mouth itches and you try to scratch it with your tongue. So finally I just reached across the table and dug in with my fingernails and gave it a tug, peeling it free and flicking it onto the floor.

Apparently I must have scratched him a little, or maybe the crust of hardened snot had attached itself to one of his nose hairs that got yanked out or something, because as I pulled it off, Steve screamed and slapped my hand and his eyes welled up with those little tears you get whenever you sneeze too hard. And Ms. Bixby asked us what was going on, and I told her I was just help-ing Steve get a booger out, which apparently was *not* the thing to say as it caused everyone in class to groan and make faces and prompted Ms. Bixby to say that, from here on out, everyone was responsible for picking their *own* boogers, thank you, *and* disposing of them in a discreet and sanitary manner, which did not include flicking them in other people's hair, sliming them across the bottoms of desks, or rolling them into doughy balls to be played with, which caused half the room to groan again but at least provided some distraction, as everyone was looking at Ms.

Bixby and no longer looking at me. Except for Steve, who stared at me with watery eyes.

"You don't have to thank me," I told him. He didn't.

Still, it proves my point. You *can* pick your friend's nose. But there's a difference between *can* and *should*.

It isn't the last part of my father's saying that I wonder about, though. It's the first part. About friends. Because I'm not entirely sure about them either. It's not exactly as if I *picked* Steve and Topher to be friends with. And it's not like they picked me. It's more like I just glommed onto them somehow. And got stuck there over time, like dried snot.

We don't have all that much in common. I mean, all three of us like video games, and we live in the same town, and we think ordering pizza should be an at-least-twice-a-week thing, but I have that in common with every guy in my school. In fact, I probably have more in common with just about every *other* kid in school than with those two.

For starters, Steve is a certifiable genius, boogers or no boogers. He has, like, one of those photographic memories. He can recite the Gettysburg Address, and he knows the names and stats of every Transformer ever invented. And he's really good at math. I still struggle sometimes with long division, and he's already mastered algebra. His head is full of numbers and statistics and names of books and world records and who knows what else. I sometimes think he might be a cyborg.

Topher's a genius too. Not like Albert Einstein genius, but in that creative sort of way. He's a better writer than me, and don't even get me started on his drawing. That kid has more stories inside his head than you could check out of the school library.

I'm no genius. I can't draw. I don't know what the capital of Montana is (Butte, I think—but that can't be right, because nobody would just tack an *E* onto the end of that word and make it their capital city). I'm not really great at anything, actually. I've played soccer and baseball—and rugby once. Suffered through tennis camp. I get Bs and Cs on everything, whether I try or not. I suppose I can cook a little bit, but that's only what I've taught myself, and only because I've had to. I can make a decent omelet, though it's usually easier to just heat up a burrito in the microwave—two if Dad's hungry.

Point is, I'm not like them. We're not like peas in a pod or anything. But sometimes you just need a place to sit and eat lunch.

This was last year. I transferred over to Fox Ridge for the fifth grade because we moved into a smaller house—there was no way my dad's disability checks were going to cover the cost of our old one. Besides, it had too many steps and no shower on the first floor, so it just wasn't practical anymore. So we moved, and I changed schools, and on my first day I stood in the doorway of the cafeteria and looked around at all the full tables, a hundred backs to me as I scanned for a place to eat. There was an empty chair at Topher and Steve's table. The two of them were huddled over a notebook, looking at one of Topher's sketches; they didn't notice me until I was standing right in front of them. I asked if there was anyone sitting in the empty seat. Topher said no, Steve said nothing, and that's how it started.

So maybe Dad was right. Maybe I did pick them. Or maybe there just wasn't anywhere else to sit.

I didn't pick Ms. Bixby, either. Just dumb luck, I guess. Or maybe she picked me, though I doubt it. I'm not sure how students are chosen for classes at the start of the year, but I'm pretty sure that the teachers don't gather around a list of names like dodgeball captains and take turns drafting whichever students they want. If they did, I would probably be one of the last ones picked. Not because I'm a troublemaker or anything—just because I don't stand out. Maybe you could say it was fate, but I don't think so. You start believing that things were *supposed* to happen a certain way, you start to ask questions that nobody has answers for.

When I found out that I would be in Ms. Bixby's class for sixth grade, I was dizzy with relief. I knew Topher and Steve were going to be in her class, and after nearly an entire year at a new school, they were still the only friends I'd made. The other sixth-grade teacher was Mr. Mackelroy: a balding, fortysomething Dungeon Master (according to the Topher Taxonomy) who smelled like stale cigarette smoke and vanilla air freshener and scowled at everyone who walked by. *Every* soon-to-be sixth grader was hoping for Ms. Bixby. Besides, Ms. Bixby had a reputation: For streaking her hair pink, which the girls thought was cool even if they made fun of it. For letting students make videos about what they did over winter break instead of writing essays. For secretly smuggling in her candy-bowl leftovers from Halloween and dishing them out, even though she knew our backpacks were already crammed full of chocolate. And for having a python as a class pet, because, as she put it in a devious whisper, "Our class pet could eat Mr. Mackelroy's class pet for breakfast." Which was true: Mr. Mack had a warty, bulbous brown lump named Jabba the Toad.

There were other things, too, little things. Like how she always chose *The Hobbit* as the class read-aloud and had different voices for every character. How she could be strict when she needed to be and sweet when she wanted to be and kind of a smart aleck all the times in between. But mostly there was the way she listened to you, giving you her full attention. All the other teachers, they'd keep looking around the room when you talked, but Ms. Bixby fixed you with her eyes and waited for you to finish no matter how long it took you to figure out what you wanted to say.

None of that mattered at the time, of course. At the time, all I cared about was that I would be in the same class as my friends. That was the cake. Ms. Bixby was just the icing.

There was no way of me knowing what would happen between us, after all.

There was supposed to be a party. That was the problem, really, because if there had been a party, I could have said what I needed to. If there had been a party, I wouldn't have this hole right in the center of my chest, threatening to eat away at me from the inside out. I wouldn't feel like throwing up every time I walk into room 213 and see that quote on the wall, the last one she left there, just for me. The sub tried to erase it, but I wouldn't let her. I knew what book it was from.

It was supposed to be a "sort of" farewell party. Sort of, because she insisted she'd be back. Probably not till next year, but she'd be back. It was a temporary good-bye. More of a "see you later." The party was scheduled for Friday. Her last official day. It was to take place during lunch. She was going to order pizza for the whole class, and McKenzie's mom was bringing cupcakes. We had leftover juice boxes from our Valentine's Day celebration a few months ago. There would be a more professional gathering with coffee and pound cake in the teachers' lounge after school, a chance for Ms. Bixby to say "see you later" to the other teachers, but this party was just for us.

Except it didn't happen.

That Monday, with only five days left until her last day, we all shuffled into the room to find someone else waiting for us beside Ms. Bixby's desk. It was Principal McNair, wearing a navy business suit, black hair corralled into a bun, purple bags under her eyes. "I'm sorry, kids," she began. "But I'm afraid Ms. Bixby isn't coming in today. It looks like she won't be back for the rest of the year, in fact."

Standing beside me in his stupid Gap sweatshirt, Kyle Kipperson blurted out, "Is she dead?" I turned and glared, wanting desperately to punch him square in that giant, upside-down-lighbulb nose of his. Principal McNair looked like she was about to have a heart attack.

"Oh heavens, no!" she choked. "No. Not at all. She just isn't feeling well. And we all thought it best if she started taking her leave of absence early and concentrated on taking care of herself."

There were groans from all over. Most of them were for Ms. Bixby, though I'm sure some were just disappointed that there wouldn't be a party. Part of me just wanted to scream at them. Topher told them all to shut up, which raised the principal's eyebrow but at least stopped the groaning.

"You should know that she fought us over it, but we insisted,"

Principal McNair continued. "She wanted to be here. She even recorded a message for you."

Principal McNair turned around and fumbled with Ms. Bixby's computer for a moment, trying to get the smartboard to work. She wiggled the mouse and the screen flashed to life, revealing Ms. Bixby, looking much the same as the Friday before, except like she'd just woken up, her eyes not as bright. She smiled that smile of hers, though: The one that lets you know that *she* knows what you're really up to. The one that I'd gotten more than once.

"Hello, class," prerecorded Bixby said, pulling the pink strand behind her ear, her face filling the camera. "Sorry to leave you all in the lurch like this, but it turns out Principal McNair doesn't want me hanging around the school anymore. She's afraid I'm contagious."

"Absolutely not true," the flustered principal whispered, but we all hushed her so that we could hear the rest of Ms. Bixby's message.

"Turns out I'm going to take my time off a little earlier than expected. Relax in my hammock with a good book and some mint tea, catch up on my to-dos, and, of course, get healthy. But before I leave, I want you all to know how proud I am of you. It has been wonderful getting to know you and watching your minds evolve and expand, and I only hope that you've learned as much from me as I've learned from you." Video Bixby paused, looked down and then back up. "I *will* be back next year," she said finally, "and you will all come back and visit me, I'm sure, and we will have that party we planned on. So be good for Principal McNair and the sub, and thanks for being such an awesome class. Remember me and smile, for it's better to forget than to remember me and cry. Au revoir."

The picture froze and Principal McNair hunched back over the computer. In a blink, Ms. Bixby was gone. The room was completely silent. It was a long time before anyone made a move or a sound. Even Kyle Kipperson managed to keep his big mouth shut for once. Then finally Sarah Tolsen timidly raised her hand.

"What about *The Hobbit*?"

Principal McNair looked confused. "What about *The Hobbit*?" she asked back.

"Ms. Bixby's been reading it to us after lunch. We only have twenty pages left," Sarah explained, pointing to the hardback copy sitting on the desk. "We were supposed to finish it this week. We have to know how it ends."

Principal McNair smiled unconvincingly. "I'm sure the sub can finish reading the book to you."

"But will she read it like Ms. Bixby reads it?" Carlos Menzanno asked.

"Yeah, will she do the voices?"

"And what about our field trip to the duck pond? Ms. Bixby said she'd take us on Thursday."

"And we never got around to finishing our unit on the coral reef."

"Is there a chance she'll be back before the year ends?"

"Can't she just come back for the party at least?"

It was a flurry of questions. Everybody was just shouting them out, nobody bothering to raise their hand. Even with the principal in the room, the class soon dissolved into a muddle, twenty uncertain voices burbling at once. I didn't raise my hand. The questions I had, I was sure Principal McNair couldn't possibly answer. Neither Topher nor Steve raised their hands either. The principal looked from one face to the next, clearly overwhelmed, reaching out to steady herself against the desk. Then I heard McKenzie ask if she should still bother to bring in cupcakes on Friday.

Next thing I knew, Principal McNair was walking quickly out the door, one hand over her face, just leaving us alone in the room with a blank screen, an unfinished book, and so many questions.

I'm no genius, but there is one thing I do know: I know that Ms. Bixby isn't coming back this year. I know a thing or two about hospitals and medical procedures and recovery times. I know that sometimes it's easier to tell somebody what they want to hear or tell them only part of the truth.

There's a difference between the truth and the whole truth. The truth is Ms. Bixby is sick and she is leaving. The whole truth is that I have something I need to tell her. Something she already knows, but I feel like I have to say it out loud, in person, just in case she's forgotten, because she needs to hear it just as much as I did.

Which means, somehow or another, I've got to see her again.

Topher

DATE: FRIDAY, MAY 7. TIME: 0730. LOCATION:
Outer perimeter of Fox Ridge Elementary School, just south of
the bus drop-off, and unfortunately behind some bushes with
potentially poisonous berries and prickly thorns.

Special Agent Sakata and I have snuck behind enemy
lines. The drop zone is clear; no sign of enemy patrols. Agent
Sakata is armed with a Carhartt multitool, complete with pliers,
unworkable scissors, and Phillips head screwdriver. I have my
sketchbook—don't leave home without it—and a regulation-size
box of raisins. The raisins are almost gone. The air is sharp with
the smell of diesel and mown grass. We are already five minutes
behind schedule. Special Agent Walker is late.

"Where is he?"

"How am I supposed to know?" Agent Sakata answers.

"What's his bus number?"

"I don't know that either."

"But you know everything!"

"I don't know what bus he rides. I've never even been to his house!"

I shrug, letting Steve off the hook. It's true. Neither of us has been to Brand's house. Not because we wouldn't go. Only because we've never been invited. He's been to both of our houses tons of times in the past year (mostly mine—we aren't allowed to run on Steve's carpet because we might mess up the vacuum lines, so we don't go there much, and my parents are usually too busy to care what we're up to). Brand says he can't invite us over because his father doesn't like guests. It seems like every group of friends has one kid whose house you never go to. Plus I've heard a few things about Mr. Walker. I know about the accident and everything. I guess I'm not in any hurry to get an invite.

"If he's not here in the next five minutes, we should give up," Steve says, looking at me nervously.

"What, you mean abort the mission and go to *school*?" Agent Sakata shrugs.

I peer out from the hedge, spreading the branches carefully— it wouldn't pay to get stuck by a thorn and bleed out here on the school lawn before this operation even got underway. It's business as usual out on the Ridge. The convoy is dropping off load after load: platoons of half-dead zombies marching in line, filing through the blue double doors in a shuffle step. I see lots of faces I recognize, but not the one I'm looking for. Special Agent Walker is MIA.

"I told you this wasn't a good idea," Steve says.

I give him a dirty look, but he's probably right. This mission is already fritzled. That's a Brand word, but we all use it. It's one of the words we use so we don't get in trouble for using *other* words. If something is *really* fritzled we say it's *gefragt*, which Steve says is just the German word for "asked," but it certainly sounds like something that is screwed up beyond repair. We aren't all the way to gefragt yet, but if Brand doesn't show up soon, we will be.

It wasn't supposed to go down like this. We had a plan. The plan was for Saturday. The plan was to lie to our parents and say we were all meeting each other at the park to play Frisbee. The plan was not to skip school. Of course, that was before we intercepted a key bit of intel between two high-ranking officials. Intel that called for a revised plan.

"I think I might vomit," Steve says, holding his stomach, though I know it's just for dramatic effect. I've only seen him blow chunks once, and that was coming off the Whiparound at the state fair.

"Pull it together, Agent." I slap him on the back and use my tough-guy voice, even though I feel the same. Neither of us has ever skipped before. It's against regulations. We could be court-martialed. Thrown in the brig. Taken before the principal. If found guilty, we might even be executed. At least, Steve might. His parents are pretty strict. Like marine-drill-sergeant-meets-Catholic-nun strict. I don't want to think about what would happen if they catch him skipping school.

"There's still time," he says shakily. "The buses are still unloading. We can make it before the tardy bell and just forget the whole thing."

I grimace and shove my last handful of raisins in my mouth, chewing them determinedly and thinking I probably should have rationed them, just in case we get stranded deep in enemy territory or something.

"Besides, we can't go without Brand. He's bringing the blanket," Steve adds.

It's true: Agent Walker has the blanket. Our load-outs were issued the night before. Brand was in charge of the blanket. I would bring the map, the directions, and the paper plates. Agent Sakata had the music. We would all contribute the funds necessary to complete the rest of the mission, which explains the big bag of change weighing down my backpack. Most of the stuff we really needed, we still had to acquire on the way. That was the plan.

"We can do without the blanket," I say. The blanket wasn't a necessity. We could sit on the grass if we needed to.

Agent Walker was the necessity.

This was all his idea, after all.

Brand's idea, though I guess it was actually the sub who started it. The same temporary sub who we had had the whole week. Mrs. Brownlee was her name. Like brownie, she told us, except it sounded more like her ancestors just couldn't choose between last names. A nice enough lady, but ditzy, and a rambler, and, like all teachers, a huge gossip. You can't walk down the halls of Fox Ridge for ten seconds without hearing one teacher whispering to another about what "What's her bucket" said to "What's her face." Except Mrs. Brownlee had no one to gossip with, so she confided in us, room 213. She told us everything she knew the minute she showed up that Monday: namely that Ms. Bixby was *not* at home reading novels and sipping tea in her backyard. She was in the hospital, earlier than expected, undergoing a "rigorous course of treatment," whatever that meant. And she would likely be there for a while. Maybe weeks. I looked over at Brand and saw his face had gone white.

We were silent for a moment, and then Susan Sonders said, "We should make her a card." Mrs. Brownlee thought that was a great idea, so out came the construction paper and the glue that we hadn't used since the first week of school, and we got to work as a class, making two dozen Get Well Soon cards, complete with self-portraits and bad poetry. Steve's was a little awkward, consisting of a checklist of everything Ms. Bixby should and shouldn't eat (apparently broccoli was in and fried chicken was out, which made me feel even worse for Ms. B.). I drew her a picture—a scene from *The Hobbit.* Then we stuffed the cards into a big manila envelope, and after a phone call to the secretary, Mrs. Brownlee scrawled an address on it, hospital room number and all. Steve volunteered to carry it down to the front desk. He memorized the address on the way; it's one of his things. When he got back, Mrs. Brownlee reluctantly started trying to teach us how to divide fractions but quickly gave up when she realized nobody was paying any attention—we were all thinking about Ms. Bixby in the hospital and what "rigorous treatment" meant—and sent us out to recess early.

That's when it happened—the plan. Brand was draped over the monkey bars, looking down at Steve and me through the spaces, both of us sitting in the mulch, throwing pieces of it, try-ing to get them into each other's collars and down each other's shirts. It was a stupid game, and notoriously one-sided as Steve had terrible aim, but the slides were all too crowded and none of us had the energy to play kickball. I had scored my third goal when Brand spoke up.

"We should go."

I looked at Steve, who was emptying the mulch out of his shirt, then back up at Brand.

"To the mall? To the moon? Back to bed? Where are you headed with this, Shakespeare?" I sometimes call Brand Shakespeare because of the making-up-words thing. We had to learn a little bit about the Bard this year. Namely that he made up words, wrote poems, and was in desperate need of a comb-over.

"To the hospital," Brand said, still talking to us upside down. "To see Ms. Bixby. I want . . ." He paused, licked his lips, and took a deep breath. "I think it would mean a lot to her if we paid her a visit."

"I'm not sure they would let us," Steve said, scratching at his neck. "Not the whole class."

"I don't mean the whole class," Brand replied, looking out over the playground. "I just mean us. The three of us."

"The three of us?" Steve repeated. It was clear he wasn't too hot on the idea.

"I don't think it's enough to send her a stupid construction-paper card, do you?"

Brand looked at me when he said it.

"Actually, my card was pretty good," I said, thinking about my drawing of Bilbo and his ring, but I knew exactly what Brand meant. It didn't feel like enough to me either. It felt like a shortcut. Just something you do because you feel compelled to do *something*. Ms. B. deserved better.

Brand flipped down from the monkey bars and joined us in the mulch. "I feel like—after everything we've been through this year—we owe her, don't you?"

Steve made a face, but I nodded. "What do you have in mind?" I asked, thinking that it should be the other way around, that Brand should be asking me for ideas. I was the creative one, after all. But he clearly had given this some thought already.

"Do you remember a few months back, we had that one prompt on the board? With the french fries? The day I called Trevor a butt zit?"

I snapped my fingers. I knew exactly what he was talking about, and not just the butt zit part, though it was hard to forget the look on Trevor's face. Ms. Bixby had us write in our journals at least once a week for fifteen or twenty minutes. Sometimes we got to write about whatever we wanted, but most of the time she scrawled a prompt on the board for us to respond to. *Describe a time when you discovered something surprising about yourself* or *Tell me about a person you admire.* Sometimes they were *Would you rather*s and sometimes they were just off-the-wall suggestions, like *Pick a new flavor of bubble gum that you think nobody would ever want to chew and then write an ad for it.* (I picked pickle.) I knew exactly which prompt Brand was thinking of. It made perfect sense, and it made me a little jealous that I hadn't thought of it first.

"And you remember what-all she said?" Brand asked.

"I remember," Steve said.

"Of course you do," I told him.

"So . . . ," Brand prompted, hands out, "we could totally do it. The park. The music. All of it. Or almost all of it. We could do it this Saturday. Surprise her. Just the three of us."

I nodded, but Steve groaned. "It won't be easy," he said. "Or cheap." He wasn't saying no. He was just pointing out the potholes.

"Nothing worth doing is easy," I said, using a Bixbyism against him.

Steve leaned against the ladder of the monkey bars, arms crossed, still not convinced. "I don't think it's a good idea."

"C'mon, man. We can't do it without you," Brand said. "It wouldn't be right. It would be like two musketeers leaving the third one at home to babysit."

"There were technically four musketeers," Steve said. "Plus what you're suggesting . . . parts of it . . . I'm not sure how we could even go about *getting* some of that stuff. And I don't think my parents . . ." He let his voice trail off, and he and Brand

45

stared at each other for a few seconds. Then Brand fell backward into the mulch, arms across his head.

"Lame," he groaned.

"Lay off, Brand," I said.

"Sorry," Brand said. "But it's always the same thing. It's always, 'I don't think my parents would go for that,' or 'I'm probably not supposed to.' Some things are more important than following the rules."

"Easy for you to say," Steve countered. "You don't have to live with them."

Brand looked like he was about to say something to that, something about what he *did* have to live with, but ultimately he just murmured, "Whatever."

I looked at Steve. Sometimes that's all it takes. I just have to look at him and that will be enough to convince him. "He's right, you know. It would be pretty cool. If we could pull it off. Think about how surprised she would be. And your parents would never have to know."

"*If* we could pull it off," Steve repeated, then sighed before saying, "But you're right about one thing. You couldn't possibly do it without me."

Brand bolted back up. "So you're in?"

Steve nodded reluctantly. I smiled. Brand started rubbing his hands together, super-villain-like. "But only if you can promise that we won't get into any trouble," Steve said.

I gave him my Indiana Jones smile. "When have we ever gotten you into trouble?"

"Three days ago," he replied. "And twice last week."

"I swear I thought Mrs. Samuelson's dog had an Invisible Fence," I said, remembering the three of us running like mad down the street, that wannabe-ferocious little schnauzer yapping at our heels, threatening to chew Steve's shoes off his feet.

We spent the rest of recess making a list of what we'd need, using a pen stolen from Melissa Trotter and Brand's arm as paper. As his forearm filled with ink, I grew more and more amped. It was pretty epic, the plan. Dangerous, yes, and maybe a little illegal, but also fantastic. We went back to our room with a blueprint of how we'd spend the coming Saturday afternoon tattooed all over Brand's arm, Steve frowning, me smiling, and Brand looking serious as ever. Then Brand suddenly stopped in the hall. He was listening to two teachers talking, having a whispered conversation outside the room next door.

"It's getting worse," Mrs. Lamos, one of the fifth-grade teachers, said. "They are transferring her to a new hospital all the way in Boston. She's flying out Saturday morning. She has family there, apparently."

"God bless her," Mr. Mattison sighed. "I just can't imagine. I feel so bad. And for the kids too."

Then he turned and saw the three of us just standing there, eavesdropping. Normally Mr. Mattison would as soon rip your head off as pat you on it, but this time he just gave us an awkward look that I can only assume was supposed to be a smile, except his muscles didn't know the pattern. He didn't say anything.

Brand turned to me. "Do you think?" he whispered.

"Yeah."

"Saturday morning? *This* Saturday?"

"I know."

"So now what?" he asked, reinstating me to my rightful place as the Games Maker of our little group.

"Now," I said, "we'll have to accelerate the plan."

Date: Friday, May 7. Time: 0738.

The raisins are all gone.

Over at the Ridge, the last of the buses spits out a handful of students. I can see Mrs. Thornburg, the assistant principal, ushering them inside, face set in her morning scowl. She looks my way, and I duck back down behind the bushes.

Still no sign of Agent Walker.

"He's a loose cannon," I say. "He's jeopardizing the mission."

Steve shakes his head. "Cool it with this secret agent act, all right?"

"Fine," I say, a little annoyed. Steve usually goes along with

48

whatever scene's playing in my head. He's been a paralyzed soldier, a stranded astronaut, a captured sidekick, a flaxen-haired princess, a zombie shoe salesman, and a raging Wookie. Of course, he's probably right. Skipping school for the first time ever is exciting enough without me having to pretend. I just can't help it. Comes with having to entertain yourself all the time.

I shut up and scan the parking lot, looking for any sign of Brand, while Steve fidgets with the Velcro on his shoe, doing and undoing the same strap over and over. *Scritch.* Fasten. *Scritch.* Fasten. I've never known him to wear shoes with laces.

"Did you know that kids with perfect attendance throughout their primary school years are three times more likely to go on to college than those students who have missed a day or more of school?" he tells me.

I'm sure he just looked that up this morning. Either that or it's something his parents told him. Or it's written on his sister's bedroom wall. "You already missed three days this year with the flu," I remind him.

"I'm just saying. If we go through with this, we dramatically decrease our chances of growing up to be successful, educated adults."

I start to say something about all three of those things being overrated, especially the adults, when I feel a tap on my shoulder. I spin around, striking what I'm hoping is an intimidating, kung-fu action hero pose. I've never taken karate, but I've seen enough movies to know how my hands should go. Brand looks at me like I'm nuts.

"Don't hurt yourself," he says. He's wearing faded blue jeans and a T-shirt with a picture of a scarf-wearing cartoon tiger telling me how great *they* are. Whoever they are. He crouches down next to us so we are all hidden behind the bushes.

"You're late," I tell him. "And what's with this?" I point to his outfit and then to the camouflage pants and green T-shirts that Steve and I are both wearing, looking like twins whose parents dress them alike, except Steve is Japanese and I'm white as a wedding cake. "I thought we decided on a uniform."

"I got out of the house late," Brand says, shrugging. "And I don't own any camo."

"Loose cannon," Steve mutters. I can't tell if he's mocking me or not. Steve's sarcasm sounds exactly like his normal voice.

"Well, did you at least bring your supplies?"

Brand sets his backpack down and opens it up, pulling out a large picnic blanket, red-checkered felt on one side and slick vinyl on the other. There is something wrapped up inside it, something small and delicate, judging by the care he takes in the unfolding. With a magician's flourish, he pulls it free. "Check it out."

He holds up the long-stemmed glass, clear as a raindrop.

The morning sun glints off the edge.

"Oooh," I say, and Steve finishes with an "Ahhh." Again, fifty-fifty chance he's being sarcastic.

"We're going to need one, right?" Brand asks.

I nod. Obviously I hadn't thought of everything. Brand carefully wraps the glass back up in the blanket and stuffs it in his bag. "So. We ready to make the call?"

I take another glance over the hedge. The parking lot is starting to empty out. There's probably still time. We could easily make it to our lockers and then to room 213 and sweet, oblivious Mrs. Brownlee before the second bell rings. I look at Steve, who shrugs, though I have a guess what he's thinking. He's thinking that things that look good on somebody's marked-up arm don't always turn out good when you put them into practice. He's having second thoughts, or, by this point, probably thirds or fourths.

I get it. I'm nervous too. But then I think about Ms. Bixby and her magic tricks, and her looks, and her quotes. And that day I found her rooting through the trash. The day she showed me what was in her bottom drawer and told me she'd hang on to it forever.

"All right. Let's do this," I say. "Communicator?"

I snap my fingers, and Steve reluctantly reaches into his pocket and pulls out his phone, handing it to Brand. Steve is the only one of us who has a cell phone. I technically *have* one—it's sitting on top of my dresser at home—except it stopped working the moment it accidentally fell in the toilet. I learned an important lesson about trying to pee and play Five Nights at Freddy's at the same time. My parents said I could have another one as soon as I save up a hundred dollars in allowance.

I currently have fifteen bucks, all of it sitting in the front flap of my backpack.

Steve recites the number for the school's front office. Brand dials and clears his throat, but then Steve reaches over and grabs the phone, ending the call.

"Wait. What about caller ID?"

"Have you seen the phones they use in the front office? Those things are, like, thirty years old. Trust me." I take the phone from Steve and hand it back to Brand, who takes a deep breath and hits redial.

This time, though, *I* snatch the phone away, frantically fumbling for the end call button.

"What now?" Brand says.

"Let me hear your voice," I say. "Your grown-up-mom-with-two-kids voice."

"Let me hear your voice," Brand echoes, sounding whiny and irritating, "your mehmehmeh with mehmehmeh meh."

"That sounds nothing like my mother," I tell him.

"So?"

"So. My mother's on the PTA. She knows everybody in the school. You have to sound like her."

"How am I supposed to imitate your mother? I don't even remember what she sounds like."

"She's got, like, a squeakier voice. Higher pitched."

Brand takes the phone back and clears his throat. Pretends like he's talking. "Hello, this is Mrs. Renn, and I just wanted to let you know that my annoying and paranoid son, Topher, won't be coming to school today. He has to spend the day giving his good friend Brand a hard time, as usual." He gives me a challenging look.

"Now you just sound like a mad Mickey Mouse."

"Forget it then. You make the call." Brand tries to hand the phone over, but I push it back to him.

"No," I say, impressed. "It's perfect. I just never realized that my mom sounded like that."

Brand dials the number again and this time we actually let him talk. He lets the front desk know that I won't be coming in today. Stomach bug. Then he waits three minutes and thirty-seven seconds, which Steve says is just random enough, and calls again, this time as Steve's dad, which is easier for him because the voice is lower. Brand hands the phone back to Steve. "Done."

"What about you?"

"I called from home." He says it like it's no big deal, like he's done it before. Sometimes I get the impression that there are lots of things Brand doesn't tell us.

From across the parking lot, we hear the first bell ring. The last stragglers shuffle inside for seven hours of menial-worksheet completing and sweaty-gym-sock smelling. But not us. We are on a mission. A pilgrimage. A quest.

"This is it. We are officially skipping school," Steve says. Now he looks like he really might spew. I'm sure he's thinking about what will happen if his parents find out. They can be a little hard core when it comes to school stuff. They won't really kill him, but they *will* torture him. That I'm certain of.

"Don't worry, Agent," I tell him. "I promise I won't let them take you alive."

He has reason to worry. Mr. and Mrs. Sakata are helicopter parents, except they're more like military-grade helicopters— complete with chain guns and antitank missiles. Hovering. Waiting to strike. Then there's his sister, who I'm pretty sure hates me. Maybe because that's how she is, or maybe because I'm always making faces at her and calling her Chris-mean-a Psycho-ta. I don't think she's really psycho. I know her parents give her just as hard a time as they do Steve, maybe even harder, but she kind of asks for it. His parents are always holding her up as some holy golden model of behavior, but Steve and I both know better. We've been spying on her since we were eight.

I don't have Steve's parent problem, or his sister problem. My sister Jess is only three, almost four, and it's hard to hold someone up as a model of behavior when she still pees her pants from time to time. My parents aren't helicopters either. They don't hover. They skim. They're flitters, darting from one thing to the next, from work to meetings to after-school events, never settling anywhere for long—like those water striders you find jumping across the pond—they drop a kiss hurriedly on the top of my head on their way out and blow extras as they walk out the door. My parents sometimes talk like those guys at the end of prescription drug commercials, so fast you can hardly hear them: *Sorry I gotta split your dad will be home in an hour don't eat too much before dinner and keep an eye on your sister love you so much be home late love you love you.*

It wasn't always that way. For a while I was the center of the universe, and everything I did was incredible. Every picture I ever made went in the scrapbook and every Play-Doh pot went on the shelf. We spent whole weekends together, the three of us, Friday to Sunday, having picnics at the playground and sitting in the third row at the movies, stuffing our cheeks with popcorn like squirrels storing for winter. They used one of my drawings once as the front of our Christmas card—a sketch of the three of us entrenched in a free-for-all snowball fight. I think I was six years old.

Then they had my sister and time suddenly got scarce. Mom went back to working nights at the clinic so that we would still have enough money for our three-story house and our annual vacation to the Outer Banks. We bought a minivan and put up baby gates. My father got a promotion requiring him to work extra hours at the office. Mom would sleep during the day, and I would sit and read stories to Jess.

Still, every now and then, when my mother has the night off and after my sister is in bed, the three of us will sit down on the couch together with our microwaved popcorn and a movie on demand, though my mother always falls asleep about halfway through, and we have to turn it up to drown out her snoring. Most nights I just watch TV by myself.

Some days I wonder if they have the slightest clue what's going on in my life. Steve says maybe it's because I live in my own little world and they aren't invited, so it's easy for them to just assume everything's okay. There's probably something to that. But there are days I wish I got half the attention from my folks that Steve gets from his. The good half, of course.

I still show them my drawings sometimes, but the responses are all pretty much the same. "That's great, T. Why don't you put it on the fridge?" "Cool, man. Leave it on the table and I'll take it to work." "I love it. Do me a favor and take the trash out, will you?" It's not that they don't look. They always look—for three seconds, every time, as if they were counting in their heads—but I'm never sure they really see what I want them to.

I guess it happens to everyone. You get pushed off to the side, or you just learn to blend in, stay out of the way, merge with the crowd. And you start to think that maybe you're not the center of the universe anymore. Maybe you're not as awesome or creative or talented or worthy of attention as you originally thought.

But in your head, at least, you can still be all those things. You can be the hero at the center of it all. The man with the plan.

The one who leads the way.

We saddle up and head away from the school toward the bus stop, me out in front.

"It's about twenty clicks from here," I say, though to be honest, I have no idea what a *click* is. It could be a yard. Could be a mile. I just heard it in a movie. For once, Steve doesn't know either, so he doesn't bother to correct me. Brand just laughs.

"What must it be like?" he asks.

"What?"

"Living inside your head?"

"It's pretty frawesome," I tell him.

Brand blinks, working through the combination. "Freaking awesome?" he asks. I nod. He doesn't have a lock on being Shakespeare. "Frawesome," Brand mumbles, as if he's chewing on the word. "I like it." He repeats the word to himself as the three of us make our way across Talbot Street, ignoring the looks of the drivers, who are probably all wondering why three boys are walking *away* from school on a Friday morning. *It's all right,* I want to tell them. *We're on a top secret mission for our teacher. Go about your mundane little lives.* Still, all those glances make me nervous. Adults have a way of making you think you're doing something wrong even if you aren't . . . though technically, we are, which makes it even worse.

"We should probably get off this street," I say. "Someone could ID us." Someone on the PTA, for example, one of a dozen meetings my mother manages to flit to.

"What? You mean your black-and-green camouflage isn't helping you to blend in?" Brand asks as we cut across a parking lot between two redbrick apartment complexes. I give him a dirty look, taking little satisfaction in the fact that if we were in the jungles of Cambodia, he'd be toast in his little tiger T-shirt. I unfold the map to make sure we are still headed toward the bus stop. We learned map reading this year in Ms. Bixby's class.

Legends and keys and Never-Eat-Spoiled-Watermelons and all that stuff. We had to, she said, because it would be on the test. The big, ugly, standardized, pass-this-or-you-will-be-sentenced-to-death-while-your-teachers-are-flayed-alive test. Ms. Bixby hated that test, so we hated it, but we took it anyway. Sometimes you have to suck it up and get it done.

"If we just make a right up here, then another left at State Street, we will be at—"

I'm suddenly cut off. Not just cut off; I'm actually thrown against the side of the apartment building beside us. Brand has one hand in my chest and another dragging Steve backward against the wall.

"I think we've been spotted," he whispers. It sounds exactly like something I would say.

"What?"

"Our cover has been blown," he repeats. He indicates that there's someone around the corner. Someone we know. I quickly steal a glance, swallow hard, then pull back.

"Oh, gefragt. Big Mack attack." I press back against the wall. Brand nods gravely.

"What? Mr. Mackelroy?" Steve squeaks. Mr. Mackelroy. The other sixth-grade teacher. The master Dungeon Master if ever there was one. Dressed in his tweed jacket and carrying his briefcase—the only teacher at Fox Ridge who bothers to carry a briefcase, like it's still the twentieth century—cigarette dangling from the corner of his frown. Thankfully he was on the phone and distracted, or he probably would have seen me sneaking a look. "Shouldn't he be at school already?" Steve whispers.

"He might say the same thing about us," I point out. I wonder what Mr. Mack is doing walking to school, but then I remember hearing that some of the teachers who work at Fox Ridge live in the nearby apartments. Mr. Mackelroy—divorced and with no kids save for the students he's constantly torturing—is probably one of them. I look down at my camo. I don't have any pants the color of red bricks.

"What do we do?" Steve asks. "We can't let him see us. He will report us to the front office. They will call our parents." Steve's face is puffing up like a blowfish, his eyes bugging out of his head. The whole mission is in danger and we've just gotten started. We are about to tunk big time. It's suddenly clear what must be done.

"We have to silence him," I say.

"Huh?" Brand says.

I glance around, scanning the ground, struggling to come up with something, thinking out loud. "You know. Take him out. Eliminate the threat. We can use a shoelace to strangle him. Or a belt." I can hear Mr. Mack's voice now, still on his phone, getting closer. "Or, here." I bend down and pick up a chunk of brick that has broken free from the wall, pushing it toward Brand. "Just smash him over the head with this. Then, while he's unconscious, we can drag him behind those Dumpsters over there."

"*Or,*" Brand suggests, lowering my brick-holding hand calmly and pointing to the parking lot we just walked across, "we could just go hide behind a car."

I look at the brick. Then at the cars. "Right," I say, and set the brick down as the three of us sneak behind the gray Toyota parked closest to us. We huddle just below the window as Mr. Mack emerges from behind the apartment building, walking quickly, talking loud enough for us to hear. His voice is raspy. Cold morning air and way too much smoking.

"I will, all right? Listen. I'm running late yet again, and if I'm not in that room by the time the second bell rings, Principal McNasty is going to have my butt in a sling. Yeah. I swear that witch has it out for me. I don't know. Maybe she was dropped on her head as a child. Right. Call me next week."

I peer over the door through the car windows, taking in briefcase, coat, and grimace. Mr. Mack clicks off his phone and takes one last long drag of his cigarette before smashing it under his loafer. He looks like a gangster, or at least a gangster's weaselly accountant. He pockets his phone and heads toward the parking lot, making straight for the Ridge.

Just keep walking. Don't look this way.

He's passing right by us. Completely oblivious. We are in stealth mode. Under the radar. No problem at all.

Beside me Steve sneezes, and Mr. Mack turns. I duck down as fast as I can, leaving my heart in my throat. It isn't fast enough.

"Christopher, is that you?"

"Stay down!" Steve hisses.

"Don't sneeze!" I snap back.

"Christopher Renn?" I can hear Mr. Mackelroy's voice growing even louder. Closer. Can hear his footsteps slapping the asphalt.

Ten feet.

Eight feet.

I look down at my shoes. There's no way I could unlace them in time. Steve is clawing frantically at my shirt, as if that's going to help.

Six feet.

Five.

We are so totally gefragt.

Then everything gets quiet. Quiet and still. I'm afraid to breathe. I'm afraid not to. I can't hear a thing. Beside me Steve is huddled into a ball. Brand is crouched, bouncing on his heels, ready to spring, ready to bolt. He's faster than Steve and me. He says it's because he walks almost everywhere he goes.

"Boo!"

All three of us jump. My backpack scrapes along the car, and Steve actually slams his head against the driver's-side mirror and yelps like a kicked puppy. We fumble and spin and press together, merging like conjoined triplets as Mr. Mackelroy casts his ample shadow across us, one hand on his forehead like he's just developed a headache, the other pointing his phone at us like a pistol. He hasn't shaved in days. We all three stand, backs pressed up against the car now.

"What are you boys doing here? Why aren't you in class? It's almost eight o'clock."

Mr. Mackelroy's eyes are bloodshot. The corner of his mouth twitches. We need an excuse and we need one fast. I fumble for something, maybe a lie about carpooling, and my mother's van running out of gas, and us having to walk the rest of the way. Trouble with that is that Mr. Mack would insist on walking to school with us. Then I would still have to knock him unconscious with something before we got there. On my left, Steve is muttering under his breath. A prayer, probably. Mr. Mackelroy looks like he's trying to develop laser vision so that he can just incinerate us with his eyes, he's staring so hard. Thinking that there is no other recourse, I'm about to just make a run for it when Brand steps forward.

"Why aren't *you* in class?" he says. I turn and stare at him.

I've never heard him talk back to a teacher like that before. Other kids, yes, but not Brand. He barely talks when you call on him.

"*Excuse* me?" Mr. Mackelroy growls.

Steve groans. That's it. It's over. Mr. Mack will drag us back to school by our earlobes. We will be marked as tardy. Worse still, we will have to call our parents and explain that we were caught trying to skip school. Likely there will be detention. Two hours in the brig. No snacks. No phones. No drawing. Just torturous silence and evil teacher eyes burrowing into you.

"What did you just say to me?" Mr. Mack points at Brand with one finger. He has yellow fingernails. Pretty gross.

"It's okay. I get it," Brand continues. "It must be hard to go work for Principal McNasty every day."

Mr. Mack's face blooms bright red; his jaw drops like a drawbridge with a busted hinge.

"That witch really has it out for you, huh?" Brand presses.

"*What?*"

"Can't blame her with all that childhood brain trauma. I didn't know she was dropped on her head as a baby. Or were you just making that part up?"

"I never said—" Mr. Mack stumbles.

"No, it's all right. I understand," Brand continues. "She's your boss. You're allowed to say terrible things about her behind her back. But if she really has it out for you, you probably shouldn't be late again either. What will this be, the fourth time? The fifth? And it's already what time again?"

Brand points to Mr. Mack's watch—he actually still wears a watch. Nobody wears watches anymore. Mr. Mackelroy glances at it.

"Oh crap," he mutters, glances at it again, just to be sure, then turns and starts running in the direction of the school, briefcase flapping at his side, looking like a bird with one wing broken. He slows once, looking back at us as if trying to figure out what to do, how best to punish us. Then he gives up and keeps running, across the street, past the baseball diamond, toward the school parking lot.

I can't help it. I have to laugh. Part relief, part amazement, part just watching Mr. Mack trying to run. You can almost hear the echo of his wheezing in the breeze. I give Brand a high five. "Did you see the look on his face?"

He's smiling smugly. Steve looks less enthused. His whole body is shaking. "We are going to pay for that later," he says.

"Yeah. Well. Lucky for us, Mr. Mack isn't our teacher," I say.

Our teacher's sitting in a hospital bed, probably reading twenty-plus construction-paper cards from her students, completely unaware of what three of them are up to.

"And Big Mack's probably opened his big mouth wide enough for one day," Brand adds. He grabs his pack and heads off in the direction of the bus stop again. "Aren't you guys coming?" he asks.

He takes the lead, but it's all right. He earned it.

"Now what?" Steve asks, still watching Mr. Mack in the distance, waddling across the empty bus lanes toward school.

"We stick to the plan," I say.

"Yeah, but—"

"But what? Today isn't about Mr. Mack. What we're doing is more important. Plus now at least we have a new name for Principal McNair."

I smile at him and he returns my smile at half strength. He's not convinced, but I know he's not going to back out now, not to go on his own. I turn and follow Brand, and after three seconds Steve jogs to catch up. "Still wasn't smart," he huffs from behind.

Yeah, but don't you ever get tired of being smart all the time? I want to ask him, but I don't, because I know the answer. I've known Steve for longer than I haven't, and unlike Brand, almost nothing he does surprises me.

STEVE

CHANGE IS THE ONLY CONSTANT.

I came in to find that written on Ms. Bixby's board one day. It was said by a Greek philosopher named Heraclitus over 2,500 years ago. I know. I looked it up. Of course, Heraclitus was a recluse who rubbed himself with cow manure before he died because he thought it would cure his swelling, so his wisdom is questionable. Still, I've found the quote to be frustratingly true. Just when you think you've got something pinned down, it shifts on you.

Take Pluto. I was devastated when I found out Pluto wasn't a planet anymore, and all because it's not gravitationally dominant in its own orbit, which is suddenly what's important. Not that I think Pluto should be a planet. I just think people should be consistent in how they define things. You can't suddenly stop being a planet because a bunch of scientists say so.

The diorama on my headboard has nine planets. Astronomically inaccurate, I realize, but it gives me comfort seeing little Pluto sticking out on the end. Topher says I worry about this kind of stuff too much. He once said to me, "The more things change, the more they stay the same." I told him that may be the dumbest thing I've ever heard.

The problem is that you get used to things being the way they are, and then you wake up one day to find that they've rearranged the aisles at the grocery store so that you can no longer find the individually packaged applesauce cups, which have moved from the canned fruit to next to the crackers. Or your sister, who used to let you sleep in her bed with her when you were little and your parents were arguing, suddenly starts whispering to boys on the phone and screams at you to get out of her room when you are just stopping by to see if she wants to play Scrabble. Or your teacher disappears with only a month left in the school year, leaving you with a sub who doesn't even know the capital of Syria and doesn't call on you because she's afraid you'll politely point out when she's wrong.

Or the empty chair at the lunch table you've been sitting at for years is suddenly not empty anymore. And instead of the two of you, like usual, there are three of you. And even though you know that nothing has changed, not really, that your best friend is still your best friend, you still feel uneasy, because it *could* all change, your whole relationship. Because, as the saying really goes, "No man ever steps in the same river twice."

That's actually what Heraclitus said, 2,500 years ago—the exact quote—probably just before he covered himself in cow poop. I'm sure his fellow Greeks wished *he'd* stepped in a river once or twice.

One thing I am certain of: Bus 142 smells like a wet dog.

The bus picks us up at State Street and then heads east, stopping seventeen more places before it hits Woodfield Shopping Center. It has two sets of doors, one at the front and one in the middle. It holds approximately forty-eight people. Forty-nine if you count the very large woman driving it. She stares out the front window as we drop our coins into her box. I actually drop mine in one by one because I like the sound they make; it reminds me of wind chimes.

We head to the back, and I'm a little surprised when Brand and Topher take a seat together. Not that they aren't allowed to, exactly, it's just that typically Topher and I sit together. We take the same bus to school, Bus 17, and every day he saves me a seat. He saves me a seat toward the back, and then he copies off of my math homework while I eat some of the prepackaged cookies his mother gives him for lunch. My parents don't pack me sweets. They don't want me to be one of those fat American kids the TV is always complaining about. Unlike my Tupperwares full of fresh fruits and vegetables, everything in Topher's lunch box comes in its own foil wrapper, which is a very tidy if environmentally unsound way of doing things. The cookies usually come four to a pack, which makes two for each of us, though Topher usually lets me have three.

Today, though, on this strange, new bus that smells awful, Brand and Topher sit together, and I stand in the aisle for a moment, uncertain. Then the bus lurches forward and I spin on my heels, toppling into the seat in front of them, my backpack containing my portable speakers slamming against the side. The speakers are for the music—a mix that I put together especially for Ms. Bixby. The plan called exclusively for Beethoven, but I added a few extra tracks, things I think she would appreciate. I listened to them all last night. She won't be able to hear them if the speakers get smashed, though.

I manage to right myself and immediately get up on my knees and turn around so I'm facing them. The vinyl covering of the seat sticks to my fingers. I try not to touch it.

"You okay?" Topher asks. I must look worried.

I nod. "According to the US Department of Transportation, bus accidents resulting in injury have gone down steadily over the past twenty-five years. I looked it up."

"Good to know," Topher says, then huddles over the map with Brand, the two of them tracing our route with their fingers, even though I was the one who did all the research and marked all the points along the way, from school to the mall to downtown to the hospital to the park and back again. It's Topher's map and Brand's idea, but it's my route.

I wait a moment, then say, "It should take us twenty-three minutes to reach Woodfield Shopping Center."

Brand turns and says something to Topher, but I can't quite hear it because of the rumble of the bus engine and the squawk of traffic right outside my window. Too much noise makes me fidgety. When I get anxious, I sometimes have a tendency to talk more.

"The first-ever school bus was invented in 1827. It was drawn by horses," I say. Last night's research might have gone a little bit off topic. Bus schedules led to accident statistics, which led to the history of mass transit. Before I knew it, an entire hour had passed.

"That's really great," Topher says, finally looking up at me and putting down the map. "Hey, instead of using our only working phone to memorize every page of Wikipedia, maybe you could send a text to someone in our class and see if Mrs. Brownlee has said anything about us being absent yet."

"Or if Mr. Mack ratted us out," Brand adds.

"I don't text anyone in our class," I tell Topher, though he already knows this. "Except you. Until you dropped your phone in the toilet." I don't mean it as a joke, but Brand laughs anyway. Topher gives me a dirty look.

"It was an accident," he says.

"Yeah. Those toilets are death traps," Brand remarks, then starts to snicker again. The bus stops rather abruptly, sending me rocking backward. Three people get on. Nobody gets off. I turn back around, my back pressed up against the sticky seat now, and look out the window. I hear Topher laughing at something Brand says behind me and tell myself it's not important. I don't need to know everything. It doesn't matter who sits where or by whom. Topher's my best friend, and nothing is ever going to change that.

We met in the first grade, Topher and I. He pointed to my Lego Star Wars lunch box and asked me if I had any of the actual Lego Star Wars sets. I told him I had four, all complete, all sitting on my dresser at home, the instructions carefully packed away in case I ever needed to rebuild them, like if an earthquake happened. He said he had a few of them, too, but they weren't put together; as soon as he built them, he tore them apart and mixed the pieces in with his other pieces. Also he lost Lego Boba Fett's legs when his dog ate them. I told him that was the craziest thing I'd ever heard. Not the dog part, which was troubling, but the mixing pieces part, which was even more troubling. I asked the obvious question: "If you mix up all the pieces, how will you put the ship back together?"

Topher shrugged. "Guess I'll just build my own ship," he said.

In that moment, I knew the most basic thing I needed to know about Topher Renn.

It took a few weeks of building—with his Legos, obviously, as I refused to separate mine—but after that first month of school we clicked. We spent every afternoon together, playing Pokémon and lightsaber battles and at least a dozen games that Topher invented but all involved us running around his backyard, saving the world from mummies, zombies, vampires, or giant robots. We acted out movies without cameras, mostly jumping straight to the fight scenes and skipping over the sappy parts. We would get into his parents' car and pretend it was a starship, laying on the horn until one of his parents—whichever one was at home—opened a window and yelled at us to get out. It was all Topher's idea. It was always Topher's idea. I just followed his lead.

Every day after school we would set off on one of his adventures, making couch forts or digging holes in the park to bury our treasure in, a quarter or a packet of Smarties that we would forget to go dig back up. The best was when we pretended we were secret agents and would spy on my sister, using my iPod to record her conversations or just hiding in her closet until she heard us breathing and screamed at us to get out. I spent more time with Topher than with my own family. I'm sure they weren't thrilled with the idea, this kid with the wild, scraggly blond hair and even wilder blue eyes monopolizing my carefully allocated free time, but Topher was polite around my parents and earned "decent enough" grades, so I was allowed to keep him as a friend. Friends were important to my parents, provided I didn't have too many and they didn't interfere with the quest for accomplishment and recognition.

We managed to stay in the same class as each other every year. Topher says it's because we are a duo. Like Batman and Robin or Finn and Jake. Other students, mostly boys, would sometimes make fun of us, sing the tree song, or just give us dirty looks. I'd learn about other things they said behind our backs eventually. I know Topher did too, but he never said anything to me. It didn't matter. All that mattered was that we stuck together. And saved the world from the giant robots after school.

Topher is a constant, like pi or radical two. He was there when I had to have my appendix removed, showing up at the hospital afterward with strawberry milk shakes and comic books. He was there when my father and mother both had to go out of town on separate business trips and I spent four agonizing days with Christina bossing me around, acting like my mother even more than usual. He was there when Tyler Fisk threatened to "beat the living snot out of me" because I snitched on him for cheating off my math test. We both ended up with bruises that day and compared them on the bus ride home. Mine was bigger by a quarter of an inch, which made Topher jealous for some reason.

Constants are called that for a reason. You can take them for granted. Like sunrises or breathing or the hissing sound a can of Coke makes when you open it. Like the quote your teacher puts on the board every morning.

Or your best friend saving your seat on the bus.

"Woodfield Mall."

Operator 57 calls out the stop in her gruff voice, and I stand. Topher and Brand shuffle behind me as we step off into the dewy grass, which thankfully isn't quite long enough to reach the cuffs of my socks. On our side of the street is the mall, a Sears and a JCPenney tethered to each other with strings of shops that my sister, Christina, could probably describe in detail. On the other side is another row of shops, punctuated by half a dozen restaurants. One of them is a McDonald's, but we aren't ready for that yet. We are going to the bakery three shops down, the first red circle on the map. That's where we will find the first item on our list.

This is all part of the plan. The plan that we cooked up on the playground and then had to change when we found out Ms. Bixby was going to Boston. The plan that had us meeting up outside the school and calling in sick. The plan that calls for us making our first stop here to purchase item number one and then boarding bus number 37 downtown. There we will pick up item number two, though I'm still not sure how we are supposed to pull *that* off. It's illegal, for one. And probably expensive. Topher says he has an idea, but he won't tell me what it is, which means it's an especially bad one. Item number three on the list will be obtained last, because otherwise it will get soggy, which is why we don't need the McDonald's yet. After item three, we will walk the six remaining blocks to the hospital. Just like the three kings in the Christmas carol, Topher says. We break Ms. Bixby out of the hospital, take her to the park circled on the map—the one I looked up last night along with the bus schedule—and then . . .

I'm really not sure what happens then. I just know I wasn't about to let Topher go without me.

"There's Michelle's," Brand says, pointing. I remember what he said last Monday under the monkey bars as we penned notes on his arm. *Michelle's is a must have; there can be no substitutes.* Topher told him he sounded like a commercial, but he was right. Ms. Bixby mentioned Michelle's by name.

"Come on." Topher gives me a tug and we run across the street, dodging potholes and cars. Brand leads the way, me in back, as the bus rumbles off, letting off one last odiferous cloud of exhaust.

Michelle's Bakery is a medium-sized stone building with tall glass windows filled with cakes. Most of them are probably plastic—either that, or cardboard pieces pasted together with thick, crusty icing, hard as limestone. My father told me once that all vanilla ice cream in photographs is actually mashed potatoes, because mashed potatoes don't melt. One reason why the real thing is never as pretty as the picture.

The sign for Michelle's is also white with rolling green letters, all pressed close together. The blinking blue light says *Catering Available.* Another sign advertises *Open Till 8 on Weekends.* There is a poster for a missing cat named Princess Paw Paw. I'm not fond of cats. My family doesn't own any pets, which is only odd because my sister is planning to become a veterinarian. I suspect she just wants to become a doctor but doesn't want patients that can argue with her. We walk in and a bell on the door jangles.

"Hello. Welcome to Michelle's," says a man with an accent

77

that catches me off guard. I look around and spy him standing behind a counter, the only other person in the bakery besides us. The man is large—not overweight like Mr. Mackelroy, but large like a wrestler, thick muscled and bulky. He has dark, bronze skin and black hair. In keeping with my expectations, he at least has a mustache.

"Are you Michelle?" I ask. I'm not trying to be rude. I'm just curious. He doesn't look like a Michelle. Topher says that sometimes I say things that can easily come off the wrong way. I'm wondering if this is one of those times. Beside me Brand is already shaking his head.

"Not Michelle," the man says. "I'm Eduardo."

"Eduardo," I repeat. It's another habit of mine, echoing people. I just want to make sure I heard right. He looks like an Eduardo.

"Michelle's just the name on the sign. I'm the guy who bakes the cakes."

I nod. Then I look around. The bakery, at least, smells much better than the bus. Everything in here is white, except for Eduardo and me. There are rows of cupcakes in the glass display in front of us, each of them curlicued with thick whips of frosting. My mouth waters looking at them. At my house, the closest we get to dessert are chewable vitamins. My parents have a lot of rules.

"So you mean you, like, run the joint?" Brand asks the man behind the counter.

"I own this bakery, yes." Eduardo offers an impatient-looking smile. I get the sense this isn't the first time he has explained this.

"So then why not just call the place Eduardo's?" Topher asks. Sometimes, I think, my curiousity rubs off on him.

The large man behind the counter sighs. His mustache actually curves up at the ends. I'm tempted to reach over and tug on it to see if it's real or if it's like the cardboard cakes in the window, but I don't, because people don't like it when you pull on their facial hair. I know this from experience.

"Let me ask you something," Eduardo begins, draping both large hands over the cash register in front of him. "And be honest. Would you rather buy a big, fancy, expensive cake from a place called Eduardo's or from a place called Michelle's?"

I don't actually see where it makes any difference so long as the big fancy cake tastes good, so I just shrug. Maybe it's a trick question. Ms. Bixby would ask trick questions sometimes just to make sure we were paying attention. My favorite was: Before Mount Everest was discovered, what was the highest mountain in the world? Everyone in class got it wrong but me. Eduardo doesn't wait for an answer. "Would you go to a Mexican restaurant named Michelle's?" he prods.

"I don't eat Mexican food. The beans make me f—" I start to say, but Topher elbows me in the side, so I don't finish the sentence. It doesn't matter. Eduardo knows.

"Me too," he says, patting his stomach. "It's nothing to be ashamed of. It's what beans do. What people do. The natural order of things. It's to be expected. We are creatures of habit. Most people, they prefer to buy their cakes from a place called Michelle's. That's just how it is."

I look at the sign for Michelle's in the window and try to imagine it saying *Eduardo's* instead. Maybe he's right. I know exactly what Ms. Bixby would say if she were here, though. She'd say when you are content to be simply yourself, everyone will respect you. It's something she borrowed from Lao Tzu. I know because I looked it up too. Lao Tzu wasn't so wise, though. He was also the one who said that the journey of a thousand miles begins with a single step, not bothering to mention the five million more steps you have to take after that. I've done the math.

I look back at Eduardo and consider telling him about Lao Tzu and suggest maybe he change the name of his bakery, but I'm guessing he probably wouldn't take the advice of a twelve-year-old Japanese kid named Steve.

"So what can I do for you gentlemen?" Eduardo asks. Behind us Brand has wandered off already, looking at the enclosed glass cases, heading to the refrigerators on the other side. I fill in the gap he leaves behind, shuffling closer to Topher.

"We are looking for a cake," Topher says, raising one eyebrow and using one of his make-believe voices. He's done this as long as I've known him. I guess he's pretending we are police detectives or something. Police detectives who hunt down suspicious desserts. "White-chocolate raspberry supreme cheesecake. Maybe you've heard of it?"

Eduardo who owns Michelle's nods appreciatively, stroking his mustache, playing along. "Yes. I know this cake you speak of," he says.

"So you know how we can get it?" Topher nudges.

"That depends," Eduardo says. "Do you want it whole or by the slice?"

Topher looks to me. Probably he senses a story problem coming on, and I'm the math genius among us. "How much?" I ask, thinking of the original plan, which was to get a whole cake and split it among the four of us, but then thinking about how much money we have between us.

Without even batting a lash, the man behind the counter says, "Seven ninety-nine for the slice. Fifty-four ninety for the whole enchilada." The word *enchilada* strikes me as funny for some reason and I almost laugh, but Topher is not at all amused. You can tell by the way his eyebrows jump into his bangs.

"Fifty-five *dollars*?"

The baker with the curly mustache shrugs. "At Eduardo's you could probably get it for forty. But this is Michelle's, so it's fifty-five." He gives us a wry smile, and I count two silver teeth. Topher looks physically pained.

"I thought you said it would be three bucks," he whispers at me.

"I said it had three dollar signs in the review online. That means it's expensive," I explain. Behind us, Brand is still standing at the freezer, staring at his reflection in the frosted glass. Topher throws his hands up.

"Forget it," he says. "No way. No cake is worth fifty bucks."

I nod in agreement. It does seem like a lot for creamy cheese and sugar. Eduardo leans over the counter and clears his throat. His cheeks are pocked. I can see now that his mostly coal-colored hair is shifting to gray by his ears. He beckons us closer with one finger and Topher and I lean in.

"Excuse me, *mijo*, but have you ever *tried* Michelle's white-chocolate raspberry supreme cheesecake?" He's speaking to both of us, but it seems as if he's looking right at me. His eyes are spooky. They are brown, but so dark that it looks like he just has two giant pupils. I shake my head.

"*¿Crees en Dios?*" Eduardo asks.

"I don't speak Spanish," Topher says.

"I can only count to twenty," I say, though I'm pretty fluent in Japanese and I know a few Russian curses that Topher and I learned off the Internet. But I'm guessing Eduardo is not going to call me a *glupo mudak*.

"Are you a religious person?" Eduardo translates.

I'm not sure what that has to do with anything, but Topher is looking at me like I'm supposed to answer. His parents are atheists. I take communion, at least, so I nod.

"And have you ever been to heaven?"

Obviously another trick question, but I don't have a trick answer, so I don't even bother. Eduardo points his finger at us in triumph. "That's because you've never tried my white-chocolate raspberry supreme cheesecake." Then he slaps his hands on the counter with a tremendous thump, and my knees knock instinctively. "Trust me, amigos, eight dollars a slice is a bargain. Heaven should be so cheap."

"Fine," Topher groans. "We'll take two slices." I'm not sure what kind of math he's doing. I'm guessing he thinks we will split each of them in half, though if it comes to sharing with Brand or even Ms. Bixby, I will probably pass. I'm not comfortable sharing my food with just anyone. Topher asks me for money, and I fish for the ten that I brought. He digs in the front pocket of his backpack and pulls out a paper clip holding a ten and two fives. He adds the fives to mine and slaps the cash on the counter. He keeps the other ten in reserve. "Two slices," he repeats.

Eduardo is about to take the money when Brand's voice stops him.

"We're getting the whole cake."

I turn to see him standing right behind us. He has his wallet out. I didn't know he owned a wallet. I don't own a wallet. I don't even have a paper clip. Brand produces a twenty and lays it on the counter, making it forty dollars. I'm not sure about his math skills either.

"Dude, what are you doing?" Topher hisses.

"It has to be the whole cake," Brand says. "No compromises."

Eduardo eyes the bills suspiciously with his brown button eyes. "The *whole* cake is fifty-four ninety," he reminds us. Topher starts to say something, but Brand puts a hand on Topher's shoulder.

"Why don't you two wait for me outside?" he says.

Topher hesitates, but I head for the door. I'm used to following directions.

My father said the same thing not too long ago: told me to wait outside. And I would have, because I am in the habit of doing whatever either of my parents asks of me. Maybe I should have, but then I would have missed the look on his face when Ms. Bixby finally called him out.

It was a parent-teacher conference, but it wasn't the regularly scheduled parent-teacher conference that only comes once a year. This was an impromptu meeting, arranged by my father almost immediately after seeing my last report card, most notably the B in language arts. Not a B plus, which is disappointing but can be tolerated due to its close proximity to something better, but a pathetically ordinary B, like a boil, ugly and bumpy and sticking out amid the array of As, impossible to ignore. I was afraid to bring the report card home. The B was an abnormality, I knew, and it called for an explanation. I offered the best one I could, which was that I struggled with some of the reading quizzes and writing assignments. My mother nodded and told me I would do better next time, but my father wasn't satisfied.

Which was how I found myself standing outside room 213 with my father the next evening after dinner, my mother at gymnastics with Christina, whose report card was blemish free and already magneted to the refridgerator. Ms. Bixby appeared in the doorway, looking cheerful despite being stuck at school so long. She asked us to come in. I started to go, but my father grabbed my shoulder, holding me back.

"Wait out here," he said, pointing to the chairs teachers keep in the hall for students who need time to "reflect on their choices," like when Trevor Cowly blew his nose in his hand and then wiped it on the back of my shirt. I started to head toward the chair when Ms. Bixby interrupted.

"It's all right, Mr. Sakata," she said evenly. "Steven is welcome to join us."

My father looked at Ms. Bixby, then at the empty chair, then at me. Finally he bowed his head and Ms. Bixby ushered us both inside. I noticed him staring at her hair. He did the same thing at Back to School Night. Ms. Bixby reached up and touched the strand of pink self-consciously.

You think that's something, you should see my tattoo. That's what Ms. Bixby usually said whenever someone, usually a new student, commented on her hair. Of course, she had confided in all of us that she didn't really have a tattoo; it was just something clever to say. Ms. Bixby didn't use the imaginary tattoo line on my father, however. She just touched her hair and asked us both to sit down. He retrieved the report card from the inside pocket of his suit and set it on the desk between them, then immediately launched into a prepared speech on the topic of "The Recent Decline in Steven's Evaluated Performance," complete with a painstakingly accurate account of my elementary career thus far, which had been B-less, though dotted with a few near-miss A minuses. Somewhere in the speech I heard the words *surprising*, *error*, and *inexcusable*. Ms. Bixby listened patiently, waiting for a breath, keeping her eyes on my father, who concluded by asking her how it was possible for his son to be given such a grade.

"Your son *earned* a B," Ms. Bixby said. "I didn't give it to him. He did very well on all his spelling tests, and his reading comprehension has improved steadily from the beginning of the year. He's an excellent student."

"Exactly. Excellent," my father said, repeating the part that interested him. "Excellent is A work."

"Bs at Fox Ridge Elementary signify above-average work," Ms. Bixby clarified.

"It is below *his* average," my father retorted, the corners of his mouth tightening. "He studies two hours a day after school. He takes Japanese. He reads every night before bed. His mother and I quiz him about what he's read. It seems impossible for him to get anything less than an A."

"It sounds like you keep him very busy," Ms. Bixby replied, though it didn't sound like a compliment. Then she pulled up a screen on her laptop. "It looks like Steven struggled a little through our fiction unit this year and missed some questions on his reading quizzes. That's all. It's only a third-quarter grade; there are plenty of opportunities left in the year to improve, though I think he should be happy with what he's accomplished so far." She turned and smiled at me. I smiled back, then quickly readopted the look of self-disappointment that I came in with before my father noticed.

"I'm sure my son is only satisfied with doing his very best," my father answered.

"I'm sure he is too," Ms. Bixby said. "But a B is a perfectly acceptable grade."

Already it had gone from above average to perfectly acceptable. My father had that effect on people. He would soon have her convinced that the B was a stain on my record that should be removed before it ruined my chances of ever getting into a decent college. "Perhaps for other students in your class," he responded coldly, "but not for Steven."

Ms. Bixby's cheeks turned pink to match her shock of hair. Suddenly the two of them started talking over each other.

"Mr. Sakata, I appreciate what you are trying to say, but I think what's more important is that Steve feels like he is being challenged and that he is growing, socially and intellectually, making connections and—"

"But in my son's case it represents a breakdown in the learning process, either on his end or on yours, and signifies—"

"—grades are just one way to reflect and measure that growth, and that one—"

"—his sister certainly never earned a B in her life, and both of his parents are quite well educated—"

"—spend too much time focusing on end results and not enough time on the process, the journey that your son is taking—"

"—feel that the real problem is that you aren't challenging

him *enough,* or maybe your system of evaluation is flawed and needs—"

"—simply don't think one little B is really worth worrying about."

My father cleared his throat. "My son is a straight-A student, Ms. Bixby," he said, straightening up himself, his voice rising to match.

I looked up to see Ms. Bixby smiling.

"Is that what your bumper sticker says?"

I laughed. I couldn't help it. I might have only smiled if it wasn't for the fact that there actually is a "Proud parent of straight-A students!" sticker pasted on the back of the Volvo. I'm not sure how she knew, or even *if* she knew. Maybe it was a lucky guess. Or maybe she had had this same discussion before with someone else's father, bickering over someone else's B.

"Excuse me?" my father barked.

Ms. Bixby blushed again. "I'm sorry. That was uncalled-for. You're absolutely right. You should be proud of Steven. Incredibly proud. He is one of the brightest students I've ever had the honor to teach. He surprises me every day with how much he knows, and his curiosity is insatiable. I will make sure that he and I work hard the next several weeks to ensure that all his grades reflect the kind of student he is." She gave a polite smile. My father stared at her hair again.

"That's all I'm asking," he said gruffly, reaching out and retrieving my report card, holding it with two fingers like a used tissue. "Thank you for your time."

He rose, and Ms. Bixby rose too. They shook hands politely. I wasn't at all sure who the victor was. I was still laughing inside at the bumper sticker remark. Then, as we were walking out the door to room 213, Ms. Bixby called my name. I turned and she stretched out her index finger, her look asking me to do the same. Our fingers touched lightly at the tips, and her eyes brightened. "Be. Good," she said.

It was a line from *E.T.* I know because Topher and I had seen that movie four times already. But I also knew she was making a joke. Thankfully my father didn't get it, or maybe he just didn't hear. Then she said, "See you tomorrow," and "Thanks for coming," and I couldn't be sure, but I think she closed the door to her classroom with a little more force than usual.

Back in the Volvo my father shook his head. "Never have these problems with your sister. *Her* teachers understand."

"I think Ms. Bixby understands," I murmured.

"Doesn't matter," my father grumbled. "Only eight more weeks." Meaning only eight more weeks in the semester. Eight more weeks to bring my grade up. Eight more weeks with Ms. Bixby. Eight more weeks to deal with this woman with the crazy hair who obviously didn't know how to teach or at least didn't appreciate Sakata greatness when she saw it. Eight weeks.

Except his math was wrong. He didn't know what was growing inside her. None of us did.

There were really only four.

The bells on the door chirp at us on our way out, leaving Brand and Eduardo huddled over the counter. Topher and I sit on the curb next to each other, knees almost touching. Topher reaches down and plucks a pebble from the street, rolling it back and forth between his fingers. I take my phone out and type in *why is cheesecake so expensive*. The answer, according to the first website I check, is "Because it is yummy." That hardly seems scientific. The real answer, I suspect, is because people are willing to pay that much for it.

"What if it were Topher's?"

I put the phone down and look at Topher. He's looking at the pebble, smooth and gray, barely the size of an M&M. "It's just a rock," I tell him. "You can probably have it if you want it." I'm also not sure why he's talking about himself in the third person.

"Not the rock. The bakery," he says, looking up at the sign. "What if it were called Topher's? How much do you think I could charge for that cheesecake?"

Now I understand. It's a game. How much is your name

worth? "Would it be called Topher's or Christopher's?" I ask back, not that it would make a difference to me. I'd shop there regardless, though I know for a fact Topher doesn't know how to bake. The one time we tried to make cookies at his house, we set off the smoke detector.

"I don't know. I guess Christopher's sounds better. Topher's is more the name of an ice-cream parlor, don't you think?"

I don't actually think about things like this. That's why I like to have Topher around. "I guess so," I say. "What about Steve's?"

Topher scrunches his nose. "Sorry, man. I'm not sure you could charge more than twenty bucks. Nobody wants to buy cheesecake from a Steve. No offense."

I'm not offended. It takes a lot more than that. Especially coming from him.

"But I'd *totally* buy comic books from one," he adds, then smiles, his dimples surfacing. He has a great smile.

I try to imagine what my parents would say if I told them I was going to skip college and open up my own comic book store. I picture their heads exploding. The thought makes me smile too. "What's he doing in there, anyway?" Topher says, craning his neck. Brand's back is to us, but Eduardo is nodding over and over.

I shrug. I can tell it bothers Topher, being kicked out, sitting out here on the curb while Brand is in there, carrying on the mission or whatever he's doing, but it doesn't bother me. I think about all the times the two of us have sat together like this. On the bus. On the floor in his basement. In the cardboard fort we built in his backyard. Always side by side, never across from each other. Topher flicks the pebble with his thumb. I watch it skitter across the parking lot and bounce into a drain. I could never make that shot on the first try. Or the second. "You think this is a good idea?" he asks.

"It's a lot of money for a cake," I say.

"I don't mean the cake. Not *just* the cake, anyway. I mean all of it." He stretches his hands out to indicate the *all* of all of it, his shoulder bumping into mine. "I mean, do you think it's weird? Do you think *she'll* think it's weird?"

The word *weird* just sits there between us. I think about Ms. Bixby, who made us all memorize monologues from our favorite movies instead of famous speeches from history (though I still memorized the Gettysburg Address because my parents insisted on it, claiming that it was also, technically, from a movie, and had greater educational value). Ms. Bixby, who once came to school wearing her bathrobe over her normal clothes because it was twenty degrees outside and she couldn't find her coat. Ms. Bixby, who kept books scattered all around the room in the most unusual places—tucked in with the hand sanitizer, sitting on the windowsills, stacked on top of the python's terrarium—because, as she put it, stories are everywhere, just waiting to be found.

"I think *she's* a little weird," I say.

"She probably thinks you're a little weird," Topher says. "*I* think you're a little weird. Don't worry. It's a good thing. It just means you're remarkable."

"I think you're weird too," I say.

"Come to think of it," Topher continues, "I think the word *weird* is kind of weird. Just say it out loud a few times. Weird. Weird. Weird . . ."

I start to chant it along with him, the two of us sitting on the curb saying *weird* over and over again. I suppose if you say anything over and over again, it starts to sound strange.

About twelve *weird*s in, the door behind us jangles again and Brand comes out of the bakery carrying a square white box, holding it with both hands. The box doesn't have one of those see-through windows that birthday cakes from the grocery store always have, but I can only guess it's the whole enchilada.

"What was that all about?" Topher asks. I can tell he's miffed, and he's letting Brand know.

"No big deal," Brand says. "I took care of it."

"You 'took care of it'?" Topher repeats. "What, are you the Godfather now? How much did he charge you? Did you actually get it for forty?"

Brand shakes his head and smiles. He hands the box to

Topher, who nearly drops it, grunting at the weight. Then he hands me back my crumpled ten and one of Topher's fives. Somehow he got the cake for less than half the price.

"Turns out it's teacher appreciation day," he says with a shrug.

Through the window of Michelle's, I see the baker shrug at us too.

"Welcome to Eduardo's," Brand says.

Brand

EVERYBODY LOVES A GOOD SOB STORY, SO LONG
as it's not their story.

I don't know why. I'm not sure if people honestly care about other people or they just want a way to confirm that they've got it better than someone else, someone they can point to and say, "It could be worse. I could be *that* guy."

Don't get me wrong. I don't think people are really like that. Not most people anyways. But I think we're all guilty of it sometimes. Just like we're all guilty of doing the opposite, looking at everyone else around us and thinking that none of 'em understand. That they are living in a fantasyland full of birthday cake and sunshine and can't possibly get what we are going through.

I think that all the time. I can't help it. Because, as it turns out, nobody knows what I'm going through.

Then again, maybe that's because I haven't told them.

Eduardo didn't sob when I told him my story, but he did get quiet. He knew Ms. Bixby, he said. He remembered the pink hair, or was it orange? He couldn't quite recall, but she had definitely been in the shop before, and he was very sorry to hear about her diagnosis. He was even sorrier when I told him my side of the story—the truth, if not the whole truth—and why it was so important for me to see her today. Then he asked what this all had to do with cheesecake, and I explained that part too. He nodded to himself several times, tapping his fingers on the counter before telling me to just take it. The whole cake. Gratis. No charge. We argued about it for a few minutes more, and then I finally made a compromise, taking the cake and leaving twenty-five bucks on the counter. Nothing free is worth having.

That's not one of Ms. Bixby's sayings. My father actually taught me that one. My father, who keeps most of his money—most of our money—in the bread box by the refrigerator, and tells me to take whatever I need. I watch it slowly diminish, dwindle down to a few bills over a couple of weeks, and then I walk to the ATM by the Village Pantry and make a withdrawal and the bread box is suddenly full again, like magic. I'm sure he keeps track, but he doesn't say anything. Most days it's just lunch money. A couple of bucks to rent a movie. Cash and tip for the pizza delivery guy.

Fridays are different, though. Fridays are the best. Fridays I take at least a hundred bucks.

Today I took twenty. I guess I should have taken more. Of course if my father knew that I spent twenty of his dollars on a cake for my teacher, he would flip.

Of course, if he stopped and thought about, he'd realize he probably owes her as much as I do. Nothing worth having is free.

There's a used-book store just down the street, and Topher insists on going. He says there's something he wants to look for, something he should have thought of earlier. We still have some time before the right bus comes to pick us up. The bookstore's not part of the original plan written across my arm a few days ago, but I can tell Topher's a little peeved at me for leaving him out of the whole cheesecake getting, so I go along.

First things first, though. We have to figure out some way to shove this cake in one of our backpacks. It weighs as much as a watermelon, and the box is the size of a microwave. Steve's pack is the biggest, so we empty it out, putting the speakers in Topher's, and wrapping the backpack around the box as best we can. It doesn't zip all the way, but the cake isn't going anywhere.

"We should have brought a cooler," Steve says. "Cheesecake should be kept refrigerated."

"I think it'll be fine for a couple of hours," Topher says, though I can tell by the look on his face that he doesn't know the first thing about cheesecake. If it doesn't come slathered in ketchup or have a picture of Cap'n Crunch on it, Topher's not interested.

Steve carefully slides his arms through the straps, grunting at the weight. He looks like he's about to tip over backward and I wonder if I shouldn't be the one to carry it, but I know if I say something to Steve, he will think I'm hinting at something. That he's not strong enough. That he can't handle it. So I let it go and we walk over to Alexander's. That's the name of the bookstore. And maybe the guy who owns it. Then again, maybe not.

We push through the curtain of dust that greets us at the door, followed by the smell of pinewood and Old Spice cologne—the same kind my father used to wear, back when he took showers every day, before even going to the bathroom counted as exercise. The place looks just like one of those creaky old libraries you'd find in a Goosebumps book, jammed with books from floor to ceiling, stacked sideways, spine-ways, slanted, two and three deep on shelves that lean in every possible direction, like Jenga blocks about to fall. The floors creak when you step on them and even when you just stand there, but that's not the spookiest part.

The spookiest part is the owl sitting on one of the high-up shelves by the door. Stuffed, obviously, except whoever stuffed it did it with its head twisted around, looking backward. Owls can do that, I know, but it's still freaky. A sign on the wall below the twisted owl says *Caveat Emptor* in fancy gold letters and then, smaller underneath, *Buyer Beware.* Beware of what? I wonder. The owl's clearly missing some feathers; I guess it's seen better days.

The door swings shut behind us, no chimes or ringing bells to give us away. Topher calls out a "Hello?" There's no answer. "Bizarre," he says.

"Yeah," I say.

"And creepy," Topher adds.

"That too."

"You ever been here before?"

I shake my head. "Didn't even know the place existed."

Topher inches a little closer to me. I can't imagine what he's thinking. His imagination must be in overdrive. "Reminds me of the bookstore from *The Neverending Story*," he says.

"Never read it," I say.

"That's all right. It's practically impossible to finish anyway."

Any other time I'd laugh, if I wasn't feeling so weirded out. We stand by the door, none of us wanting to take a further step inside. There aren't enough lights—at least a third of the bulbs are burned out—and that makes for a lot of shadows on the walls. I get a chill, and it seems to be contagious, because Topher and Steve shiver too. Then, just as I'm about to suggest turning around, heading back, and waiting at the bus stop, Steve sneezes so hard he gets a blob of snot in the crook of his elbow. A huge yellow glob quivering there like Jell-O. I think about the time I picked his nose. This is way grosser.

"I meed a missue," he calls out desperately, more snot snaking down his upper lip. Topher says to just rub it in, but Steve looks horrified at the idea. I look around and find an antiquey-looking sign that says *Powder Room*, pointing down a dark hallway. Steve looks at the hallway, looks at the snot, trying to decide if it's worth the risk. Then he finally stumbles off.

"Messy," Topher says.

"Yeah," I say.

The upside is that Steve has broken the invisible force field that was holding us in place by the door, at least. We take a few timid steps, me leading the way. Save for the three of us and the freaky, backward-glancing owl, the place seems deserted. I stare at the mountains of books leaning against each other along the crooked wood shelves. Now that we are inside and surrounded by them, though, I feel a little better. It reminds me a little of room 213 and how there are books everywhere you look. Ms. Bixby would like it here, I think. This is the kind of place she would go. A place you could get lost in. A wooden placard dangling by twine from the ceiling says we are in the literature section.

I run a finger along one shelf, leaving my trail in the dust, then pull out a copy of a book by someone named Alfred, Lord Tennyson. Never heard of the guy. Sounds like a blowhard. The gilded letters on the cover say *Idylls of the King*. I open it up to the middle, see that it's actually poetry—really *long* poetry—and quickly put it back. I don't mind reading literature when I have to, but it's almost summer and I have my limits.

Suddenly the books start to speak.

"'Theirs not to make reply, Theirs not to reason why, Theirs but to do and die.'"

Topher and I instinctively step close together. From the dark hallway with the powder room I hear a sound—not quite a scream, more of a squeak, but definitely Steve's voice. Before I can even take a step toward it, though, a man not much taller than me peeks his head around the corner of the shelf, looking at us from behind thick silver-framed glasses. I nearly trip over Topher as we both stagger backward.

"Aha!" he says.

The man who emerges from behind the bookcase looks like Yoda . . . if Yoda were a nearsighted, five-foot-tall white man in khaki pants and a frumpy gray sweater. Pointy ears jut out of a melonish head, topped with little wisps of white hair tufting out like pulled cotton. And he's got Yoda wrinkles too, the kind that come in waves crashing down to his eyebrows. His gray wool cardigan reaches nearly to his knees. He has a haunted expression on his face, eyes wide, dangerous looking. "'Boldly they rode and well,'" he bellows. "'Into the jaws of Death, Into the mouth of hell . . .'" With the last word, he slaps his hand down on the bookshelf beside him. I jump.

Then the man's expression suddenly softens. "Tennyson," he says brightly.

Topher mumbles something like "Mmwha?" I don't say anything. I'm starting to think there is a good chance we are about to be murdered.

"'The Charge of the Light Brigade'?" the man says. "Surely you've heard it. 'Cannon to right of them, Cannon to left of them, Cannon in front of them, Volley'd and thunder'd; Storm'd at with shot and shell, Boldly they rode and well.'" His voice grows thunderous, then gravelly, then thunderous again, and he pounds one fist into the other hand and grins. I shake my head. The man frowns. "What are they teaching kids in school these days?" I maneuver a little—small steps, just so I have a clear path to the exit. I'm not sure he realizes it, but Topher is holding on to the sleeve of my shirt. "Sorry I didn't hear you boys come in. I was down in the basement, eating a body," the old man adds, licking his lips.

"Um . . . *what?*" Topher asks.

"Biscotti," the old man repeats, holding up a half-eaten biscuit. "They are really quite good dunked in tea."

Crazy-five-foot-tall-Yoda-who-could-still-very-well-be-an-ax-murderer circles around us, blocking our path, heading toward the front of the store, probably to lock us in. "I think we should get out of here," I whisper to Topher, but then I remember that Steve is still in the bathroom.

The old man is standing at the entrance now, looking up at the stuffed owl on the shelf above. He calls back over his shoulder. "Normally Scout warns me when we have guests, don't you, Scout?"

The name strikes a chord, and I feel a a little jolt of electricity shoot through me. "The owl's name is Scout?" I ask. I know a Scout. Ms. Bixby introduced us not too long ago.

The man nods. "A good name for an owl, don't you think?" He cocks his head, as if listening to the stuffed bird. "Scout's wondering what brought you in here today."

My eyes dance from the owl to the old man and back again. I elbow Topher. This was all his idea, after all.

Topher clears his throat. "We were . . ." I step on his foot. "I mean, *I* was, um, looking, um, you know . . . for a book."

"Then you've come to the right place, hasn't he, Scout?" The old man snorts and snaps his fingers. Maybe he's not a cannibal, but he's clearly nuts. "No shortage of supply here, though I should warn you: I don't carry comic books. I don't have any diaries written by wimps. And the only novel I have about vampires was written over a hundred years ago. So if you are looking for anything like that, you might as well leave."

"Funny. That's what *I* said," I say to Topher through clenched teeth. I look back toward the hallway to see if Steve has come out of the restroom yet.

"Actually," Topher says, ignoring me, "I just need to know if you can point me to your fantasy section."

The old man puts a finger to his nose and then points to Topher. "Fantasy. Of course. I could tell just by looking at you." And in a flurry of his flapping cardigan, he comes and takes Topher by the shoulders, leading him through the maze of shelves. Topher glances back at me, begging me with his eyes to come along, but I hear another door open and look to see Steve finally emerging from the hallway, face ghostly. He approaches slowly, glancing back over his shoulder with every other step. When he gets to me, he takes a deep breath.

"There's a shark in the toilet," he says.

If it were Topher, I'd laugh. Or give him a dirty look. But this is Steve. Steve doesn't make things up. He researches them carefully and then commits them to memory so he can bore you with them later. His eyes are as round as cheesecakes.

"Show me," I say, leaving Topher to fend for himself.

We head down the dark hallway to the restroom, and I flip on the light. Steve stands by the open toilet, pointing with both hands, just in case I don't know where to look.

"Huh," I say.

Sure enough. Someone has painstakingly painted the inside of the toilet bowl to look like a great white shark's gaping mouth. Pretty much just the mouth and that triangle snout, like in the movie poster from *Jaws*. Rows of jagged teeth, red gullet, deep dark pit leading to who knows where.

"Who paints a shark in their toilet?" Steve wants to know. Of course he hasn't met the crazy, wispy-haired man who talks to stuffed owls and shouts about the jaws of hell yet.

I stare at the shark. "I wonder how the paint even stays on," I say. "You'd think it would wear away by now. You know. Erosion or something."

"Probably because nobody ever uses it," Steve mutters.

I guess it would be a little disconcerting, sitting there, picturing those teeth right below you, that long snout reaching up to take a big bite out of your you-know-what. "Didn't you?"

"Are you kidding? In that? Even if I *had* to I wouldn't."

I look down again at the great white.

It makes me think of Dad.

I point to the door.

"If you'll excuse me," I say.

Who paints a shark in their toilet?

My father would. Or at least it seems like something he would do. Or would have done. Before.

Dad was a prankster. A gag master. He used to play practical jokes all the time on his buddies at work. Not on actual construction sites, of course—that would be stupid dangerous. But back at the office or right after work. Whipped cream in the desk drawers. Shaken cans of beer. Switching the contents of sack lunches. It was the same at home for a while, except at home, I was the only target. And they were always sneak attacks. Except for one day out of the year. The one day I could see it coming. April 1st.

Next to Christmas, April Fool's Day was the best holiday at our house. We even made up a mascot for it: the April Fool's Jackass, a magical donkey who would sneak through your window on March 31st and dump a basket of goodies in your bed. Old-school stuff. Joy buzzers and whoopee cushions and fake parking tickets. Flies for your ice cubes and dollars on retractable string. And rubber dog poop. You always woke up with a big pile of dog doo, there on the pillow, right under your nose.

Of course he always played a prank on you as well, that clever little donkey. One time he replaced my toothpaste with Elmer's glue. Not as bad as it sounds—I'd tasted it before—but hard to brush with. Another time he pasted a fake mustache to my face in my sleep that I had to wear to school all the next day, earning me the temporary nickname Luigi (my fault for also wearing green). If you've ever taken a bite out of a caramel-coated onion that you expected to be an apple, you might have had a visit from the April Fool's Jackass.

"It's all in good fun," Dad would say, and then he'd laugh while you picked the fake maggots out of your cereal bowl. You'd vow to get him back, of course, but he would suddenly look innocent and claim it was the donkey that did it. And you wouldn't eat, even though it was kind of funny, because maggots, fake or not, will make you lose your appetite.

But I did get him back. Sometimes. Not on April Fool's, of course. Not when his guard was up, but later. Put a rotten banana in the toe of his work boots. Stuck a fake roach in his grilled cheese. Sprinkled hot sauce on his french fries. He never got angry. Not once. "Well played, son," he'd say, wrapping his arms around me, halfway between a hug and a wrestler's hold. Then he'd give me a grin full of wickedness and the promise of retaliation, and I'd spend the next three days opening every door slowly, inch by inch, and sniffing all my food before taking a bite.

That was all before. Before the accident and the surgeries, the disability checks and the medications. The hours spent at home, in his chair or on the couch, cemented in place, like a nickel superglued to the sidewalk. After a while it just wasn't funny anymore. Any of it. There were no more pranks. No more gags. He would still make jokes sometimes, tell me something he heard on late-night TV. And I would laugh, not wanting to disappoint him. But it wasn't the same.

I said a prayer not long ago. On April Fool's Eve. It's not something I do often, praying, because I feel like if you do it too much, it loses its effect. Like building up a tolerance—God just starts to tune you out. But on March 31st I prayed that the April Fool's Jackass would appear and leave a big basket of gags on my bed and a pile of dog poop on my pillow. Not because I wanted to play a prank on anyone, though it would have been fun to see the look on Steve's face when he bit into a piece of hot pepper gum. Just because I didn't want to stop believing in him yet.

The next morning there was no basket. No poop. No joke.

Nothing to get him back for. Nothing to look forward to.

Dad would really have loved this toilet.

Sitting there, thinking of the great white about to take a bite out of my skinny white bottom, I think of a new word, or at least a new way of thinking about an old one. *Squaring.* As in

"I just squared one." Pretty much the same as "going number two" or "dropping a deuce" except even more scientific. It's going potty to the power of two. Plus it's more appropriate for dinner conversation than "making fudge nuggets" or "birthing a Baby Ruth."

I finish and flush and wash my hands, and then I step out to see Steve and Topher huddled over the checkout counter, which is really not much more than another rickety wooden bookshelf with a cash register balanced precariously on top of it. The old man with the bushy eyebrows is standing behind it, one eyebrow raised. Topher and Steve have concerned looks on their faces too, and I wonder if something's happened. Wonder what trouble they've gotten themselves into, wonder if the old man and his owl have caught them stealing, though I can't imagine either of them doing such a thing. Buyer beware. It's not till I get closer that I see that they aren't worried—they are deep in thought.

"Seven seconds," the old man says.

"Hang on," Topher shouts. "I've almost got it. 'Put me in a bucket, and I'll make it *lighter*.'"

"Four."

"No. Wait."

"Two."

Topher snaps his fingers repeatedly. "A hole. A hole. You're a hole."

"Exactly," the old man says, his eyes brightening. Topher throws his arms up in triumph.

"Boo-ya. Who da man? I'm the man." Leave it to Topher to talk trash over solving a riddle. Steve shakes his head.

"All right, 'da man.' Try this one, then. 'You use a knife to slice my head and weep beside me when I am dead.'"

"I don't know," Steve says in his mopey voice. "I told you. I suck at riddles. Why can't we do sudoku or something?"

"Seven seconds."

"It can't be that hard."

"Five."

"I'd like to cut my sister's head off sometimes," Steve says.

"Three."

"I don't know!" Topher shouts as I step up behind him.

"You're an onion," I say, with one second to spare.

The old man points at me and grins. "Excellent."

"I was just about to say that," Topher huffs.

So that's what they were doing while I was in the restroom. Playing a riddle game. "Come on, Mr. Alexander. One more," Topher pleads.

His name really is Alexander. He seems a lot less frightening than before, when he was shouting about the jaws of death and eating bodies down in his basement. In fact, he looks completely harmless now, standing behind his cash register with his cup of tea and biscuit crumbs caught in his sweater. In the time it took me to square, Steve and Topher have made a new friend.

"Aren't you going to miss your bus?" Mr. Alexander asks.

"Yes. Probably," Steve says.

"Just one more," Topher insists. "And make it a tough one."

I step up so I'm standing in between Topher and Steve now. I see Topher's already found the book he was looking for, and I almost hit myself for not thinking of it. It's a brilliant addition to the plan. It's perfect, actually. A great finishing touch, even if it's not one of the things she asked for. The copy he's found is well loved, cover torn, pages yellowed and warped, but she won't care. Knowing her, she will probably like it better that way.

"All right," Mr. Alexander says. "But after this you need to either buy more books or get out of my shop. Scout can't abide loiterers." The old man puts a finger to his chin, then grins mischievously. "'You can run from me, but you can never escape. You can beg for me, but I don't always listen. To most I am a thing worth waiting the longest for.'"

"You can run from me . . . ," Steve echoes.

"Eight seconds."

"The sun?" Topher guesses.

"I don't always listen?" Steve says.

"Five seconds."

"Maybe it's time. Is it time?" Topher asks.

"Three."

"Don't look at me!" Steve shouts. Topher is hopping up and down. He looks at me instead, desperate.

I know the answer, but I don't say it. The old man fixes me with his cloudy blue eyes and I suddenly feel transparent, like he's staring right through me. He knows I know. Topher bangs his hands on the counter. "C'mon, c'mon, c'mon!"

"Time's up," Mr. Alexander says triumphantly. Topher growls in disgust.

"Well, tell us then," Steve says.

"Yeah, Mr. Alexander," Topher adds. "You can't just leave us hanging like that. What's the answer?"

The bookseller smiles at me. It's a lonely smile. I know because I see that same smile every day. I open my mouth, start to say something, when the growl of an engine grumbles by, shaking the windows, knocking a couple of books over, rattling Scout on the shelf where she's perched.

Mr. Alexander frowns, and we all run to the door and look out just in time to see our bus shoot by.

The April Fool's Jackass disappeared on a cloudy day in mid-October, well over two years ago.

He was working along a scaffold three stories up. Something snapped or slipped or just popped loose, and the scaffolding collapsed, folding in on itself. He collapsed with it, folding in on himself too.

He only fell thirty feet, which isn't that much, if you think about it. Steve tells me that a flight attendant in Europe once fell out of an exploding jetliner, miraculously surviving a fall of thirty-three thousand feet. She became a hero. But it's not always how far you fall. Sometimes it's just how you land.

Dad landed badly. Broke his arm in two places, a compound fracture tearing a gash through his forearm that looked like something out of a slasher movie. He chipped a shoulder blade and cut his ear, too, but those were nothing. The real damage was done to L2 and L3, otherwise known as Lilo and Stitch. That was what the neurologist called them, the two vertebrae that had fractured and dislocated in my father's spine, causing untold damage to the cord inside. Lilo and Stitch did a number on my father, gnawing and pinching through the fabric of nervous tissue that give marching orders to his lower half. They didn't rip off his legs, but they might as well have.

There were surgeries, of course. Procedures. Medications. Tirades. Prayers. An extended hospital stay. I missed a lot of school—my old school, not the Ridge. I spent a lot of time with my great-aunt Tracy, who had flown in from Oregon, the only relative on my mother's side who still kept in touch after she died. Aunt Tracy promised to take care of me until Dad got out of the hospital, but she couldn't stay forever. Within a month she was gone and my dad came home, transferred from ambulance to wheelchair and from wheelchair to couch.

The surgeons did what they could. Now it was all up to him. With enough physical therapy, they said, he would probably walk again, but it was going to be the hardest thing he'd ever done in his life. He said he was up for the challenge. He had lost my mom when I was only two and raised me all by himself. He taught me how to ride a bike. He could teach himself how to walk.

He made it to his first nine physical therapy appointments and didn't make much progress.

On the tenth one he said he wasn't feeling well and would reschedule.

On the eleventh he said he just forgot.

After that he stopped picking up the phone.

Thankfully, we didn't want for money. The company my father worked for ponied up. They didn't really have a choice. They covered his medical bills and kicked in a sort of workers' compensation package that would probably support us for the rest of his life, provided we pinched our pennies. Then they turned around and sued the company that made the scaffolding materials. The scaffold makers sued some company in China that produced the bolts used to hold the scaffolding together.

Which means somehow or another there is a big manufacturing corporation in China that pays my father to sit on his butt all day and watch *Ice Road Truckers*. There's a joke there, somewhere, about a screw loose probably, but it's not funny anymore. The whole story is this: My father fell and he doesn't have the heart to stand back up.

There are days he just comes out and says it. That thirty feet wasn't far enough. That it would be better if he had fallen farther. Thirty thousand feet. A million feet. Clear off the face of the earth. He says, then it would be better for both of us. I never know what to say when he says that, so I just go hide out in my room or sit on the back porch and watch the fireflies blink on and off. Later he always says he's sorry, that he didn't mean it. He was just feeling down.

I never know what to say to that either. So instead I just tell him I'm going to go make us dinner.

We run as fast as we can, but it's pointless; the bus is already half a mile away. So we walk slowly back to the bus stop, Steve shifting under the weight of his shoulder straps, Topher with his new used book under his arm. It's not the end of the world. There will be another bus, but it does set us back on the schedule. Another kink in the plan. I kick at the curb and stare down the road.

"Make it a *tough* one?" I say.

"Hey. I wasn't the one dropping anchor in the back," Topher replies.

"It's called 'squaring.' And it's not every day you get to go inside a shark's mouth."

There is a splintering bench by the bus stop, advertising the latest extra-value menu item, and the three of us sit next to an old lady and her lapdog, a little yappy thing that looks like a dirty Muppet and snarls at Topher when he plops down beside it. Steve immediately takes out his phone to check the bus schedule and see when the next one is due. I'm surprised he doesn't have it memorized. I fiddle with the zipper on my backpack and think about the wineglass wrapped up in the blanket inside, think about nerves encased in bone, wrapped in muscle and sinew and skin, think about the walls of room 213, layered with watercolor paintings and science reports. Safe things. Secure things. All wrapped up. All enclosed. Until they're not. Until they are out in the open, exposed and fragile.

Topher opens his pack and puts the book he just bought inside, then pulls out his sketchbook. A thick spiral job with rough, cream-colored paper that only people who are serious about drawing have. He flips to a blank page near the front and starts to draw something. I lean across Steve to get a look. If I were anyone else, any of the other kids from our class, I'd get a flash of teeth and a protective growl. Topher's sketchbook is his prize possession, like Batman's utility belt or everyone else's iPhone. Steve and I are the only ones allowed to look, as far as I know, and I've only recently been added to the list. I watch him sketch out the rough outline of a few bookshelves, followed by a figure huddled between them. The head, the ears, the glasses, the marching wrinkles. It's a pretty good likeness. Topher makes the head much too large, caricature style, but he manages to get Mr. Alexander's mischievous expression right.

"That's pretty good," I say.

It's actually *really* good, as usual, but Topher's a dude and my friend, so I'm not about to gush on him. Not that I would gush on anyone.

"Yeah," Topher says, which is kind of like *thanks* and *I already knew that* all at once. "I just wanted to get it down while I could still picture what he looks like."

"There's another bus that will take us within a block of where we need to be that's supposed to be here in seven and a half minutes," Steve says, but I'm busy watching Topher flesh out his sketch of Mr. Alexander. It's mesmerizing, watching him make something out of nothing, like he's got a direct wire going from his brain to his hand, through the pencil and straight to the book. It's something I wish I could do. One of many things I wish I could do.

"Don't forget Scout," I say.

"Right."

Topher etches in the headlight eyes and crooked beak of the owl, fills in the feathers and the hooked talons, then pauses to review his handiwork.

"Cool," I say.

"Yeah," Topher says again, studying his sketch intently, shading in a few spots. That's the difference between artists and the rest of us, I think. Artists know where to put the shadows. "At first I thought he was a deranged psychopath who opened a bookstore to lure in little kids. But then we started talking about the book, and he asked us if we like riddles, and you . . . well, you were squaring, I guess."

"Exactly."

"Though cubing sounds better. Shape-wise."

"Cubed is to the *third* power," Steve says. "Nobody goes to the bathroom to do a number three. There is no number three."

I smirk with satisfaction. It's not often he takes my side over Topher's. Steve dives back into his phone, and Topher tucks his pencil behind his ear and riffles through the first half of his sketchbook. I've seen most of these pictures before. Mostly superheroes and their nemeses. A few landscapes. An unfinished drawing of a caveman being eaten by a dinosaur. A picture of Kyle Kipperson getting eaten by a dinosaur. Then a picture of someone who looks a little like me pinning someone who looks a little like Trevor Cowly to the ground, except I'm dressed up like a ninja and Trevor looks like Doctor Octopus. I look good as a ninja.

"That's me, right?"

"No way," Topher says. "This guy is infinitely cooler than you. Did you miss the part where he's a ninja?"

"Yeah, but it's *based* on me, right?"

"Inspired by real-life people, perhaps," Topher says, "but artistically enhanced for pure, unadulterated frawesomeness."

"Hey, look at this alligator coming out of this toilet. That can't be real, can it?"

Steve shows his phone to Topher. While he's distracted, I reach over and grab the sketchbook to get a better look. Maybe it's *not* me. It's hard to tell with the mask on. Topher grabs Steve's phone and presses his face into it as I flip through a few pages, pausing at some other stuff I haven't seen before. There's a drawing of a person in a gladiator getup battling a six-headed dragon and another of a winged fairy decked out with machine guns and hand grenades, like *Die Hard* meets *Peter Pan*. Topher lets out an "ew" as he and Steve find more things crawling out of toilets. I reach the front of the sketchbook and go back the other way.

The pages after the riddle-posing bookstore owner are blank: home for the future works of Christopher C. Renn.

Suddenly, flipping through, I feel a hole open up inside me. So many pages left. All that potential he's got. I have nothing like that. Nothing I can do that makes me stand out. I am about to close the book when something catches my eye. About three-quarters of the way in, as if tucked away.

Surrounded on both sides by pristine pages is a portrait of a woman. But not just any woman. Even in black and white, you can tell exactly who it is. It's the hair—the one lightly shaded stripe that strikes down across her bangs. The slightly snub nose and shallow cheeks. The inquisitive eyes. She looks sad in the picture. It's actually beautiful, the way he's captured her. All the details, the silhouette. He must have spent a lot of time on this drawing. A *lot* of time.

"Hey, where'd my book . . ."

I glance over at Topher. He seems frozen in place. He sees the sketchbook, the open page, the portrait. Then all at once his face flares bright red and his hands shoot out as he catapults across Steve's lap, nearly knocking the phone out of his hand. I pull the sketchbook out of reach before he can grab it, scooting to the edge of the bench.

"Is that—?" Steve starts to ask, but he can't finish the

question because Topher shouts over him.

"Give it back!"

"Hang on," I say, holding it up over my head, still studying the portrait, wondering why it's even in there.

"You're squishing me!" Steve shouts as Topher nearly crams an elbow in his mouth reaching for me, scrabbling for the book, clawing at my shirt. Muppet dog goes crazy, erupting in a fury of yaps, and I see the old lady grunt and stand, muttering something about "juvenile delinquents."

"Give it back, Brand!"

"I will. Just hang on! I'm still looking at it."

"Screw you. Give it back, now!" Topher stands up and I stand too. Steve hastily stuffs his phone in his pocket and slides his backpack with the precious cheesecake out of the way.

"I will, all right? Just chill."

But Topher doesn't chill, and I don't let go. There's something about this picture. Finding it here, secreted away in the back of his sketchbook. I'm not sure what it means, why it matters so much, but all of a sudden I'm sweating, nerves humming, irritated. I feel like something's been taken from me without permission, even though it's *his* drawing. Obviously he can draw her. She's his teacher too. But she can't possibly mean the same thing to him as she does to me. I hold up the sketchbook even farther as Topher steps in. He's not grabbing for it anymore. I see his fingers clinch.

"Give. It. Back." His jaw is tight. The words barely make it out between his clamped teeth.

"All right, I will," I say, lowering the sketchbook to where he can get it, except I still can't let go, I'm still looking at the picture, and Topher only manages to grab hold of half of it. I hear the rippled unzipping of the thick pages tearing free from the metal coil. See one half of the sketchbook come loose in Topher's hands. My half, the half with her face, flies out of my hand, rustling in the air for a moment before slapping against the pavement, pages spread.

Topher screams. Then I feel the weight of him on my chest.

We hit the sidewalk, cold and rough, and all my breath escapes me. I keep my head up, but my shoulders slam home, my elbows scrape along the concrete, rubbed raw. Topher lands on top of me and I'm surprised at how heavy he is for how skinny he looks. He raises his half of the sketchbook above my head like it's a giant stone slab that he intends to bludgeon me with. I reach out and just manage to reach the other half, holding it between us like a shield.

"Fine! Take her!" I say.

I meant take *it*, but that's not how it comes out, so I try again. "Just take it and get the hell off me!" I'm grunting. He's got one knee pressed into my gut. I can hardly breathe.

Topher doesn't move. He doesn't grab the other part of the sketchbook. He doesn't hit or kick or yell. He just holds me down. His lip quivers. Out of the corner of my eye I see Steve point and say something about a bus.

And that's just what we look like when it pulls up. Me on the ground. Topher on top. And Ms. Bixby in between.

STEVE

IT'S A TWENTY-SEVEN-MINUTE BUS RIDE FROM Woodfield Shopping Center to the corner of State Street and Third. Twenty-seven minutes, barring extraneous traffic, blown tire, or hostile takeover. Twenty-seven minutes can feel like hours when you are caught in the middle of two friends.

Topher is slumped in the seat next to me, his sweaty head pressed against the seat. Brand sits across the aisle, checking his elbows. They're pink, stripped of skin and spotted with blood from where they hit the pavement. I can't look at them for more than a second: blood makes me queasy. So do brussels sprouts, millipedes, and mayonnaise, but blood especially.

This bus smells like ammonia. Or that stuff they use when someone vomits in the halls at school, which also makes my stomach turn. The bus driver is a man this time. His name is Bob, and he has shaggy hair and a beard that reaches to his chest. He looks like he belongs on a motorcycle, or at least in an advertisement for motorcycles. I've never actually met anyone who rides a motorcycle. My parents think they should be outlawed because they are too dangerous, along with cigarettes, horror movies, and any boy who might want to date my sister. The thought of my father on a motorcycle is funny to me.

Topher has both halves of his sketchbook in his lap, the cover creased and torn on one corner. More of the pages are coming loose from the binding, which is also bent. I feel bad. I know how much that sketchbook means to him. The drawing of Ms. Bixby is tucked away in there somewhere.

I glance from Topher to Brand and back again. There's nothing worse than being stuck between two people who are mad at each other.

That's not true. Dying of starvation is worse. Being stranded in the void of outer space with only ten minutes of oxygen left in your suit is worse. Earthquakes. Alzheimer's disease. Ductal adenocarcinoma. These are all worse. But being stuck in between is still bad. When my parents argue, they will sometimes put my sister or me in the middle, use us to prove a point, to try to admit that one or the other of them is right. When that happens, Christina often ends up trying to negotiate peace. I usually find some reason to escape to my room or go call Topher.

There's nowhere to escape to when you are stuck on a bus, jerking along cracked city streets, heading south toward downtown. I'm not excited by the idea. Just yesterday a postal delivery worker found a dead cat stuffed into a mailbox downtown, presumably not Princess Paw Paw. It doesn't sound like an ideal place to spend the day, but unfortunately everything we still need is downtown, including Ms. Bixby.

Up near the front a mother with two toddlers is spilling crackers all over her lap. Judging by the dark-purple stain on her blouse, she isn't having a good day. The two kids complain about being thirsty and having to use the bathroom. Then they start to fight over who has more crackers. She flashes me an apologetic smile. I'd like to tell her that I understand how she feels, but I don't talk to strangers.

Brand and Topher continue to pout on either side of me. I wish I knew what to do in these situations, but I don't, so instead I take my phone back out, boot up Minecraft, and go crush some creepers, ignoring the warnings that my battery is already starting to run low. That's the nice thing about phone batteries, I think. They at least *warn* you when they are about to fail. They give you time to prepare. Topher and Brand, on the other hand—I didn't see that one coming. It was just a picture, hardly worth fighting over. It wasn't even Topher's best work. I like his dinosaur drawings better.

This bus really smells bad. And those kids are loud. Brand winces every time he pokes his sidewalk burns. I wonder if taking this second bus is going to put us too far behind schedule, if we will be able to get back to the school in time to get home. I don't want to have to call my sister for a ride. We shouldn't have gone to the bookstore. I shouldn't have told Brand about the shark. I wish I could get the rest of the snot off my shirtsleeve; I guess it's just going to dry there and be crusty. I still think the cheesecake should be in a cooler. Things are not going according to plan, and I feel a little light-headed because of it.

I'm in the middle of making some Minecraft explosives when Topher finally stops chewing on his lip and says something.

"It's not what you think."

I'm not sure if he's talking to Brand or me, because he's still looking straight ahead. I go with me because he's mad at Brand. I'm not sure if Brand is even listening; he's staring through the dirty glass at the blur of buildings now, his elbows cradled in his hands. Of course if Topher is talking to me, I'm not sure what to say, because I'm not sure what he thinks *I* think.

"It's just a picture," Topher continues, which *is* one of the things I was just thinking. "It doesn't mean anything. It's not like I have a crush on her or anything."

A crush? On Ms. *Bixby*? That wasn't at all what I thought.

Now, suddenly, it's all I can think.

I pause my game. "Oh," I say. "Right." I still stare at the phone. I'm sort of afraid to look at Topher.

"It's not like that at all," he continues, looking at the seat in front of him, refusing to look at me too. "I just . . . I don't know. I thought that if I drew a picture of her, she would, you know . . . always *be* there somehow."

"Uh-huh," I say.

Uh-huh is what my parents say to each other at the dinner table when they pretend to be listening to each other. Except I'm not pretending. I'm really listening. I'm just not really understanding. Ms. Bixby is a thirty-five-year-old woman. And our teacher. Topher is twelve. And my best friend. These two things are incongruent.

"I thought it would be like a way of, you know . . . preserving her," Topher says. He looks over at me finally, waiting for my response, to say something reassuring. To *get* it.

I think I got it. "Like formaldehyde," I say.

My sister had to dissect a frog last year in biology. She said they kept the frogs in formaldehyde, which is this chemical that preserves living tissue so that it rots slower. Unfortunately, formaldehyde causes cancer. Not that the dead frogs care. Judging by the look on Topher's face, I obviously don't get it.

Topher groans and slumps up against the window, and now

I'm afraid he's mad at me too for thinking the wrong thing, even though he's the one who made me think it in the first place.

"I get it."

Brand's voice is barely more than a whisper. And I'm not entirely sure I hear him right. But then he turns and looks at us. Actually, he looks past me and directly at Topher. "It makes perfect sense," he says. Topher looks over my head at Brand, and I feel like I'm suddenly in the way. "It's like Shakespeare," he adds. "How he wrote all those poems and thought that it would make him immortal or something." Ms. Bixby taught us a little about Shakespeare. We read a sonnet by him in class.

It didn't work, I want to say, Shakespeare still died, but Brand keeps talking. "You draw her and she's, like, with you forever. I think it's cool."

"Really?" Topher asks. He looks at me for confirmation.

"Hmm," I say. *Hmm* is what you say when you can't say the thing that the other person wants to hear. I learned that from my parents too.

"Seriously," Brand says. "I was just jealous 'cause . . ." It takes a few seconds for him to finish the thought. "Honestly, I just wish I could draw half as good as you."

"Half as well," I correct. Brand ignores me. I turn around to Topher. "I get it too," I say. "Totally." I really don't. I still think it's a little strange to be drawing pictures of your teacher. I'm just

130

glad that Topher doesn't have a crush on Ms. Bixby. That would be worse.

There is a long, quiet moment, and then Brand reaches across the aisle with his fist. "I'm sorry about your sketchbook."

I look at Brand's fist, hovering right in front of my face. For a moment I think Topher is going to leave him hanging. For a moment I hope he does, but then Topher rolls his eyes and finishes the bump. I have to lean back to avoid getting punched.

"You're a total dufkus," Topher says. *Dufkus* is a Brand word. Like *dork* and *doofus* and a few other things all rolled into one. It's not a good thing, but it's not near as bad as being a flipwad. "And you're *so* buying me a new one."

"It was fourteen ninety-five," I say. I know because I'm the one who bought it for Topher's tenth birthday. That and a set of charcoal pencils. He told me it was the coolest present he ever got and promised his first sketch would be of me. It wasn't.

"In that case, I regret to inform you," Brand says, "that I just spent all *my* money on cheesecake."

"It's all right. You can just owe me," Topher says.

Up ahead the bus driver finally calls out our stop. The lady with the juice-stained shirt collects her children and ushers them out the door, trailing cracker crumbs behind them. The three of us stand, Topher tucking both halves of his sketchbook in his bag, zipping it tight, me shouldering the cheesecake again, taking my place in the back of the line as I follow the path of crackers off the bus, trying hard not to think about the thing Topher told me I was thinking, about Ms. Bixby and how he didn't feel about her. About crushes and living forever.

Cecelia Flowers had a crush on me once. I know because she gave me a folded piece of pink construction paper with a strawberry scratch-and-sniff sticker on the front and a message inside. The message read: *I lik you*.

We were five, so I didn't hold her spelling against her. Instead I told her I liked her back, in part because her pigtails reminded me of tornadoes, but mostly because it seemed like the polite thing to do and I was taught to use good manners. We held hands during recess that afternoon, and I let her borrow my favorite Transformers Optimus Prime pencil. The next day, I tried to hold her hand again and she stuck out her tongue at me. I assumed that meant she didn't like me anymore. I asked for my pencil back and she said she lost it.

She was my first and only girlfriend.

I understand Newton's laws of motion, and HTML, and basic trigonometry, but girls are confusing. They don't follow set patterns. They are an equation full of variables: $x + y = z$, where $x = q$ and y is constantly changing and z is whispering about you behind your back. I know because sometimes I catch girls whispering about me behind my back. I know because I overhear my sister on the phone complaining about all the kids at her school, even the ones she insists are her friends. Except she doesn't whisper, which is good, because otherwise it might be hard to hear, even with my ear pressed up against her door.

From my experience, boys are easier to get along with. We have basic needs: potato chips, video games, and movies where national landmarks blow up. That makes us compatible. Compatible means going together without conflict. Strawberries and whipped cream are compatible. Sunshine and swimming pools are compatible. Hydrogen and oxygen. Han Solo and Chewbacca. Cereal and milk.

My sister and I are not compatible. Only five years separate us, but she sometimes pretends it's more like twenty. Ever since I was born, I've literally felt her standing over me, starting when I was first learning how to walk and she followed right behind with both hands on either side, ready to catch me. When I was growing up, she quizzed me and corrected me, told me when I was coloring outside the lines, and pointed out words I didn't know. My parents thought it was sweet the way she hovered over me, tying my shoes, correcting my homework, saying, "No, Steven," the same way my mother did. They thought it was her way of showing affection, but I knew it was her way of letting me know which one of us was in charge. From those first moments stumbling through the kitchen as a toddler, unsure of my footing, wobbling and having her arms wrapped around me—I've never questioned it.

Dad says there are tigers and there are sheep. My sister is a tiger. I can only assume I'm a sheep. Not compatible.

My parents aren't either. That's why my mother spends the weekends in her garden, weeding the flower beds, tending to the strawberry plants, or just sitting on the patio looking at the sky. My father spends that time indoors. They are like vinegar and bleach: highly toxic when combined. It doesn't take much to trigger a reaction—an unemptied dishwasher, a random remark—and the shouting begins.

Topher knows. He's been over when my parents are arguing. That's usually when we sneak out the door and bike through the neighborhood. Sometimes we go back to his house. Sometimes we walk down to the pond and try to capture tadpoles, armed with nets and empty margarine tubs. That's where we were the day Topher swore off marriage forever.

My parents were arguing over the credit card bill. We could hear them from my bedroom. Christina popped her head in, giving me a look that was both annoyed and concerned. "I'm going to Nat's house to study. You dweebs want me to drop you off somewhere?"

I shook my head, hoping to leave it at that, but Topher said,

"We would, Chris, but I really doubt there's room for three on your broomstick." My sister drives a Subaru, actually, purchased for her sixteenth birthday. She also hates to be called Chris. She and Topher have that in common, at least.

"You're such a turd," Christina said, then looked at me. "You okay?"

I nodded again and she left, but not without trading glares with Topher again.

"How do you stand her?" Topher asked.

"Could be worse," I said. "The sand tiger shark eats its own siblings while it's still in the womb."

"Yeah, well, it's a good thing you two aren't twins," Topher said. Then he suggested we go hunt for tadpoles.

We grabbed our stuff, cut across several backyards, and walked down to the water's edge, avoiding the nettles and whacking at the cattails with sticks. Topher insisted they were sprouting swamp monsters, and I went along.

"They sure do fight a lot," Topher said, meaning my parents, not the swamp monsters, which just stood there and let us decapitate them, like cattails would.

"Just when they are in the same room," I joked.

Topher didn't laugh. He sometimes didn't get my humor. "People who get married are asking for it," he said.

It seemed like a strange comment, coming from him. In the

pictures on his living room walls, Topher's parents were always smiling. "Your parents get along," I said.

"Yeah, if you can somehow manage to get them together."

Topher's father worked most of the day; his mother worked most evenings. One of them was almost always at home whenever I came over, but seldom both. For the most part they stayed out of Topher's business. I envied that, though I think it bothered him.

I followed Topher down to the stones that crossed the creek and we found the least wobbly ones to stand on. It was too early in the year to find tadpoles. The water was still too cold, and the frogs were just now laying their eggs, but I didn't want to tell Topher that. He'd call me a know-it-all. It was better to just let him discover it himself. I stood beside him, crouching down, pretending to study the slowly rippling water.

"If movies teach us anything, it's that you absolutely should *not* get married," Topher continued. "Take *The Princess Bride*, for example."

We had just watched the movie two nights before. For the fourth time. It was one of Topher's favorites. He could quote most of it on cue. Whenever we had a stick-swordfight he would always start with his left hand, just so he could say he knew something I did not know, even though I knew exactly what he was going to say next. Topher poked at the water with a tree branch. "Sure Westley and Buttercup get together in the end, but they don't get married. They just kiss. That's it. The one time she even *thought* she was married, she tried to stab herself in the heart. What's that tell you?"

"That there's a shortage of perfect breasts in the world?" I ventured. I knew quoting the movie would make Topher smile, and it did.

"What it tells you is that love is okay, but marriage sucks."

That's the moral of the story, as Ms. Bixby would say. "What about the old couple? Miracle Max and the witch? They were married."

"Are you kidding me?" Topher said. "They *hated* each other. Called each other names. Chased each other around the hut. And not just them. Look at Anakin and Padmé. They got married, then he tried to choke her to death using the Force. Superman. Indiana Jones. Katniss Everdeen. All happily unmarried."

"Actually, Katniss gets married," I corrected. I'd read the entire Hunger Games trilogy over Christmas break. It was good, but I couldn't picture Christina ever taking my place in the reaping. Or maybe she would, just to show me up and score some brownie points with Mom and Dad.

"Epilogues don't count," Topher said. "They're just a way for authors to tack on a happy ending. She was probably still miserable." Topher dropped his stick in the water, and I watched the ripples work their way back to the edge. "Nothing here." He sighed and set his empty Blue Bonnet tub on the bank and collapsed next to it. I sat beside him. We watched the clouds for a moment; then Topher turned and put both hands on my shoulders.

"Promise me that you will never, ever, *e-ver* let me get married."

I couldn't tell if he was being serious or not. With Topher it was always a toss-up. "Okay," I said. Either way, it seemed like an easy enough promise to make. We were only twelve.

"No, man. You have to promise. No matter what I say. Promise me you won't let it happen. In fact, promise me you will never let any girl get between us, no matter what."

He let go of my shoulders and put out his hand. In the past he used to spit in his palm, until I confessed to him that I thought it was a little gross, but we still shook on our promises.

"I swear," I said.

And for half a second on the banks of a tadpole-less pond in early spring, Topher and I held hands.

The bus leaves us in another cloud of swirling dust and exhaust. We turn and cough and choke and find ourselves staring through the haze at the steaming sewer grates and dirty brick faces of downtown. The streets are dotted with broken bottles and yesterday's news crumpled and tumbling about. The mail collection box is banged up, paint peeling. I'm not about to go anywhere near it, mostly because of the dead cat thing. The walls in this part of downtown are scrawled with graffiti. I'm sure if I asked him, Topher would say that the red and white spray paint you see everywhere is actually ancient Elvish, and that the symbols point the way to some magical world, but this place looks anything but magical.

"The hospital is that way," Topher says, checking the map. "And the park's just beyond it. But the place we are looking for should be just down the street."

The place we are looking for is called What Ales You. It's one of fifteen liquor establishments we have to choose from; it just happens to be the one closest to this bus stop. Also it carries a wide selection of wine, at least according to its website. I've never been in a liquor store before. My parents don't drink, not even sake. They probably believe alcohol should be outlawed too, along with motorcycles and Halloween. Ms. Bixby, obviously, feels differently.

The cheesecake is pulling the straps down on my shoulders, which already feel bruised. I don't know why Brand can't carry it. His backpack's not much smaller than mine and he's the biggest of the three of us, big enough to call Trevor Cowly names to his face, at least.

"Tell me again how three sixth graders are going to acquire

a bottle of wine?" I ask, stepping around a shard of broken glass. This, after all, was the hazy part of Topher's plan, the one he was saving for later. It's certainly the only part we could get arrested for. As far as I know you don't have to be over twenty-one to buy a cheesecake, but a bottle of wine is different.

Topher shrugs. "It's simple," he says. "We just hang around outside the liquor store until we find someone who is willing to go in and buy it *for* us."

Brand turns and stands in front of Topher, blocking the sidewalk.

"That's it? *That's* your elaborate master plan?"

"What? They do it all the time in movies!" Topher protests.

"Not in any of the movies *I've* seen," Brand tells him.

It's true. I hate to side with Brand, but I don't remember Harry Potter bribing Hagrid to buy him a beer at the Leaky Cauldron.

"Well, what did you think we were going to do? Slip the bottle under our shirt and walk out with it? That's illegal!"

"So is purchasing alcohol for minors," I point out.

"But stealing is *more* illegal," Topher counters.

I shake my head. I'm fairly certain there aren't levels of this sort of thing. Something is either legal or it's not, and this is definitely not. But Topher is insistent. "It will work," he says. "All we need is a good story."

"Want to know what's *not* a good story?" Brand mumbles. "Three Fox Ridge sixth graders were arrested earlier today for attempting to illegally purchase a bottle of wine. Tune in at six for details."

Topher huffs impatiently. "Listen. Nobody said this would be easy. You knew that when you signed on. But you said yourself, if we are going to do this, we are going to do it right or not at all." He's looking at Brand, who nods. "Then you guys are just going to have to trust me on this one."

Topher smiles, and I'm sure it's supposed to be reassuring, but I can tell he's just as uncertain as I am.

The sign for What Ales You hangs over the front door. There is actually a drawing of a man holding a bottle of something with *X*s on the labels. He looks exceptionally happy, judging by the bubbles coming out of his mouth and ears. The walls of the building are cracked. There are bars on the windows. I feel the need to point this out. I think about the kinds of places that put bars on windows. Prisons. Insane asylums. Gun stores. I check the time on my phone. It is 11:18. If I were still in school, I would be in writer's workshop right now, finishing my story about the astrophysicist who won the Nobel Prize and called his less-accomplished, underachieving older sister to rub it in her face. Instead I'm here.

"Now what?" I ask.

"Now we just find the right mark," Topher says. I just assume *mark* means *person who is stupid enough to buy alcohol for minors.*

We all sit there on the corner, out of sight of the barred windows so that it doesn't look like we are loitering, and scan the scattered pockets of people crossing the streets. I point at a few passing pedestrians, but every time Topher shakes his head. *Not him,* he says. *Nope, him either. Nobody in a suit. Not her. Nobody with kids. Nope. Too old. Too young.* I point to one lady carrying several bags, moving slowly down the sidewalk. Topher looks at me funny.

"She's expecting a baby. Use a little common sense."

I glare at him. Common sense says I should be in room 213 right now, listening to Ms. Brownlee tell me about her pet dogs, rather than sitting on this curb, looking for someone willing to risk incarceration to help three kids get their hands on a bottle of booze.

"Hold up," Topher says. "What about that guy?"

He points to a man, midthirties, though I'm not a great judge of age, wearing torn jeans and a blue T-shirt. He wears scuffed cowboy boots, which makes me nervous. I don't really know anyone who wears cowboy boots. My father wouldn't be caught dead in cowboy boots. Unlike the other people, who either walk in pairs or have their ears pressed to their phones, this man looks like he's got nowhere in particular to be. I'm not sure that's a good thing.

"What about sparkling grape juice?" I ask. "We could pick some up at a grocery store." But Topher dismisses me with a wave of his hand.

"Nope. That is totally our guy," he says. "Just let me do the talking." We wait for him to get closer before Topher stands up and calls out. "Hey, mister. In the blue shirt. Over here."

For a moment the man in cowboy boots looks like he's just going to keep walking, and I'm relieved, but then Topher calls out again. "Excuse me, sir. You got a second?"

The man turns. "You talking to me?"

I shake my head vigorously, but Topher nods and takes a step closer so that he doesn't have to shout. Brand and I immediately flank him. Now that he's close enough, I can see the man has a large scar on his chin running almost up to his lip. Most likely from a prison knife fight or a barroom brawl, if I had to guess.

"Yeah. Listen," Topher says, "this is going to sound strange, I know, but I have a favor to ask. My mother's fortieth birthday is tomorrow, and I wanted to get her a bottle of wine. Except, as you can see, I'm not quite old enough."

The man has a tattoo running the length of his left arm. A green-and-gold dragon whose tail disappears into the sleeve of his shirt. I don't know anybody with tattoos either. Even Ms. Bixby's is make-believe.

"Not quite," the man repeats, fixing on Topher through squinting amber eyes. "What are you, ten?"

"Thirteen," Topher says, feeling the need to embellish everything. "So like I said, her birthday's tomorrow, and we have money. We just need some assistance in the, um . . . acquisitions department."

The man in the blue shirt looks at each of us—I can feel his eyes on me—but I can't bring myself to look back. "Why don't ya ask your dad to get it for you?"

"He's dead," Topher says without missing a beat. "Plane crash. Six years ago. On his way home from a dental conference in Albuquerque."

I can, however, look at Topher, who somehow says this all with a straight face. His father's an accountant.

"Albuquerque?" the man echoes, clearly not buying it.

"New Mexico," I interject, trying to be helpful. Topher nudges me with his elbow. The man with the dragon tattoo shakes his head.

"Just get her some flowers, boys," he says.

He turns and starts to walk off, and I take a deep breath, but then Topher says, "Wait," and reaches out for the guy, which is a terrible idea. The man stops.

"All right," Topher says. "That's not at all true, what I just said about my mom. It's not for her. We really need the bottle of wine for our teacher, who is sick in the hospital battling pancreatic cancer. She's leaving tomorrow for Boston, and we've skipped school just to go see her because they canceled the school party we were supposed to have and we didn't get a chance to say good-bye." He says it all in one breath, as if he was afraid he'd never get it all out otherwise.

The man stops to consider it. Then shakes his head. "Your first story was better," he says. He doesn't walk away, though. Instead he eyes all three of us in turn. I make the mistake of making eye contact this time. His eyes look almost like golden coins with black holes in the middle.

"You say you got money?" he asks, still looking at me. I nod. Swallow. Nod some more. He snaps his fingers impatiently, and I dig in my pockets for the bills left over from the bakery. Topher does the same, finding the ten that Brand gave back to him. "Twenty-five bucks." The man coughs. "That's it? That's everything?"

"Why? Is twenty-five not enough? We only need one bottle," Topher says.

Dragon Man scratches the scruff on his chin. He's got scabs on his knuckles. Knife fights *and* fistfights probably. "All right. Here's the deal: You get ten to spend on your dying mother's bottle of birthday wine. The rest I keep. Understood?"

We all look at each other. I'm not sure what the going rate is for bribing adults to break the law for you. I'm also not sure if ten dollars is enough to buy a bottle of wine that will complement a fifty-dollar cheesecake. I kind of doubt it, but we aren't in a position to negotiate. Topher nods and I nod along with him. Brand doesn't move.

"All right," the man says. "Give me the cash. You just wait out here."

I start to hand over the bills, but Brand stops me, grabbing my wrist. "No," he says.

"Excuse me?" the man says.

I try to step on Brand's foot, to let him know that I don't think arguing with this tattooed stranger is a great idea, but he ignores me.

"No. We have to go in with you. We have to pick it out ourselves. It has to be perfect."

For some reason, this makes the man snort, and the snorting makes his face turn ugly, his mouth screwed up at the corners. "The perfect ten-dollar bottle of wine. All right, then," he says. "We all go. But if anyone asks, I'm yours and yours dad." He points to Topher and Brand. "And you," he says, pointing to me last, "were adopted from China."

"I'm Japanese," I tell him, then shut my mouth and stare

again at my shoes. The man takes the cash from Topher and me and folds it together, stuffing it in the back pocket of his jeans. Then he starts toward the door of What Ales You.

Topher turns to me and grins. He obviously wants me to tell him what a genius he is. To admit that he was right. Instead I watch as Brand hesitantly reaches out and tugs on the back of the man's blue T-shirt again.

"What's your name?" Brand asks. "What do we call you?"

The man stops to think. "You can just call me George," he says. "George Nelson."

What Ales You is a lot like Alexander's, except substitute bottles for books and brown stains on the floor for dust on the shelves. And the man standing behind the counter looks nothing like Mr. Alexander. For starters, he's big, almost Eduardo sized. He's dressed in a red polo shirt that's way too tight around his thick neck. He's reading a magazine about baseball. He looks up and nods at George Nelson, then frowns when he sees the three of us in tow.

"All right, kids," George tells us, loud enough that even people in the next building over could probably hear. "Go pick out a nice, *inexpensive* bottle of wine for your mother." He turns to the man behind the register. "It's her birthday tomorrow. The boys are making her dinner."

"That's nice," the giant black man behind the register says without conviction, then buries himself back in his magazine. I take one more look at the bars on the windows and follow Brand down the middle aisle, leaving our chaperone standing on the end.

"Let's hurry," I say. "I don't want to be here any longer than we have to."

"What are we even looking for?" Brand asks as we scan the legions of long-necked bottles that comprise the wine section.

"I don't know jack about this stuff," Topher says.

Ms. Bixby didn't say what kind of wine she liked. It's probably not the sort of conversation you get into with sixth graders. I get out my phone, thanking my parents for splurging on unlimited data. The warning says my battery is only at eight percent, but this is important. Behind us, George Nelson has started wandering the aisles, picking up bottles of brown liquid and eyeing them carefully. Every second that we are in this place makes me more anxious. The huge man behind the counter peers at us occasionally from over the top of his magazine. The Cubs have a great shot at winning their division this year, according to the cover.

"Let's just get this one," Brand says, holding up a bottle of something called Zinfandel. "It says it's white. The cheesecake is white. It matches."

"I don't think it works that way," Topher counters. He looks at me, and I Google white-chocolate raspberry cheesecake and wine. Turns out I'm not the first person to want to know. It's a question of compatibility. So many things are.

"Do you see a Moscato or a Brachetto anywhere?" I say, hoping I'm pronouncing them right. We all scan the shelves.

"There's this one. Robert Mondavi Napa Moscato d'Oro," Topher says.

"Did you say 'da Oreo'?"

"D'Oro. It has little leafy symbols all over it."

"They all have leaves on them," I point out.

"This one's called Bo-de-gas-val-de-vid-ver-de-jo-con-de-sa-ee-lo," Brand says, as if he's singing a scale. "I think."

"Too long. What about Asti spumante? I've actually heard of that, and it's only six bucks," Topher suggests.

I thought spumante was a kind of ice cream. My parents ordered it for me at an Italian restaurant once. I had to eat around the chunks of cherry.

"If it's only six bucks, it's no good," Brand says. Behind us, George Nelson is walking up and down the aisle by the door.

"Since when did you become a wine connoisseur?" Topher looks at me. "What does it say about this one?" He holds up a bottle with another long Italian-looking name. I punch it into my phone and find a website full of wine descriptions. I read it out loud, keeping my voice at a whisper.

"'Mild citrus and pear aromas combine with floral notes of rose, honey, and candied violets to create an intense yet delicate profile. Finishes fresh with just a hint of ginger.'"

"Sounds disgusting," Brand says.

"Yeah," Topher concurs, putting it back. "How about this one?" We all stand around my phone as I type it in.

"'Black currant, cocoa, violet and smoky aromas, complemented by undertones of raspberry and loam, culminates in a silky and prolonged finish.'"

"God. Gross. Who *drinks* this stuff?"

"And what the heck is loam?" Brand wants to know. I start to look that up too, but Topher interrupts me.

"Here. This one is exactly ten bucks and I can pronounce it." He holds up a bottle of wine called Woop Woop. Brand shakes his head.

"'Look, Ms. Bixby, we got you a bottle of Woop Woop'? Let's try to find something that sounds a little classy at least," he says. "Just get the first one. The one without the loam."

As Topher and Brand stand there arguing, I follow a whim and type the name George Nelson into my phone. There are no George Nelsons who live nearby, at least according to the social networking sites or the online white pages. I do learn that George Nelson was the name of a famous American furniture designer. He invented the family room—which is basically just the room with the biggest TV.

George Nelson was also the nickname of one of the most infamous bank robbers and known murderers in American history.

I put the phone down. Brand and Topher are debating what a candied violet might taste like, holding bottles in each hand. "Hey, guys," I whisper, waving the phone at them. "Guys. I think I found something."

Suddenly the guy behind the counter calls out to us.

"Boys?"

We all turn, and he points to the door.

"Your *dad* just took off without you."

Topher

GEORGE NELSON IS GONE. AND ALL OF OUR CASH with him.

Guess I'm probably not the first person in history to say that.

We are out the door in seconds, the bottles of wine set totteringly back on their shelf. Behind me I can hear the guy from What Ales You yelling at us—words that Brand would have to make up safer ones to replace—but we don't stick around to hear the whole thing. Something about us never stepping foot in his store again, I think. And a word about our mothers.

Outside now. Look left. Right. Scan the area. Blue shirt. Torn jeans. Black hair. There. On the corner. The thief looks back at us, then takes off down the street, moving fast.

"There he is! After him!"

I've always wanted to say that.

Brand is first, me right behind, Steve bringing up the rear, saying something about a backpack and bouncing and heavy, but I just yell for him to keep up. George Nelson is getting away. I catch up to Brand and huff out the play-by-play.

"Suspect is a Caucasian male. Five nine. One hundred eighty pounds. Fleeing on foot. Last seen at the intersection of whatever street we are running down and whatever street we are about to turn onto." I wait for Brand to contribute something, ask if he's armed and dangerous maybe, if we should proceed with caution, but instead he just adds that the suspect is a freaking jerk. He's so angry he can't even come up with his own word.

We tear around the corner like zombies are chasing us, though the only one behind us is Steve, who already seems on the verge of collapse. Up ahead, George Nelson runs into the street, chancing another glance behind him as he launches himself into the intersection. A car screeches to a halt, tires peeling, and George slams into it, catching the bumper with his knee. He spins once but keeps on running, causing more screeching and honking. The driver of the car that nearly flattened him rolls down his window and starts cursing as Brand and I catapult ourselves into the street. You don't look both ways when you're chasing the bad guy.

Brand circles around the car that nearly ran over the thief, but on an impulse I put both hands on the hood and more or less vault over the front of it. It's not the same as jumping on the thing and leaping from the top of one car to the next, which is what I *want* to do, but it's as close as I'm going to get. The guy in the car yells something about my mother, too, and lays on his horn. As we make it to the sidewalk I glance behind me to see Steve on the pavement at the edge of the intersection, leaning against a mailbox, waving us on.

"You guys . . . go on . . . without me," he yells. Then he collapses, legs pretzled beneath him.

"Man down!" I say, but Brand doesn't stop. He can't stop. George Nelson is still at least thirty yards ahead of us. We fly past grimacing pedestrians. I'm surprised at how fast Brand is; it takes everything I've got to keep up with him. We cross in front of bars and restaurants, underneath the forest-green awnings of old hotels. The perp is less than fifty feet away now. We are gaining on him. The loose gravel kicks up from my shoes. My backpack pistons up and down with each step. Somebody I nearly run into tells me to watch it. I apologize, even though heroes never apologize. They are too busy saving the day. "We're catching up," I yell at Brand.

Suddenly I feel a sharp pain in my side. I've been shot, obviously. Sniper on the roof, covering the criminal's escape. I reach down under my rib cage and hitch a breath.

No blood. No bullet. Just a cramp. I'm not used to running this much. I leave my hand pressed against my side and keep running. From somewhere far away I'm almost positive I hear helicopter blades. Or it could just be the sound of a car engine.

Up the street, the perp glances backward and sees that we are right behind him. He knocks over a metal trash can, tipping it onto the middle of the sidewalk with a reverberating *gong*. It's a classic move, I think. It's exactly what I would have done.

Brand simply goes around the trash can, just like he did the car. Practical.

I'm not Brand.

I'm James Bond. I'm Jason Bourne. I'm Super-freaking-Mario come to life. I'm the caped crusader, sans cape. I don't go around, I go over. I leap. I practically fly.

I catch the edge of the aluminum can with my back foot.

I fall, twisting, my front foot turning underneath me as I try to catch myself.

I hit the sidewalk hard, sprawled out, chin scraped, backpack catapulting up over my head. I cry out, completely un-007-like.

A few feet away, Brand hears my cry of pain and stops, looks back at me, then up at George Nelson, who is turning another corner.

"Go," I wince, holding my chin with one hand, reaching for my foot with the other. "I'm all right."

But he can see I'm not all right. My ankle screams. I can feel it pulsing. I can't even begin to try and move my foot, let alone stand. Maybe it's broken or maybe it's just sprained, but it shoots needles of pain up my leg. I try to crawl. I close my eyes and will myself to my knees. *Get on your feet. What kind of caped crusader are you?* I scrabble upward, but the instant I put weight on my left foot, I tumble right back down, whole leg throbbing, blood pounding in my ears. The whole city swirls around me. I close my eyes.

This is so stupid. It was a stupid idea, giving our money to some total stranger. I bite down on my lower lip and pound the sidewalk with my fist, which only serves to make it hurt as well. Then I feel a pair of hands underneath my sweaty armpits.

"Come on, soldier," Brand says.

Brand lifts me and pulls one of my arms over his shoulder, propping me up. He half carries, half drags me past the bags of trash over to a nearby bench, then bends down to inspect my ankle. I scan the street ahead of us. George Nelson is nowhere to be seen now. We've lost him. And our twenty-five bucks. Our mission is officially gefragt.

I wince as Brand pokes at my ankle, gingerly peels down my sock. "He got away," I tell him.

"Yeah," Brand says, unlacing my shoe and carefully slipping it off.

"He's got our money."

"Yeah," Brand says again, gently moving my foot by fractions of an inch, watching my face to see how much it hurts. I try not to show him. He slowly moves my foot in a circle and I suck in a breath and scrunch my eyes, blinking back tears. Heroes don't cry. The pain is shifting from a butcher-knife stabbing to a hammer-blow aching.

"I don't think it's broken," Brand sighs. "Probably just twisted it."

I look back at the metal trash can lying impertinently in the middle of the sidewalk. "I guess I shouldn't have tried to jump it."

Brand nods. "You're not Superman, you know."

I look away. I know that. Of course I know that.

I just don't need to hear it from him.

It's true I sometimes imagine my life is different. That I'm somebody else. Maybe more than sometimes. But I'm not the only one around who makes stuff up.

Adults are always telling you you can be whatever you want when you grow up, but they don't mean it. They don't believe it. They just want *you* to believe it. It's a fairy tale. Like the tooth fairy. Something they tell you that gets you excited about something not so fantastic. If you think about it, it's pretty gross—your teeth just falling out of your head, leaving bloody sockets for your tongue to poke through. But the story makes it better and the dollar makes it worth it.

Then one afternoon you sneak into their bedroom and open the drawer of their nightstand, looking for the DS that they confiscated as punishment for your jumping on the roof of the car again, and you find the little Tupperware full of a dozen jagged pearls, caked brown with your own dried blood, your name written in black Sharpie across a piece of Scotch tape, and you stare at them for a moment in disbelief, wondering if maybe they aren't what you think they are. Maybe they are somebody else's teeth. They can't be yours, because *your* teeth are in Neverland. Or Toothtopia. Or outer space. Or wherever kleptomaniac fairies live.

So you confront them, your lying, scheming parents. Over breakfast, you ask your mom about the tooth fairy: where she lives, what she does during the day, how she manages to collect so many teeth each night, and how come some kids' teeth (like Robbie Dinkler's) are worth five bucks when yours only fetch a dollar apiece. And you see her search for some explanation that is at once both magical and believable, but you know she's just making it up as she goes.

It's the same with all grown-ups. They tell you what they think you want to hear and let life tell you the truth later. You can be an astronaut or the president of the United States or second baseman for the White Sox, but you can't really because you hate math, aren't rich, and can't even hit the ball. It's just another fairy tale. So when your next tooth falls out, you figure you'll just ask them if they'd like to keep it or throw it away, because you're not buying it anymore.

Or maybe not. Maybe you won't tell them. Maybe you'll still put your teeth under your pillow.

Because sometimes it's better to believe in the impossible. To believe you are a secret agent or a private detective or a superhero and not just a kid with freckled cheeks and gangly arms who is too clumsy to leap a tipped-over garbage can in a single bound.

Until you are lying in the middle of the sidewalk, with a throbbing ankle and bloody chin, wishing you hadn't even tried.

Brand goes back for Steve. It takes longer than I thought it would. I sit and wait on the bench and poke tentatively at my already swollen ankle. It's not as bad as I first thought. I don't think it will need to be amputated. Unfortunately, there won't even be a scar to show off. But it still hurts like a mother whenever I try to move it.

When I see the two of them coming up the street, I know something is wrong. Not just that George Nelson has run off with our cash. Something else. Brand looks mad enough to punch through brick walls. Steve hangs his head in shame. He's carrying his backpack in his arms, cradling it like an infant.

"Show him," Brand says when they make it to my spot, my foot propped on my own backpack with the book for Ms. B. inside.

"Show me what?"

Steve reluctantly kneels down and opens his pack. I know what's coming. I can see the state of the white box, its corners crunched, one side caved in. He opens the lid.

There sits twenty-five bucks' worth of heaven, except it looks like it's been through hell. Michelle's formerly divine white-chocolate raspberry supreme cheesecake now looks like a giant, heaping turd of white and red Play-Doh mixed together. I'm guessing the heat and the running caused it to soften and then be repeatedly smashed into the sides of the box, taking a beating with every step. It's a deformed monster of a dessert now. The hunchback of cheesecakes. I bet it still tastes okay, but I'm not sure I'd be the first to try it. "It's lumpy," I say. Kind of like my ankle.

"It's ruined," Brand says. "The whole thing."

He doesn't look at me when he says this, but I know that it's somehow my fault; I know that's what he means. Even though this was all his idea to begin with. Even though Steve was the one carrying the cake. It's still my fault. Without me there wouldn't have been a George Nelson. Without the high-speed chase, we'd still have our money, and our cheesecake would still look more like a wheel than a mound of bloody mashed potatoes. I stare at it, sitting in its half-collapsed cardboard container. It looks nothing like the cakes sitting behind the glass back at the store.

"It's just a cake," Steve replies, closing the lid and taking a seat beside me.

"An expensive cake," I say.

Brand looks across the street. I think maybe he's looking for George Nelson still, but his eyes are glazed over, like he no longer recognizes where we are. Steve somehow wrangles the box back into his backpack, though at this point it seems we might just as well toss the whole thing in the trash. "So now what?" he asks timidly.

Even after all this, he's still looking at me for a plan. I don't know what to tell him. We've got three dollars in change, a twisted ankle, and a ruined cake. It's not as if we can run to the cops. *Excuse me, officer, but you won't believe this—the guy who we bribed to buy us a bottle of wine ran off with our money.* I can already hear the laughter. And I can't imagine Brand could work the same magic with the guy at What Ales You that he did on Eduardo and get us a free bottle, not after what that man said about our mothers. So then where do we go from here? That's what Steve wants to know. "What do you think?" I ask back.

"Well, I guess we could still do it," Steve suggests. "Go to the hospital, I mean. To visit Ms. Bixby. While we're there, you could have your ankle looked at."

I give him a dirty look. I can't help it. "Sure. That's a great idea. Let's go to the emergency room and have the nurse call my parents so I can explain how we skipped school to come downtown and I broke my ankle chasing the guy who stole all our money. Then we can call *your* parents and tell them the same thing."

As soon as I say it, I feel bad. Steve's shoulders slump, chin digging into his chest. The thought of calling his parents terrifies him. He draws something in the gravel with his toe. "I'm just saying, it really doesn't matter what it *looks* like. What matters is that we tried. Right?"

Standing beside us, Brand takes one more look at Steve's backpack, then down the street where George Nelson disappeared. It looks like he's holding his breath; his face turns red for a moment.

"It's *not* right," he says.

He turns his back to us and starts walking. But he's not headed in the direction of What Ales You or even the direction of the hospital.

He's headed back toward the bus stop.

"Hold up. Where are you going?" Steve calls out, but Brand doesn't answer. And he doesn't stop either. I try to stand, still holding my left shoe in my hand. I make it three hobbling steps before Steve is beside me, propping me up.

162

"Brand, hold on," I call after him. "Seriously. Where *are* you going?"

"I'm going home," Brand calls back angrily.

I start to limp after him, using Steve as my crutch. Then Steve mutters a "Christ," which he almost never does, and says something about the cake and leaves me hopping on one foot and I feel like I'm about to topple over. I put my weight down on the swollen ankle, take a tentative step, though it's more of a skip. Another bolt of pain shoots up my shin. Behind me Steve is grabbing his pack with the mutilated cake. I call out for Brand to stop again, except I have to yell this time—that's how far he's gotten already. "Seriously, man, hold up!"

Brand freezes, his back still to us, and I gingerly take a few more steps. Steve once again is beside me, pulling one of my arms around his shoulders. When we are only a few feet away, Brand turns around and I can see that his cheeks are smeared wet with tears. I don't think I've ever seen him cry before.

"You don't get it," he says, nearly shouting back at us. "It's over. We screwed up."

"It's just a cake," I say under my breath. It's the only thing I can think of to say.

Brand shakes his head. "No. Not just the cake. It was a stupid idea. All of it. It was stupid and pointless and a complete waste of time, because there was nothing—*nothing* we could do

163

that would make the slightest bit of difference. Not this!" he says, reaching over and practically wrenching the backpack off Steve's shoulders. "Not the wine or the stupid music or your stupid book. You can't cure cancer with a freakin' cheesecake!"

He stands there for a moment facing us, daring us, it seems, to come up with something, anything to prove him wrong. I open my mouth, but my throat is dry and nothing comes out. Brand turns and continues down the sidewalk. I totter after him.

"Brand, wait."

"For what?" he says, spinning to face us. "For things to get better? Because they don't. Ever. They just get worse. The guy took our money. It's gone. You're limping. The cake is ruined. We barely have enough cash to get back. The plan is shot. If you two want to go, go. But I can't do it. I'm done. I'm going home."

Steve and I look at each other.

"So that's it?" I ask. "All that talk about *doing* something? About how she deserved something better?"

"She does deserve something better," Brand shouts.

"And now you just want to quit?"

Brand's eyes narrow and I know I've pushed him too far. He points to me. "You can't say that. You don't understand. This was the *one* day, my one chance, and now . . ." He doesn't finish the thought, though, just wipes his nose on his sleeve

164

and repeats, "You don't understand," before turning and walking away again.

"What about Ms. Bixby?" I call out to his back. "What about Ms. Bixby?" I call again, even louder.

But I get no answer.

About Ms. Bixby.

She always wanted to be a magician. She told me that once.

She told the whole class, in fact. We had just started reading *The Hobbit* and asked her who her favorite character was. She said, "Are you kidding? Gandalf. Who else *could* it be?"

And then she told us the story of how her grandmother almost murdered her gerbil.

She wanted to be a magician, but not just some street magician pulling cards from sleeves or making a little red ball disappear. She wanted to be a master illusionist, like David Copperfield or Lance Burton. The kind who can make anything vanish before your very eyes—people, buildings, you name it. As a kid she pored over dog-eared magic books checked out of the library. She kept a deck of cards in her backpack, put on nickel shows for her parents and friends, and dazzled the lunch ladies by pulling pennies from their hairnets. Then one day she decided she was ready to try one of the classics: the pull-a-rabbit-from-a-hat trick.

She had an oversize top hat made of thin plastic and lined with black felt, a Christmas present that was much too big to fit on her head but plenty large enough to tuck a rabbit into, complete with a false bottom good for stashing anything from colorful scarfs to cottontails. What she didn't have was the rabbit. So she asked her parents.

What she got was gerbils. Two of them. She named them Siegfried and Roy. She practiced with them daily, stuffing them in the hat and waving her plastic wand, then reaching in and grabbing hold of the two gerbils to imaginary applause. When she felt she had the trick down, she invited her friends and family, directed them to the living room, and charged them each a quarter admission.

All was going well. She ran through her gamut of card and coin tricks and even managed to pull a ribbon out of her mother's nose. Then it was time for the grand finale. Twenty minutes before, she had done all the prep work, choosing Roy because he was the least jittery of the pair. She secreted him away in the hat's trick bottom, complete with small holes for air and cushioned with extra black cloth so that he wouldn't get jostled during the performance. Now, with the crowd enthralled and her father videotaping, young Maggie Bixby pulled out her hat, quickly showed that there was nothing in it, and reached inside.

Except, as she told our class, there was *really* nothing in it.

In the time it had taken her to do three card tricks and pull a ribbon from her mom's nostril, Roy had chewed a hole through both the felt lining and the outer plastic shell. The moment she reached into the hat, Roy launched himself from the table and belly flopped onto the carpet, where he proceeded to terrorize the audience, particularly Ms. Bixby's grandmother, who shrieked, "Rat!" and tried to stomp the life out of him. The young magician barely managed to save her furry assistant, throwing herself into the fray and grabbing him by his tail.

It was, as she told the class, a disaster. She was devastated. Ten-year-old Maggie Bixby took one look into her father's camera and then ran to her room, hot tears on her cheeks.

"Roy was okay, though, right?" Allison Sydner asked after Ms. Bixby told the story. "I mean, he didn't get hurt, did he?"

Roy was fine, Ms. Bixby said, but she never tried the trick again. In fact, from that point on, she said, she more or less gave up on her dream of being a professional magician. Then, in typical Bixby fashion, she asked us what the moral of the story was.

"A gerbil is not a rabbit," Rebecca Roudabush guessed, earning her a "True" from Ms. B.

"Don't save your best trick till the very end," Mason Foster offered.

"People shouldn't pull *anything* out of other people's noses," Steve said, looking right at Brand. But Brand had a different moral.

"There's no such thing as magic," he said without even being called on.

At this Ms. Bixby frowned. "Maybe," she said. "Or maybe I should have tried harder. 'The moment you doubt whether you can fly, you cease forever to be able to do it.'"

Ms. B. smiled at the class then, though I had a feeling the smile was meant mostly for Brand. Sometimes when Ms. Bixby smiled at you, you had the feeling she'd been saving it just for you, that the smile actually had your name on it, that she could read your mind and knew you needed that smile more than anyone else in the room. Then she closed *The Hobbit*, promising we'd get back to it later, stood up, and set it in her empty chair.

Brand

HE FELL. AND IT RUINED EVERYTHING.

The second fall was worse than the first. The first wasn't his fault. The first was an accident. Blame the scaffold. Blame the faulty bolts holding it together. Blame God, maybe, if that's your thing, but I couldn't blame Dad. Not for that one.

The second fall was much slower, but somehow, to me at least, it hurt a whole lot more. Unlike the first fall that broke his spine, my dad's other fall—the downward spiral that came after—was harder to measure, but I sensed it happening, every day.

The first few months back at home were right out of daytime talk shows or reality TV. Inspirational moments with Oprah or whatever. There were interviews with the paper, Dad and me on the local news, even a visit from last year's Miss Decatur County, who kissed my father on the cheek for the cameras. Neighbors we'd never bothered to get to know left casseroles on our doorstep, like peace offerings. The phone rang off the hook with well-wishers. Reverend Galbraeth of the local Methodist church stopped by for a visit, which was funny, since my father hadn't stepped foot in a church since he was baptized. The construction company my father worked for sent fresh flowers every day for a week. A local auto body shop volunteered to put a hand-controlled accelerator/braking system in our car so that Dad could still drive even without the use of his legs. The insurance company consoled us with warm smiles and promises of monthly direct deposits.

The medicine chest was stuffed.

Dad took it all in stride (ba-da-bum-*chi*). He was pretty gracious. He forgave the construction company for making him a paraplegic (though not legally, of course—legally they were still very much to blame). He ate the casseroles and took all the medicines in their proper dosages, and did his physical therapy. He made progress, recovering a little function in his legs. The doctors were pleased, full of cautious smiles and hearty handshakes. There was a good chance, with a lot more physical therapy and rehabilitation, that Abe Walker would get the use of his legs back.

It would have made a great headline for the local section of the paper: Walker Walks Again.

Then it all started to slide. The casseroles dwindled. The news reporters found something else to talk about—the women who rescued the drowning puppies, the couple with sextuplets. Appointments were missed. Some of the medications were ignored. Others were taken a little more regularly than they should have been. The voice mail filled up with doctor's office reminders.

My father adapted to his new life. We put a minifridge next to the recliner, itself sitting next to the wheelchair. Our cable plan was upgraded to add more channels. The medicine chest got moved to a big white plastic basket by the fridge.

Days passed. Then weeks. Then months. The bills got paid through direct withdrawals. The television stayed on for twenty-four hours. I started doing everything around the house. I learned how to use the stove, burning myself only once, bad enough to leave a scar on my hand. I learned how to do laundry, folding the sheets the best I could, though I only changed them on my bed—Dad slept in his chair most nights. Some weeks things didn't get done: scrubbing the toilets, taking out the recycling, writing my school science report. I changed the lightbulbs in the three rooms we used. The insurance company deposited the checks. I did the dishes. Dad sat and watched the History channel. Deposit, wash, sit, watch, withdrawal. Repeat.

For a while I tried. I asked him if he wanted to go out. I told him I would help him with the walker or even push him in the chair. We could drive to the movies or just go to the pond and let the fish steal our worms. We wouldn't have to go far. Wouldn't even have to see anyone if he didn't want to—Dad wasn't exactly comfortable around people, the way they kept looking at his legs, like they were afraid they'd leap up and bite them or something. It could just be the two of us.

"Maybe later," he said.

Maybe later came and went.

On Meet the Teacher Night this year I walked myself to school. I sat with Topher and his parents, and they bought me a Fox Ridge Wildcats bumper sticker to put on our car that never moved. We ate cheap hot dogs and cookies in the cafeteria. That night Ms. Bixby introduced herself to me for the first time. She was wearing a crimpy yellow dress that sounded like sandpaper scratching when she walked, and her band of pink hair had been tamed with a clip. She shook my hand and asked me if I was there by myself. I said yes.

She said that was all right. That she would help me. That if I needed anything at all, to just ask her.

For the record, I never did. Ask her, that is. She volunteered.

For the record, it was all her idea.

✦ ✦ ✦

I should have come alone.

That's all I can think as we board the bus. That if I had just come by myself, it wouldn't matter whether I went through with it or not. Nobody would know. Not even Ms. Bixby. But the truth is, I was scared. Afraid of what she would think if it was just me. That she would get the wrong idea. Scared of what she would look like. Scared that she might be hooked up to all those machines, tubes in her arms, snaked up to her nostrils, pulsing, beeping, wheezing. Scared that she would look like my father right after the accident, practically bolted to his bed, unable to move for fear of damaging his spine any further, drinking ice water through chapped lips, blinking at me through scared, swollen eyes, wanting to know *what happened*.

Then I remembered what she told us. About how she would spend her last day. And I thought: This is it. This will be perfect. We can *make it* perfect. But I couldn't do it by myself.

I knew as soon as I told them my idea that Topher would go for it. It was an adventure, and even if it wasn't, he would turn it into one. And if he was in, Steve was in, because if I had learned anything about the two of them, it was that Steve worshipped Topher the same way Topher worshipped every comic book hero he'd ever met. Besides, I knew Ms. Bixby meant something to them too, though it wasn't the same. It couldn't possibly be the same.

They didn't understand why I needed to go, but that wasn't their fault. I never bothered to explain. Not just about Ms. Bixby, but all of it. Why I'm always asking if I can come over to their houses on the weekends instead of the other way around. Why I always need a ride if we go somewhere. Why I sometimes punch the walls at school hard enough to skin my knuckles. I never bothered to explain why I needed to see her so bad.

Of course it doesn't matter now.

We get on the bus that will take us back to school, Steve helping Topher up the steps. It's hard to tell how much his ankle hurts him—he can be pretty melodramatic—but I can tell it's swollen. He could probably use an ice pack and some painkillers. If he were at my house, he'd be set. One oxycodone would do it. My father wouldn't miss it; he's got a three-month supply. Topher takes an empty seat and motions for Steve to sit next to him. He's mad at me. Topher. For yelling at him. For giving up. Maybe even about the sketchbook still. Steve doesn't seem angry. He just looks worried, like always. I sit in the empty seat across from them but scoot all the way over, leaving room for an imaginary fourth person between us. The fourth musketeer maybe, but really I just need some space.

Steve gets on his phone, mutters something about the battery nearly being dead, then shuts it off and stuffs it back in his pocket. Without it, his hands don't seem to know what to do, so they start fiddling with the zipper on his backpack. I shift and look out the window, press my face up against it. My cheeks are hot and wet and the glass is cool, and I can feel the vibrations of the bus's engines rattle my teeth. It's quiet, save for the bus's rumble. Nobody on the bus is talking. That's absolutely fine. I'm used to the quiet. I've learned to cope without conversation. Even on those Friday evenings with Ms. Bixby there would sometimes be stretches of silence, riding in her car, watching the sky change colors and thinking that I wasn't ready to go home, even though I knew I had to.

Those days with her just felt different. They felt better. It felt like I was in some magical space where time stood still, where nothing bad could happen. They were almost perfect.

That's what today was supposed to be. That's what hurts so much.

Across the aisle by the opposite window, Topher leans his head back. He glances over at me, as if confirming that I'm still there, then looks straight ahead. "Who do you think would win in a fight? Wolverine or Captain America?" he says.

He's not talking to either of us in particular. He's just throwing it out there. Cutting the silence. Filling the space. I keep my head pressed to the window, making wishes on passing cars.

"I mean Wolverine's claws could probably just cut right

through Cap's shield, wouldn't you think?" he adds.

I don't respond. I *won't* respond. But naturally, Steve takes the bait. "Doubtful. Wolverine's claws are made out of adamantium. Captain America's shield is made out of *proto*-adamantium, which is better than regular adamantium."

This is the reason you will never have a girlfriend, I think, but I wouldn't say that to Steve. He doesn't seem all that interested in girls anyways.

"Yes," Topher says, still looking at the seat in front of him, "but you're forgetting the awesome factor. Captain America's a goody-two-shoes dweeb with goofy little wings on his head that don't even let him fly. Wolverine has killer sideburns *and* a better backstory. Wolvie beats him on coolness alone."

"Superheroes are not traditionally rated on their coolness," Steve says.

"Everyone is rated on their coolness," Topher replies. "What about Thor versus Cap?"

"Thor's a god," Steve replies. "He can beat up anybody."

"So does that mean he could beat up Jesus?" Topher presses.

I laugh. Okay, I don't really laugh, but I sort of snort at least. Enough that Topher knows I'm listening. He doesn't look at me still, but he smiles. "I don't think Jesus and Thor would even fight," Steve says. "That's not Jesus's style." Topher nods, conceding the point.

Part of me wants to ignore them, to keep looking out the window, to shut myself out and be alone, but I can't help it. Topher has somehow suckered me in too. "What if Jesus had Thor's hammer? He was a carpenter, right."

Both of them twist around to look at me, a little surprised that I joined the conversation after storming off and shouting at them before. Steve shakes his head.

"Theologically speaking, billions of people currently believe in Jesus, and probably only a handful still worship Thor. Advantage Jesus."

I don't argue. Steve goes to Mass every Sunday, so he probably knows better. Dad had an entire church come to the house once, the whole congregation showing up in a long white bus. It was right after the accident. They stood on our front lawn and sang a song called "Rise Up!" I don't think they were being ironic. They really thought he might do it.

"All right. I've got one," Steve says. "Legolas versus Hawkeye."

"Unfair comparison," Topher says. "Legolas is immortal."

"Not if you stick him full of arrows, he isn't," Steve counters. "Especially those ones Hawkeye has that explode. You'd have little elf chunks flying everywhere."

"Elf chunks." For some reason I find this funny too.

"Doesn't matter," Topher says. "Legolas is eternal. He

doesn't get old. He doesn't get sick. Even if you kill him, his spirit comes back, like Obi-Wan Kenobi. He will live forever, no matter what."

As soon as he says it, Topher frowns. Steve pushes his glasses back up his nose.

A long silence follows, and I look back out the window and up at the sky. The clouds have cleared out now, making room for endless waves of blue. I wonder what it is about clouds that makes people think of heaven. Maybe just they are in the way, so there must be something else up there.

Suddenly there is a gurgled growl coming from Steve, loud enough for me to hear from across the aisle. "Dude. Was that you?" Topher asks.

"I haven't eaten since breakfast. It's already past noon," Steve says, holding his stomach with both hands like he's afraid it's going to pop out and go looking for food on its own.

"I guess we didn't think about lunch," Topher says. Then he turns and looks down at the floorboards, and I realize what he's looking at. Steve's backpack and the bent white box stuffed inside.

"Twenty-five dollars is a lot to waste," Steve says. "I mean— if nobody else is going to eat it." He means Ms. Bixby.

They both look at me. Because I paid the most for it. Or because the whole thing was my idea. The whole cake. The whole everything.

"She wouldn't want it to go to waste," Topher says.

That's true. She was a firm believer in making the most of things. I don't say yes, but I don't say no either. I just shrug. I already feel sick to my stomach. I can't bear the thought of eating anything. The bus pulls up to the next stop and Steve starts to unzip his pack, shimmying the dilapidated box free. Topher starts to dig in his pack for the plates he brought. We have nothing to wash it down with. Just one empty wineglass. I figure I'll try a bite though. For Ms. Bixby's sake. Just to see if Eduardo was right.

I look over at Steve, who has his hands on either side of the box, but he's not opening it. Instead he's looking up at the front of the bus. His eyebrows shoot skyward.

He drops, slinking behind the brown vinyl seat in front of him, pulling Topher alongside and hissing at me to do the same. "Get down!"

"What? What is it?" I duck behind my seat, wondering what in the name of Michelle's white-chocolate raspberry supreme cheese-cake he saw. Someone from school? A teacher? Mr. Mack? Or maybe it's his parents; they found out he's skipping and are hunting him down. Or maybe the cashier from the liquor store called the cops and *they* are looking for us. Or maybe it's just Steve's turn to be melodramatic. I peek over the top of the seat in front of me.

My jaw drops.

I can hardly believe our luck.

You could say Ms. Bixby saved me, but *that* would be melodramatic. All she did was pick me up. It was all a matter of luck.

She found me in a snowstorm, up to my knees, six grocery bags hanging from my arms and wrists. I'm not sure how she spotted me. Probably recognized my coat. Or the hat that I wore—blue with a yellow floppy fuzzball on top and giant earflaps that nearly hit my shoulders, borrowed out of the closet from Dad. She found me and she pulled over and opened her window and called my name. And I didn't want to stop because I figured she would ask me all sorts of questions. It wasn't school, we weren't in class, and I didn't have to explain, to her or anyone. So I trudged on, pretending not to notice her, but then she honked her horn and leaned over and said, "Do you need a ride?"

I wasn't sure what I needed, but I looked at the car with its heater and music both blasting and the mile of foot-high snow I still had to trudge through and figured a ride wouldn't hurt. Just this once.

And that's how it started between me and Ms. Bixby. She just happened to be passing by.

I feel a warmth surge through me. It's him. The last one in the line of oncoming passengers. Torn jeans and blue shirt. One hand holding a brown paper bag. Dragon clawing its way up his arm.

George Nelson.

The flipwad who stole our money and ruined our day.

But I don't really see him. What I see is Ms. Bixby pulling up along the side of the road and asking me if I need a ride. I see her tapping on the steering wheel to one of her favorite songs.

I see her standing over me, both hands on my shoulders, telling me that sometimes you're beat before you even get started, but it doesn't matter. You keep going. No matter what.

And I realize the day's not over yet.

STEVE

THE INLAND TAIPAN IS CONSIDERED THE MOST poisonous snake in the world, but it's not the most dangerous. The odds of surviving a snakebite from an inland taipan are one in a hundred thousand, unless you're a herpetologist and carry antivenom in your back pocket. Of course, the odds of getting bitten by one are almost nil, unless you live in the middle of Australia, and even then it's highly unlikely. You have a much better chance of getting struck by lightning or knocked unconscious by a falling coconut.

Some things are simply more dangerous than others. The odds of being eaten by a shark are one in four million, and the odds of being injured by a toilet are one in ten thousand, making toilets four hundred times more hazardous than sharks. I don't know what the odds of being injured by a toilet with a shark in it are. During my one and only encounter, I managed to get out alive.

Numbers don't lie; you can count on them. That's a joke Topher told me, though he had to stop and explain it, which can be frustrating, I know. But numbers are comforting. They let you know what you're up against. They let you know what you're getting into.

Ms. Bixby read us a poem a few months ago, about two people who were soul mates and were separated by some twist of fate. The speaker—that's the imaginary guy in the poem, I'm told—was complaining about how miserable he was without this other woman and vowing that he would find her again no matter what. Ms. Bixby agreed it was sappy—her word—but she liked it because it used lots of metaphors and she's big on metaphors. I'm not that fond of metaphors, or poetry, for that matter—I think life would be easier if everyone just said exactly what they were thinking—but Ms. Bixby loves them both, so we were forced to read about this man and woman who were supposedly destined to be together because fate said so. When she finished, I raised my hand.

"I don't buy it," I said.

"And why is that?" Ms. Bixby said.

"Because what you're describing is statistically impossible," I said.

Ms. Bixby was intrigued. She leaned forward in her reading chair, which I assumed was my cue to continue.

"There are approximately seven point two billion people in the world. You're telling me that you really believe you will find one person out of *seven billion* who's the exact right person you're *supposed* to be with?"

Ms. Bixby didn't even stop to think about it. "I'm not saying *I* will, necessarily. But I think people do, yes. The man and woman in this poem were soul mates. They were destined to be with each other. That's what the poem's about." She called on someone else as I fished in my desk for my calculator. Then I raised my hand again.

"Yes, Steve."

"All right. Assuming that it takes a minimum of five minutes to fall in love," I began. There was a chorus of giggles in the class. Brian Frey said something like *Not with you*, and Rebecca gave him a dirty look. I ignored him and started tapping in numbers.

"Actually, it doesn't even have to take *that* long," Ms. Bixby said. "Ever hear of love at first sight?" Again more snickering. A few groans. I glanced over at Topher, who was sitting right beside me, then went back to my calculator.

"Fine. Let's say *one* minute," I conceded. "Assuming that you meet a new person every minute of your life from the day you are born—which is completely impossible, by the way—and assuming that you live to be, let's say, eighty-five, which is generous, especially for boys, that means that you could conceivably meet . . . forty-four million, six hundred seventy-six thousand potential soul mates before you die. That still leaves . . ." My fingers flick along the keys. "Seven billion, one hundred fifty-five million, three hundred twenty-four thousand people you will never even *meet*." I paused to let the magnitude of the number sink in. "I'd say it's much more likely that we will never come across the person we're meant for, even if that person exists."

I held up my calculator to show her, just in case she didn't believe me. All eyes flicked from me to Ms. Bixby. She shrugged.

"'Gravitation is not responsible for people falling in love,'" she said.

I set down my calculator. "Huh?"

"Just think about it," she said. Then she made everyone take out their writing journals so we could all experiment writing our own sappy love poetry.

I looked over at Topher. "She's crazy," I said.

"You're crazy," he told me.

"But seven billion people," I repeated.

Topher shrugged. "Never tell me the odds."

The first thing I think when I see him boarding the bus holding his brown paper bag and dropping his coins in the box is: *Impossible.*

The second is: *No. Not impossible, just highly unlikely. Stranger things have happened.*

The third is: *If he sees us, he will kill us. He will strangle us in our seats.*

I duck, dragging Topher with me, then turn and whisper for Brand to do the same. The incoming passengers step up, the clink of their quarters no longer giving me a shiver of satisfaction. I can hear the riders brushing up against the seats, making their way down the aisle. The bus is only half full, plenty of space, but there is a chance—a statistically significant one—that George Nelson could come all the way to the back, sit down right across from us, right next to Brand. I listen for footfalls. Wait for the shout. To see his face appear up over the seat in front of me.

I'm not exactly sure what I'm afraid of. He stole *our* money, after all. If anything, we should be looking for *him*. But for all the adventures Topher and I have been on together—battling ninjas and pirates, defusing nuclear bombs and piloting renegade spaceships—we've never faced a real criminal before. We've never faced a real *anything*, actually.

I suddenly realize this is the second time I've had to hide from someone today.

Brand peeks over the back of the seat, one hand motioning us to stay down even as he pops his head up. He turns and whispers, "It's him!"

"I know," I say.

"Him who?" Topher says, then takes a peek himself. I can't help it—I steal another glance as well, just to confirm. George Nelson is sitting three rows behind the driver, well in front of us, looking out the window. He hasn't seen us, or if he has, he's not showing it. He's got a set of buds plugged into his ears, and his head bobs up and down. We don't have to whisper. Between the bus engine and the headphones, there's no way he can hear us.

I'm thinking maybe he will get off at the next stop. I'm thinking maybe we will stay on the bus until he leaves. I'm thinking there is no way we can let him see us.

The fierce look on Brand's face tells me exactly what he's thinking.

"It's fate," he says.

It's not fate. This is just really bad luck. But apparently I'm the only one who thinks so. Beside me Topher is nodding, and Brand has made his hands into fists. I think about the time he nearly socked Trevor Cowly after Trevor called us the Nerd Patrol for the seventh time. The two of them got into a shoving match by the swings, and Trevor ended up facedown in the mulch. There's a picture of it in Topher's sketchbook. Sort of.

Brand has that same look on his face now. "We are going to get our money back," he hisses. Topher is still nodding. Once again I'm forced to point out the obvious.

"He's a grown man," I say. "He has a *tattoo*. Of a *dragon*." Though admittedly it could be a tattoo of a baby unicorn and I wouldn't feel any better about it.

"There's three of us and only one of him," Brand says, which strikes me as faulty logic, even if it has a basis in arithmetic. Three ants are no match for one tennis shoe. "He took our money. He's gotta pay."

I shake my head. The thought of confronting George Nelson makes me want to throw up. I'm certainly not hungry anymore. "There's nothing we can do. We can't even call the police," I remind him.

Brand's face blossoms into a devious smile. "Steve, you are a genius," he says.

"What does *that* have to do with anything?"

"What you just said. Is there any juice left in your phone?" he asks me.

I look. I'm at 2 percent. Maybe a minute of battery life left.

"It doesn't matter," Brand says. "Just give the phone to Topher and be prepared to get off at whatever stop George does."

I don't want to give my phone to Topher—I know what happened to his last one. And I certainly don't want to get off at whatever stop George does. But Brand says somebody needs to hang back with the phone and stay out of the way, and with his swollen ankle, Topher's the best man for that job.

"Stay out of the way of what?" I ask. But Brand says don't worry. He has a plan.

The day Brand sat down next to us, there were six other empty seats. I know because I counted them. Of course, of the seven total empty seats, three were at all-girls tables, so I understand why he might have avoided them, but there was still only a 25 percent chance that he would sit next to us.

One in four is better than one in seven billion, but it's still against the odds.

When he sat down at lunch with us that first day, I remember looking over at Topher. It was a look that said, *Tell him to go away. I* couldn't tell him because I'm a firm believer in not saying anything that will get me either beat up or into trouble. But Topher didn't say, *Go away.* He said, "Sure. Have a seat." So Brand sat down with us and I counted the empty chairs.

That first week I tried everything I could think of to

convince him that he didn't belong with us. I tried pretending he didn't exist. I forgot to invite him over to my house after school whenever I invited Topher. I sent him a note from Mindy Winkler asking if he would sit by her at lunch instead, but that backfired when Mindy had to get her braces tightened the next day and didn't even bother to come to school, making Brand wonder who the note was from. I said I didn't know.

It wasn't that I didn't like Brand. He had never shot any spit wads into my hair. He never tried to push me down the stairs or burped in my face. All he did was sit down at our table at lunch. But at the time, I hated him, just for sitting down, because I wasn't sure what it meant. Because it had always just been Topher and me. To make matters worse, he seemed nice and he had seen all the right movies and knew lots of good jokes, and Topher obviously thought he was cool, which meant there was a chance—a good chance—that over time, Topher might choose him over me.

And that simply couldn't happen.

We are ninjas. That's what Topher says as we get off the bus. Stealth and subterfuge. Actually he says subtlety, but I think he means subterfuge. Though I suppose a ninja could be subtle too. Until they cut your head off with a katana.

We don't have katanas. I have a Carhartt multipurpose

tool that has a knife blade on it sharp enough to cut mud. We didn't even think to bring forks for the cheesecake. Topher says it doesn't matter. We just need to *walk* like ninjas. We aren't beheading anyone.

I don't know how ninjas walk, but I assume it is on their tiptoes, so I walk on my tiptoes, though after a while that hurts and I just walk regular but slow, keeping against the brick walls of the buildings we pass. I am with Topher, who walks like a ninja with his toes chopped off, limping and stumbling and reaching out occasionally to put a hand on my shoulder. I am keeping an eye on Brand, who is on the other side of the street. He's the one trailing George Nelson, staying a good twenty yards away, waiting for "just the right moment." I'm not sure what the right moment is. All I know is that he will give me the signal.

I suddenly feel the urge to pee—I didn't go at the bookstore when I had the chance—and I whisper that to Topher, who tells me ninjas don't pee. I tell him that is biologically impossible and historically inaccurate. He asks me if I've ever seen a ninja pee in a movie. I tell him I've never seen anyone pee in a movie. He says ninjas don't talk about peeing either and that we should maintain mission silence from here on out, so I just follow the sidewalk, keeping one eye on our target and the other on Brand, waiting for just the right moment.

George Nelson still has his earbuds in and seems completely

unaware of our presence no matter how we walk. Only once does he look in our direction, and I freeze, Topher nearly crashing into me. The man doesn't register us, though. He is just checking for cars before crossing—easier to do when you're not being chased. He crosses the intersection, then turns down a small alleyway behind a corner drugstore.

This, apparently, is the moment. Brand gives the signal, wildly slapping the top of his head with both hands, more *surprised baboon* than *stealthy ninja*, but unmistakable at least. Topher motions for me to go. "I'll be right behind you," he whispers. Brand points to the alley's entrance and then makes some other motion with his hand, something about a tornado or a spinning ballerina, and then he sprints around the front of the Walgreens. Topher calls out behind me. "Go. Cut him off."

I run a little faster, thinking about the lumpy cheesecake still jouncing around in my backpack, getting lumpier, and what a terrible idea this is, running to confront a grown man—a criminal named after a cop killer, no less—in a deserted alleyway in the middle of downtown. I say a quick prayer as I come to the alley entrance, pressing my back firmly against the wall, leaning to take a look.

George Nelson is there. He's stopped about twenty feet away and is looking at a poster pasted to a door. I look for Brand. Brand is the one who is going to confront him. I'm just supposed to make sure he doesn't get away. Of course if he tries to get away, I don't know how I will stop him. My parents enrolled me in tae kwon do one summer but let me quit when the school year started back up. Straight As are more important than learning to defend yourself. In three months of classes I learned four words in Korean and how to tie my belt. If George Nelson wants to get past me, he will.

I don't see Brand. I look to make sure Topher is limping up behind me—he is still a block away. I turn back around.

George Nelson is staring at me.

He looks confused for a moment. He cocks his head sideways. Then I see his eyes flash, the moment when he realizes who I am: that annoying little Chinese kid he adopted outside a liquor store.

Fifteen thousand people are murdered in cold blood each year. I don't know why I know this. Now I wish I didn't.

George Nelson holds the brown paper bag against his chest with one hand, then reaches down to the pocket of his jeans with another, and for a split second, I think, *This is it. He's got a gun and he's going to shoot me and I am going to die, right here, in this alley, without having even graduated from elementary school,* and it's strange, but my very first thought is who will come to my funeral, and will my sister even bother to wear black, and what will my father say about me. Probably something about not being able to realize my potential.

I don't have time to imagine the rest of the eulogy, because at that moment, George Nelson turns and bolts toward the other end of the alleyway. He's actually running away. From me.

Except I'm supposed to *keep* him from getting away—that's my role in the plan—so I yell, "Stop!"

He hesitates, for only a second. Then something drops out of the sky right in front of him. Maybe it's spending so much time with Topher, but my first thought is *Batman*, except this something has a dorky-looking cartoon tiger on his chest. Then I realize it's only Brand, who has jumped off the roof of the drugstore, landing first on a Dumpster and then hitting the pavement, blocking George Nelson's way, trapping him between us. I can't help it. I'm impressed.

George Nelson looks back and forth from me to Brand, still clutching his brown paper bag and whatever is inside it. I take a quick glance behind me for Topher, but now there's no sign of him. He was just there a second ago, I swear, but all I can see is another set of Dumpsters and an empty cardboard box. I want to go look for him, but I can't leave Brand alone in the alley with this man.

"Where's our money, George?"

My head whips back at the sound of Brand's voice, though it doesn't sound quite like him. I think he's making his voice deeper, huskier on purpose.

"This is a joke, right?" George says. He's not laughing or even smiling, though.

"Twenty-five bucks. Where is it?" Brand insists.

"I don't have your money."

"We had an agreement," Brand says.

George tightens his grip on his bag, takes three steps backward so he's about halfway between Brand and me. He looks unsteady, off balance, but his eyes are slits, darting back and forth. "C'mon, kid. Really? What did you *think* was going to happen? You're too young to be drinking anyways."

"But not too young for you to steal our money." Brand takes two steps toward George Nelson. I'm not exactly sure what the plan is from here. Brand didn't say. Cut him off. Don't let him escape. That was it. I take another look for Topher, but I still don't see him. With a sneer, George Nelson closes the remaining distance between him and Brand.

"Outa the way, kid."

"Give us our money back," Brand says, much cooler than I ever could. He refuses to move. I would have moved.

"I'm not going to ask you again." George Nelson spits on the pavement between Brand's feet. It's a standoff. I count in my head—one second, two, three—then the man gives Brand a shove, hands to chest.

Brand stumbles backward but quickly recovers and shoves

right back. Hard. Harder than I could have anticipated. Harder than George Nelson probably expected. Hard enough that the man staggers backward, spinning toward me, only a few feet away. Before I know it, Brand is right on top of him, pushing him into me, and the three of us are tangled together. I try to yell for Topher, his name sticking in my throat. The man stumbles, takes a step back, and I see his fist, not the one holding the bag but the other one, the one that leads to the dragon, swing out. Brand ducks at the last moment and George Nelson's left hook misses him completely.

I'm standing right next to Brand, but I don't think to duck. Three months of tae kwon do, but they never covered ducking.

The pain is instant, explosive, as George's punch lands square on my jaw—tooth loosening and intense. The brick walls spin, quickly replaced by the pavement underneath me as I bang my head. From my new spot on the ground I get a darkened glimpse of Brand swinging his backpack around, catching George Nelson across the face, distracting him long enough for Brand to tackle him at the knees, driving him backward, catching him off balance, slamming them both into the side of the building. I decide it's best to just stay on the ground.

The two of them topple over and wrestle for a moment, limbs flailing, hands in faces, though Brand actually seems to have the advantage as George fights one-handed, the other one still holding his bag out of reach, protecting it like it's the Holy Grail. George grunts, pushing Brand off him, and then the two of them wobble back to their feet. George Nelson looks like he's about to take another swing at Brand, but then he stops, staring down the alleyway, past me at something by the Dumpster.

Topher. Finally. He pops up out of nowhere, holding my phone.

"Did you get it?" Brand calls out, taking a step backward, keeping his eyes on George Nelson.

"I got it," Topher says.

"What? What did you get? What's he doing?" George Nelson huffs.

"Well, about three seconds ago, I was getting some awesome up-close video of you punching my friend. Except it's not called punching, not when you're doing it to a twelve-year-old kid unprovoked. What's that called again?" Topher asks.

"Assault and battery," Brand says, stepping over to help me up. I claw my way up his shirt and onto my feet. My teeth feel loose in their sockets. I can taste blood in my mouth. For some reason it hurts just to blink.

"Right. Video of you assaulting and battering my friend. And *now* I am calling the police," Topher says smugly.

It takes a second. Then suddenly George Nelson is stammering.

"Wait! Hold on, now. Just put that phone away. Everybody calm down, all right? You guys came and surrounded *me*. You assaulted *me*."

"Yeah, that's not what the camera shows," Topher says, tilting my phone and wincing at what he sees there. "*Ouch. Ooh.* Yeah. I'm pretty sure I know what the cops will think of this. Especially *that* part." He makes a move like he is going to dial again. I lean against Brand, slowly working my jaw back and forth. I'm pretty sure the blood is coming from my lip. I'm afraid to touch it. George Nelson throws his hands up.

"Wait! Hang on, all right? I get it. You win, all right? Just put the phone down!"

Topher looks at Brand, who nods.

"Whatever," George says, backing up, running his free hand through his hair. "I'm not going to jail, understand? That's *not* going to happen."

"In that case, we want our twenty-five bucks back, flopsucker," Brand says.

"What did you just call me?" George hisses, then catches a subtle movement from Topher, bringing my phone closer. "Right. Okay. Sure. Your money. I would. I really would, all right? But I don't have it anymore." George holds out the paper bag that he's been coddling. "I spent it, see?" He pulls a bottle out of the bag and shows us.

Jack Daniel's Tennessee Whiskey, it says. Old number seven. It looks like something from another century. Like medicine from the Great Depression.

"That's not wine," Topher points out.

"Trust me," George says, waving the bottle in front of us. "This stuff is *so* much better than wine. You just take it, all right? Take it and delete that little video and we can all forget that this whole thing ever happened." He puts the bottle back in the brown paper sack and sets it on the ground between us.

"How much was it?" Brand asks.

"I don't know. Twenty and change. Can you please just put the phone away?"

"Show me your wallet," Brand insists. Topher holds my phone out like it's a loaded pistol. I'm still working my jaw like a cow chews. I've been picked on and pushed around a lot, but I've never been punched in the face before. I find the courage to reach up and touch two fingers to my lip. It's bigger than I remembered. And wet. I don't want to look.

George Nelson sighs and then reluctantly digs into the back pocket of his jeans, pulling out a black leather wallet. "There's maybe two bucks left," he protests. He opens it up to show us. "See. That's it. The credit cards are all maxed out."

"Hand it over."

"I just showed you. There's nothing in there."

Brand looks over at Topher and nods. "Let's see here," Topher says. "Nine. One . . ."

George curses, but he throws over the wallet. Brand removes the driver's license and looks it over. "Hazel?" he says. "Your real name is Hazel?"

"It was my great-grandfather's name."

Brand hands me Hazel's driver's license. "File this for the future, will you?"

I take the license and scan it, committing it all to memory. The photo is terrible. Even in his license he looks like a criminal, much more like a George Nelson than a Hazel Meriwether Morgan. I get it all, reciting it to myself. Height. Weight. Eye color. Hair color. Date of birth—he's actually twenty-eight years old, though he looks older. Maybe it's the tattoo. Address. License number. Not an organ donor. I repeat it all three times to myself in my head, just to be sure, then hand it back to Brand, who stuffs it back in the wallet. He removes the two dollar bills before tossing the wallet back.

"All right, Hazel, here's what we are going to do. We are going to take this"—he bends down and grabs the bag with the bottle of Jack Daniel's—"and this"—he holds up the two dollars—"and we are going to walk away and forget that any of this ever happened, just like you asked us to." He points to Topher and the phone. "But we still have the video. And we have your name and address. And the police are just a click away. I'm sure they would be very interested in hearing about a twenty-eight-year-old man who goes around stealing from kids and then beating them up."

Hazel Morgan wipes his mouth with the back of his hand. "Oh, kid, I *so* promise you. Someday, when you're older, and you've forgotten all about this, we're going to run into each other again, and I am going to beat the living piss out of you."

"I don't think I'm ever going to forget this," Brand says. "And besides, that sounded like a threat. Did that sound like a threat to you?" he asks me. I nod. "We should get that on camera. Would you mind saying that again?"

Hazel Morgan stares at us. "You kids are psycho," he concludes. "You know what? Enjoy the Jack. Just don't ever come near me again, got it? None of you. Especially *you*." He points at Brand as he starts to walk backward, muttering under his breath. "Stupid, punk, psycho kids."

After four or five steps, he turns around and walks down to the other end of the alley with his head down, not even giving us a backward glance.

"Flopsucker?" Topher asks, coming to stand beside us.

"I just came up with it," Brand says, grinning. "It's even

worse than a flipwad. Like the king of flipwads."

"I like it," Topher says. Then he turns and inspects my face. "Wow. That's just . . . Ouch."

I reach up and touch my lip again and look this time. It's definitely blood. I get dizzy and nearly find myself back on the ground again, except Topher catches me and holds me up this time.

We find a stretch of grass surrounding one of the precious few trees left in downtown—they are considered landmarks now—and sit around it, legs sticking out like tire spokes. Topher digs in his backpack for a napkin and tells me to hold it against my lip. "And the award for best actor in a nonscripted fight scene goes to . . . Steven Sakata," he says. He is fond of giving out imaginary awards. Most of them go to me, I assume because I'm a Sakata kid and he knows we collect them to make our parents happy.

"Yeah. You did a really nice job taking that punch," Brand says.

"Thanks," I mumble. I fish in my mouth with one finger, counting. I correctly count twenty-six teeth. I'm still waiting on a couple of molars. "You knew he was going to punch me," I say, looking at Brand.

"I figured I could get him to swing at *somebody*," Brand says. "I was ready to take it, but at the last second I guess my not-getting-punched-in-the-face instinct kicked in. Sorry yours didn't."

I make a note not to stand beside Brand anymore. Especially not in the middle of a fistfight, though hopefully they will not become a regular occurrence.

"It worked, though," Topher says, patting me on the back. "I mean, did you see the look on his face when I said I got it all on video? A grown man punching out a twelve-year-old kid, and with glasses no less. And then you did that spinning drop, like all in slow motion, *keeyrunch, smloosh, thunk.*" Topher pantomimes my misery with his hands. "It was *so* frawesome. I actually wish I *had* gotten it. We could have made a whole movie around that one scene."

Brand and I both look at Topher.

"Wait, what?" I say.

Topher hands me my phone. The screen is black. I press power. Nothing. There is zero charge left. "You mean you were *bluffing*?"

Topher shrugs.

"Seriously, you got *none* of that?" Brand asks.

"Nada," Topher says. "No video. No confession. Nothing. I couldn't even have called the cops if I'd wanted to."

I shake my head in disbelief. The three of us stare at the dead phone in my hand, as if waiting for it to spontaneously come back to life.

"He could have actually killed us," Brand grunts, and for

some inexplicable reason, this strikes me as funny. I start to giggle. Topher looks at me and smiles, and then it catches, as it usually does between the two of us, and he starts to laugh—high-pitched and giddy. Before I know it, all three of us are on our backs, staring up through the tree boughs, bodies convulsing, laughing like lunatics—like a bunch of stupid, punk, psycho kids.

"It's really not funny," I cough, clutching my side. The laughter is somehow making my jaw hurt even more. I bring the napkin back to my lip and see that the bleeding has stopped at least, then wipe my eyes. The three of us lie there, taking shuddering breaths.

Finally Brand sits up and takes the torn paper sack and pulls out the bottle of amber-brown liquid, holding it up to the sunlight. "Better than wine?" he says skeptically.

I sit up on my elbows and look around to see if anyone is watching us. "You should put that away," I tell him. "Better yet, you should just throw it away. There's a trash can right there." I point to the corner, away from the alley. I don't want to go back in the direction that Hazel Morgan went, just in case he changes his mind and decides to finish beating me up. "It's not like we can take it home or back to school. We can't return it and get our money back." Brand just keeps looking at the bottle, though, lost in thought. "Brand?"

"You can't always get what you want," he says.

"What?" I ask.

"Sorry," he says, snapping back. "It's a line from a song," he says. "How's your lip?"

I stick it out even farther to show him. "It hurts," I say.

"'Tis but a scratch," Topher adds.

Brand gives him a smile, but not because of the line. He's obviously thinking something else. "And how's your ankle?" he asks Topher.

"It's all right," Topher says. "As long as I don't have to chase after any more robbers."

"Good," Brand says, then unzips his backpack and stuffs the bottle of Jack Daniel's inside. "Because we are going to have to walk. I'm not sure we have enough money for two more bus rides *and* the last item on our list, even with the flopsucker's two bucks."

"Wait, what?" I ask, but Topher and Brand nod to each other and stand up at the same time. And that's when I realize we aren't going back.

The thing Ms. Bixby said about gravity and falling in love? Albert Einstein said it first. Turns out Einstein said a lot of things you wouldn't expect. Like imagination being more important than knowledge, and education being what's left over after you forget everything you were taught in school. I'm not sure I agree with any of those statements, even if they come from a man generally assumed to be a genius, but I figured I owed it to both Einstein and Ms. Bixby to do what she asked and think about it.

The best that I could come up with is this: There may not *always* be a plausible scientific explanation for why humans do what they do. Not everything can be plugged into an equation or reduced to the lowest common denominator. Not everything can be summed up by a letter grade on a report card or a check in a box. Not everything has a formula, and sometimes things just happen for no reason at all, good or bad, logical or illogical. Ms. Bixby would probably say there actually *is* a reason—we just don't always understand it at the time. Father Massey would probably say the same thing.

I suppose there is some strange comfort in it—this idea that the numbers are sometimes wrong, that there are still mysteries in the universe, and that you don't always have to know why you do the things you do. Sometimes, despite all evidence to the contrary, things can go your way.

The day Ms. Bixby told us about her diagnosis, I came home, changed out of my ketchup-stained pants, and looked it up. It was more than just curiosity. This was Ms. Bixby. The woman who argued with my father and put my ribbon on the board. Who told me to be good and to be myself and to listen to rock music every now and then. I needed to know what she was up against.

I checked several different websites, just to be sure, but they all said the same thing: the one-year survival rate for individuals with advanced-stage ductal adenocarcinoma is 25 percent.

Topher

YOU HAVE TO SLAY THE DRAGON.

You can travel across distant lands. You can answer the riddles and follow the map and muster your forces, but sooner or later, you will find the dragon or the demon or the king flopsucker himself, and you will have to pull your dead smartphone from its case and slay him and steal his Jack Daniel's, even if it means a split lip and a swollen ankle.

I looked at Brand and I knew what he was thinking. Whatever it was that made him want to go home before, he was over it. Maybe it was the whiskey. I hear that alcohol makes people do strange things, but I always assumed you had to drink it first. Or maybe he took us running into George Nelson again as a sign. Maybe he needed to beat his own demon or something, and putting that thieving flipwad in his place was what did it.

All I know is that as soon as I saw the look on Brand's face, the soundtrack in my head cued, the violins swelled, and the trumpets blared, and I knew where we were headed.

"Welcome to McDonald's. Can I take your order?"

The girl at the checkout counter smiles at me. There's a hole in her nose where a ring or a stud is supposed to be, though I'm guessing she had to take it out for work, just in case it dropped in someone's Big Mac. She's obviously a few years older than me, but she has one of those sprightly round faces that make her look young, like a nymph or something. The name on her badge says *Clarisse*, a good nymph name. Her mousy brown hair is pulled into a ponytail, and she has a dimple in her chin. A chimple. I'll have to suggest the word to Brand.

I look at the menu board. *Yes*, I think, *I need a bottle of Robert Mohavi Nappy Musk Oreo something-or-other wine and a white-chocolate cheesecake that doesn't look like a four-hundred-pound pigeon just ate a berry bush and took a dump in my friend's backpack.* Unfortunately, those aren't on the menu, and even if they were, we only have four bucks left, half of it in change.

"Three waters, one with extra ice, and a large fries to go," I tell her.

The fries are the last item on the list. It might be the only one we end up getting right. After all, we are so close now. I can't imagine anything else going wrong today.

"Is your friend okay?" the girl asks. She's looking over my shoulder at Steve, with his fat bottom lip like a purple swollen leech. He's gone cross-eyed poking at it, maybe hoping that will make it deflate. He looks a little insane.

"He's fine," I say. "Just a rough day."

"We all have those," she says, then she tells me my total is $1.63, and I pay with the two bucks from Hazel's wallet. "Looks like it will be a couple of minutes on the fries." She asks me my name and hands me my waters and then smiles again. I'm sure she's just being polite because it's her job, but I linger at the counter a moment until Steve touches my sleeve.

"I think she likes me," I whisper to him. He frowns. Or pouts. With the lip it's hard to tell.

I set the waters down on the table Brand has picked out for us, and Steve immediately pops the lid off his and soaks his lip in the ice at the top, shuddering appreciatively. It's lunchtime at Chez Mac's. You can tell by the uniforms: polos with company logos and name-tagged shirts stained with oil and grime. The PlayPlace is teeming with toddlers and mothers begging them to eat one more chicken nugget. When we first became friends, Steve's mom would bring us to one just like this and let us mess around. We're well past the maximum height limit now, unfortunately. Growing up sucks.

"Does it still hurt?" Brand asks, pointing to the swollen crest of Steve's lower lip.

Steve gives him death-ray eyes and sucks on an ice cube. "Have you ever been punched in the face?"

Brand shakes his head. Of the three of us, I always figured Brand would be the first to get a fat lip. I would never have picked Steve—the boy has spent his whole life avoiding conflict. Until it socked him straight in the smacker.

"It's a rite of passage," I tell him. "Now you just need to kill a bear with your bare hands and you'll be a man."

"Bear hands?" Brand smirks. Steve isn't amused.

"At least he didn't break your glasses," I say, looking on the bright side. The last time Steve broke his glasses, his parents made him do ten hours of community service to "pay" to replace them. I helped him pick trash up from the playground near our neighborhood. I felt obligated. It was mostly my fault, after all. That was the day we tried to make a bungee rig out of some heavy-duty fishing line, an old life jacket, and a five-hundred pack of large rubber bands. It almost worked.

I glance back at the counter to see Clarisse taking someone else's order, giving them the exact same smile as she gave me.

"Think they'll notice?" Steve asks, looking down his glasses, still trying to see his own chubby lip. He means his parents, of course. They will definitely notice. They notice everything, and this is hard to ignore. Mrs. Sakata can scan the room and tell you when the throw pillow on the couch has been moved two inches to the right. "Just tell 'em you got hit by a swing at recess," I suggest.

"Probided they don't pind out that I wadn't eben *at* recess," Steve says, dunking his lip back into the cup. Brand looks past the PlayPlace toward the door. His eyes bug out and he emits a low whistle, like the sound of a dropping bomb.

"That could be harder than you think," he says.

I follow his gaze, seeing the open door and the teenage girl walking in. She's not green-skinned, wart-nosed, or wearing a cone-shaped black hat, but she might as well be. That's how I picture her most of the time.

Cue the screeching *Psycho* violins.

Christina walks in the door and Steve erupts like Vesuvius, half a cup of water gurgling back up, spit-sprayed across the table, showering Brand and me both.

"Seriously?" I say, wiping my face with my sleeve. Steve coughs twice more and then immediately ducks down in his chair, underneath the table.

Christina's coal-black hair is pulled into a tight ponytail and she's wearing a sweater the color of blood, even though it's nearly summer. She's also wearing a scowl, which isn't a surprise. I don't know that I've ever seen her smile. Even when she's playing the piano—the thing she supposedly loves doing more than anything in the world—she's frowning. I always figured it was because she was concentrating, but Steve says it's because she's afraid of making a mistake. Of course he also says that she does smile sometimes, just never when I'm around.

Maybe she won't see us, I think, maybe we just blend in with the backdrop. But Christina has too much of her mother in her; she spies us almost instantly. Her eyes narrow to razor slits.

Cue the theme from *Jaws*.

She's coming straight for us, practically stomping up to us in her black boots. Brand pushes his backpack, the one with Mr. Daniel's, farther under the table with his foot. I can hear Steve muttering from down below. My guess is he's praying for divine intervention. A bolt of holy wrath to disintegrate his sister in the middle of the restaurant. Or maybe to make himself disappear. Teleport back to the safety of room 213, where he's supposed to be.

"Steven?"

That voice gives me chills. Christina is standing by our table, hands on her hips. She looks so much older than seventeen. Steve doesn't move, even though she can clearly see him. It's McDonald's. It's not like there are tablecloths. Brand looks out the window and pretends he doesn't even notice her despite the fact that she's standing right next to him. I look at Christina and smile. She doesn't return the favor.

"Steven Sakata, get out from under the table."

Slowly, painfully, Steve emerges, pulling himself up and slumping in his chair, still trying to hide behind his cup. I scoot as close to him as I can. United front, like always.

Christina checks her phone. "What are you doing here? It's twelve thirty on a Friday afternoon. Why aren't you in school?" Her red knit sweater heaves with each breath. I hate it when people make a big production of breathing impatiently, like they're huffing and puffing to blow your house down.

Steve doesn't answer, so I answer for him. "We could ask you the same thing."

Christina raises her eyebrows. She has big eyebrows that don't really match her narrow face, probably the only thing about her that keeps her from being obnoxiously pretty, though I would never tell her that. Instead I once told her they looked like fuzzy black caterpillars somebody stepped on and pasted to her forehead. She told me to grow a brain.

"It's called work-study," Christina says. "Though you're probably not familiar with either of those terms. I was on my way to the animal clinic." She looks directly at Steve. "Do Mom and Dad know where you are? And what happened to your lip?

Is that blood?" She points to Steve's shirt, the spot of crimson on olive green.

Steve looks dumbly at his shirt and then shrugs. Christina groans in disgust. "You know what? Forget it. I don't even *want* to know. How about we just call Mom right now and tell her where you're at? She can take off work and come get you. I don't have time to give you a ride."

Steve is still speechless. Like his busted lip is blocking the words. It's okay, though. I can handle this.

"How about *you* stop being such a kiss-up, goody-two-shoes, tattle-telling little miss know-it-all and leave him alone," I say, though the "little" doesn't really apply. She's about six inches taller than me, made worse by the fact that we are all sitting down and she's hovering over us.

"How about *you* stay out of it for once, Topher. You're probably the one who put him up to this in the first place, whatever *this* is. I swear, when Mom and Dad hear that you have been skipping school . . ." She doesn't finish the thought, leaving the punishment to Steve's imagination (the rack is not completely out of the question). Instead she holds up her phone again.

Brand sucks in a sharp breath. We've just jumped from DEFCON 3 to DEFCON 1. If Steve's parents get involved, then we are totally gefragt, like a one-legged man in a kicking contest. If she calls, Steve will bail. Then we'll be forced to abort the mission. No man left behind. Christina holds her phone to her lips and commands it to "Call Mom's Work."

Calling Mom's Work, the phone responds.

This requires drastic measures.

Steve is catatonic, paralyzed by the thought of his parents coming to get him. It's up to me to do something. I quickly run through my options. I could tackle her, wrestle her phone away from her, and smash it against the table, except I know that she is crazy strong from all those years in gymnastics; I arm-wrestled her once a year ago for a dollar and ended up on the floor, both her *and* Steve laughing at me. We could simply make a break for it, all three of us, head for the fire exit right behind us and hope she doesn't pursue, except I'm not sure I can run on my swollen ankle. I could just dump my water all over her phone in the hopes of short-circuiting it, though I can't imagine what level of wrath that would incur. Steve says she sleeps with her phone underneath her pillow. I'm pretty sure she would rip my head off.

Brand looks at me as if to say, *What now?* I'm leaning heavily toward plan B, ankle or no ankle, when Steve starts muttering to himself—the word *no,* over and over again, like some religious chant. I make a head motion to Brand, something intended to mean *Let's make a break for it,* but he just gives me a perplexed look. We really should have worked out some emergency signals ahead of time. It's too late anyway. I think I can hear the sound of ringing coming from Christina's phone.

Then it happens. The unimaginable.

"No," Steve says, loud enough for Christina to hear this time, standing up abruptly, causing the whole table to shake and nearly knocking over his water.

"Excuse me?" Christina says.

"Hang up. This isn't about you." Steve's fat lower lip is trembling now, but his voice doesn't waver. His sister rolls her eyes, ignoring him, pressing the phone to her ear.

Steve explodes.

"I said hang up!" he shouts, slamming his hands against the table.

He has her attention now. He has the whole restaurant's attention. All conversation stops. All faces turn to us, midchew, midslurp, mid ketchup-packet squeeze. The toddlers in the Play-Place stop running, stuck halfway up their tubes. I look over at the counter. Even Clarisse with the pretty smile and the extra nose hole is looking at us.

Christina lowers her phone, ending the call. She glances nervously around, cheeks on fire. She leans across the table. "Stop it, Steven," she hisses, teeth clenched. "You're making a scene."

"This isn't about you," Steve repeats, softer this time, suddenly aware that he's the center of attention, which isn't exactly his favorite place to be. "Not everything is about you."

"What are you even talking about?" Christina says, still keeping her voice down, though you can tell it's a struggle. "You're being irresponsible. You're obviously hurt. You're skipping school. You're going to get in trouble if you haven't already." She says "if" as if she already knows the kinds of things we've been up to. Of course the fat lip *is* sort of a giveaway.

"I don't care," Steve shoots back, which I can't imagine is at all true, but maybe, right now, in this moment, he really doesn't. "I'm doing something important. And I really don't care if you like it or understand it or approve of it—I just need you to get out of the way and let me do it."

Our heads—Brand's and mine—swivel around to Christina, tennis match style, ready for the return volley. She hesitates. She actually seems taken aback for a second, but she quickly regains her composure, her voice cool and even. "Listen, I don't know what these two have put you up to, but whatever it is, it's obviously not good. So why don't you just let me call Mom and she can pick you up and take you back to school."

Brand winces at the word "school." I look at Steve, wondering if I need to step in, but he's not backing down. He pushes his glasses up with one knuckle.

"I'm not going back to school," he says. "Not until we're done. And you're not going to call Mom. I don't need you to tell

218

me what to do this time. I know what I'm doing."

"Obviously not," she says. "Look at you."

She looks at him. Brand looks at him. I look at him. It's just Steve. A little dorky looking in the camo, maybe, but still Steve. My best friend for all the years that matter. Who makes sure I get an A in math. Who always lets me pick the movies we watch. Who likes to keep the hall light on when he spends the night because he's still just a little bit spooked by the dark.

Except Steve wouldn't say the kinds of things Steve is saying. Not to Christina, anyways.

"I know what I'm doing," he insists. "And this isn't your problem."

"It's my problem now, though, isn't it?" Christina says. "It's my job to look out for you. Mom and Dad *expect* me to look out for you." Her voice cracks with frustration. She crosses her arms in front of her.

Steve's voice is even quieter this time. He looks up at her expectantly.

"So do it then," he says. "Look out for me."

Brother and sister stare across the table. I try to think of something to add, but I'm pretty sure anything I say will only make matters worse. Then suddenly Christina jumps, as if she's been struck by lightning. She looks down at her hand. Her phone has started to chirp and buzz. Brand, Steve, and I watch it like it's a timed explosive counting down the seconds. She lets it ring four times before she answers. I look to Steve for some kind of signal that I should go with plan A and just tackle her, but he won't take his eyes off his sister. She waits way too long before she says anything.

"Hi, Mom. Yes, I called you just now. No. It's no big deal, it's just . . ."

Here it comes. Another moment for the first daughter to prove how wonderful she really is. I wait for the confession. For Steve to be outed, turned over to the authorities, all so his sister can earn another gold star for whatever chart she thinks she's filling. She looks at Steve, who stands only six feet away, and I think about all those medals and trophies in Christina's room, more than I can count. Think about all the piano recitals he's had to sit through. The applause. The perfect report cards. The constant pressure. Steve once told me he never wanted to grow up and be like her. I thought I knew exactly what he meant.

Christina keeps her eyes locked on his as she speaks.

"Yeah, I just wanted to let you know that I got downtown all right. Yes, I'll be careful. Okay. See you tonight. Bye."

She ends the call and stuffs the phone into the back pocket of her jeans. Brand and I both take a deep breath. Crisis temporarily averted.

"Thanks," Steve says, though you can tell it takes some

effort. It's not a word that floats freely between the two of them. Christina points a finger at him.

"Can I talk to you?" She motions to the far corner by the Redbox kiosk, away from most of the people, most notably from me and Brand.

I watch Steve follow her far enough away that we can't hear, wondering what kind of lecture he's in for this time, waiting for the tirade, the wagging finger, for Steve's head to hang, but there's none of that. The conversation takes less than a minute. The two of them whisper, and since I'm not as good at reading lips as Steve, I have no idea what they are saying, but I do see Christina bend close to inspect her brother's lip, as if spending a couple of months interning at a vet clinic suddenly makes her a medical expert. She says something else and Steve nods. Then she follows him back to our table. He takes his seat next to me again. Christina's hands settle back on her hips as she eyes each of us in turn. She still looks a little bit evil.

"All right. Here's the deal. You never saw me, got it? I was never here. We never had this conversation. When Mom and Dad find out—and you know they are going to find out somehow—I don't want you dragging me into it. Then it will be my fault for not telling, and frankly, I've got enough to worry about."

"Yeah, your life is so hard," I say, instantly realizing that I was right before, about making it worse. The sharp look I get suggests I should definitely keep my mouth shut. The strange part is that the look comes from Steve, not from his sister. She just ignores me again.

"Make sure you're home by dinner," she says to him, waving her hands around, "and that this—whatever *this* is—doesn't become, like, a regular . . . thing."

"It won't," Steve says. "It's one day only."

Christina shakes her head. "So much trouble," she murmers to herself, though plenty loud enough for us all to hear. Whether she means me or Steve or their parents I'm not sure. "I was never here," she repeats. She starts to go but turns back around for one more parting shot. "And try not to do anything *really* stupid."

I'm not positive, because Steve and I are next to each other, but I'm pretty sure she's looking directly at me this time. I almost tell her, *Too late*. Instead I wave, not expecting her to wave back. She doesn't.

Steve's hands shake. I expect to see a satisfied smile, but he actually looks horrified.

"That was close," Brand says.

"Yeah," I say, "And awesome."

In all the years I've known him, I've never seen Steve stand up to anyone like that. Maybe there was something to that getting-hit-in-the-face stuff after all. Or maybe she just had it coming. Steve grabs his water with both hands and tips it back, draining

it in three big gulps. The chattering returns as the McCustom-
ers forget about the outburst. The mothers go back to watching
their kids on the slides. Steve watches his sister's Subaru leave
the parking lot. She didn't even get whatever it was she came in
here for.

She sure got something, though. Steve made sure of that.

From the counter I hear Clarisse call my name.

Our order is up.

You can't always pinpoint the moment everything changes. Most
of the time it's gradual, like grass growing or fog settling or your
armpits starting to smell by midafternoon. And even when it
does come down to one moment, it's not always what you expect.
It's not some big announcement from the heavens telling you
that you are the chosen one. It's not some magnificent charge
through enemy lines with the orchestra swelling behind you.
Instead it's something smaller. Like standing up to your sister
at the McDonalds. Or facing off against some flopsucker in an
alley behind the Walgreens.

Or even catching your teacher sifting through the trash and
seeing what she keeps tucked in her bottom drawer.

I caught her after school. Ms. Bixby. Going through the
recycling bin. Taking stuff. My stuff.

It had been an unusually dull Thursday, with tests to see

how would we do on later tests and tests to verify how we did on earlier tests, but no omens to suggest my life was about to change. No squawking crows or black cats, no dark smoky writing across the sky. It *was* pouring rain, so I suppose that counts for something, though at the time it just meant we couldn't go out for recess.

We sat in our corner of room 213 instead, the three of us, Brand messing around on one of the class iPads and Steve getting his homework done ahead of time, knowing he'd be asked about it as soon as he got home. I did what I usually do, doodled on a piece of scrap paper I found in my desk, the back of some fractions worksheet long ago graded (I was supposed to take it home to show my parents, but I wasn't sure they'd really care about a B minus in finding common demoninators). My sketchbook was in my bag by the door and I was too lazy to get it. Besides, I had spotted a spider foolishly trying to set up shop in our same corner by the radiator and didn't want to miss the chance to capture it on paper. It would only be a matter of time before Trevor or one of the other barbarians saw it and destroyed it. So I tried to sketch it, as a tribute to its brave stupidity. I drew for the whole time, and was just about finished when Ms. Bixby told us to get ready to go to gym. I showed Brand, who said it was pretty good, which is what he always says. He's a little like my parents that way.

It *was* good. But not great. Not worth keeping, anyway. So I tossed the paper in the recycling bin and didn't think another thing of it.

I was supposed to be picked up that day by my mom, who had all but disappeared that week, working three twelve-hour shifts in a row, and who wanted to make it up to me by taking me out for ice cream, just the two of us. Except the office called down to say that she was running late, which didn't surprise me at all. I went back to 213, looking for a book to pass the time, knowing Ms. B. had plenty to choose from.

That's when I spied her.

I stood in the doorway, watching her bent over the recycling tub, hair falling down in her face, a sheet of paper in her hand. She was wearing a buttery yellow sundress that day, with a white sweater so thin it looked like it might fly off to somewhere warmer.

"Lose something?" I asked.

Ms. Bixby jumped, startled, and I saw what she was holding. Not only could I see my name and the grade, but I could see the outline of the spider seeping through from the other side. She looked at me guiltily, as if I'd just caught her changing the scores on our standardized tests.

"Oh. Hi, Topher," she said, staring. "Wasn't your mom supposed to pick you up?"

I shrugged. "She's running late. I thought I'd see if you had something to read. What's that?" I pointed at her hand, knowing perfectly well what it was, wanting to know more why she was holding it. Maybe she was just double-checking my grade. Maybe she thought I deserved at least a B plus. Ms. Bixby looked at the drawing and smiled.

"It's a spider," she said. "Building a web. Obviously."

I glanced instinctively at the corner I had been sitting in only hours before. The web was still there, miraculously, but the spider was gone. I hoped it hadn't been crushed. "I guess I meant why are you holding it?"

Ms. Bixby's mouth opened and closed twice, like she was trying to figure out how to make it work. It was an awkward moment.

"I was actually going to hang on to it," she admitted finally. "I like it."

"Oh," I said.

Ms. Bixby looked intently at the drawing now, tracing the pattern of the web with one finger. "I didn't think you'd mind," she said. "I mean, you *did* throw it away."

"No. You're right. I did," I said. What did that mean, she *liked* it? Like she was going to put a smiley-face sticker on it? Like she was going to show it to the class? Or like she really, honestly *liked* it?

"Is there a reason you threw it away?"

"I don't know. I guess I just didn't know what else to do with it," I said.

"You didn't think it was worth keeping," she prodded.

I looked into the recycling bin. Stories and papers and quizzes, ripped-up cootie catchers and paper planes made out of Post-it notes, a whole week's worth of work and play. "I guess not," I said. I thought about my fridge at home—how, when I was little, it was full of papers and drawings hanging from magnet clips. Now it was covered in take-out menus and school reminders.

Ms. Bixby smiled, the smile that makes you feel like she's about to tell you a secret. Most of the time it really meant she was just going to recite one of her quotes or tell you to behave, but in this case, the smile held even more promise. She beckoned me over to her desk and sat on the edge. "Topher Renn, what I'm about to show you stays between us, understood?"

I nodded dumbly.

"That means Steve and Brand too," she emphasized. "I don't want to hurt anyone's feelings, so you have to promise."

I gave it some thought. That would be tough. I told Steve practically everything. Ms. Bixby obviously knew how things were between us.

"I promise," I said. It would probably be worth it. I felt like Lucy Pevensie lost in the wardrobe. Like Harry looking into the

Pensieve. My fingers tingled. I could keep promises if I had to, but I crossed my feet just in case. I don't think she noticed.

"Do you know Susanna Givens?" Ms. Bixby asked.

I shook my head. The name sounded slightly familiar, like something I might have heard on the radio or in a television commercial. Turns out I was way off.

"She's a former student of mine. She's in high school now. Sweet kid, very bright, but very shy. Kept to herself mostly."

"Like Steve," I said.

"Like a lot of kids I know," Ms. Bixby said, one eyebrow raised. "Susanna was a writer, probably the best young writer I've ever taught."

I nodded, feeling a little flash of jealousy. Unlike my math quizzes (which I couldn't copy off Steve on the bus like the homework), everything I wrote for Ms. Bixby's class got As. Nobody wants to hear how some complete stranger was so much better than them at something they took pride in. Then again, Ms. Bixby was still holding my spider.

"It was her poetry that got me," Ms. Bixby continued. "It was intricate and complex and full of imagery and emotion. She would write her poems on scraps of paper, just like this." Ms. Bixby held up the drawing. "Whenever she had free time in class, I would find her working on them. Some she kept. Some she threw away. But she never showed anyone, not that I know of, not even the few girls in class that she got along with.

"Except one day I found one. Same place as your drawing. And I took it and wrote a note on it and put it back into her desk."

"What did the note say?" I asked.

Ms. Bixby put a finger to her lips. "I can't tell you. That's between me and Susanna, and promises are promises. But I *can* tell you that the next day when she opened her desk, she looked at me. She didn't say anything. She *never* said anything, not directly, but later that week I found another poem, sitting on *my* desk, hidden underneath my keyboard. Then another and another. A poem a week. Sometimes two. I started keeping them in a red folder."

Ms. Bixby slipped off the desk, smoothed out her dress, and pulled opened her bottom drawer. I leaned in close. The drawer clicked and slid. Inside was a half-eaten bag of pretzel sticks and an empty bottle of Frappuccino. There was also a wire rack holding at least two dozen manila file folders, all labeled what you would expect: lesson plans and grade reports, math worksheets and tardy slips. Ms. Bixby knelt down and pushed past the plain folders to reveal a second row of folders behind, all different colors. The one in front was red.

"I can't let you read them. They aren't for sharing. But I thought you might want to see what happened after that first day."

She pulled it out and set it on the desk. The red folder labeled Susanna Givens was bursting. Even at two poems a week there was no way she could have filled it that full. Even if she were to spend all of her class time, writing odes during recess and morning work and in the lunch line, there was just no way. "Impossible," I said.

"This isn't just from when she was my student. She's been emailing me them ever since," Ms. Bixby explained. "I print them out and keep them in here."

I casually ran my thumb along the edge, ruffling the pages.

"That's hers," she said. "Yours, on the other hand . . ."

Ms. Bixby bent down again and reached over the rainbow array of folders, only half a dozen, and retrieved a green folder from the very back of the drawer. The very last one. It was thin, probably only ten sheets or so. It had my name on the front in black marker. Just Topher. No last name. She set it on top of Susanna Givens's folder and stepped aside so I could see.

Inside were drawings. My drawings. Most of them were doodles scrawled carelessly on the backs of tests or quizzes. One was a photocopy of a sketch I had made in art class when we had a sub. Another was a picture that I had sold to Kyle Kipperson for a quarter only to have him wad it up and throw it away. Ms. Bixby had saved it, unraveled it, pressed it flat, and stuck it in this folder with the rest. They were all discards. Throwaways. "You kept these?"

Ms. B. nodded. "You remember what I always wanted to be when I grew up? Before I decided to become a teacher?"

"Maggie the Magnificent," I mumbled, thumbing through my sketches, looking at them again, trying to see whatever it was she saw in them, something I must have missed the first time. "Master Illusionist."

"And my big trick, pulling my pet gerbil from my hat."

"And how your grandmother tried to step on it," I added, pausing at a drawing I'd made of Steve with his chin on his fist, styled after that famous statue of the guy who thinks too hard.

"Except I never told you *why* I gave up," Ms. Bixby said. "It was the laughter. My parents, my grandparents, my brother, all laughing about it afterward, talking about how I'd messed up the trick, like it was all a big joke. I was a comedian, not a magician. They would keep telling that story the rest of my life, with their friends, at the dinner table, and every time they would laugh all over again. I ran to my room that day and cried. They didn't get it. That was supposed to be my breakout moment. But to them I was just a kid playing pretend."

I stopped paging through the green folder and looked at

Ms. Bixby. She always seemed so confident, so one-step-ahead-of-the-rest-of-us, but now she looked different, uncertain.

"It's funny how, as kids, we get these ideas in our head about what's possible and what's not. One day we're invincible and the next day we are afraid of what's in the closet. I grew up wanting to become a magician, but I became a teacher instead. Teaching is wonderful, don't get me wrong, but it's not every ten-year-old's dream."

I shook my head. "So what? So you screwed up on one trick. You can still be a magician," I said, trying to sound as inspirational as she did sometimes when she would spout her quotes. "What's stopping you?"

Ms. Bixby laughed, and her laughter made me feel foolish for some reason, probably the same way she felt after she failed at her grand finale. "Oh, Topher. There are so many things stopping me, you have no idea," she said, as if there were a hundred secrets she wasn't about to share. "But this isn't about me. This isn't my folder. It's yours."

I looked at my drawings. Sword-wielding warlords. Masked vigilantes. But also a sketch of the willow tree outside room 213. I closed the folder and looked at Ms. B.

"We all have moments when we think nobody really *sees* us. When we feel like we have to act out or be somebody else just to get noticed. But somebody notices, Topher. Somebody sees.

Somebody out there probably thinks you're the greatest thing in the whole world. Don't ever think you're not good enough."

She reached to the desk and took up the drawing of the spider, holding it out to me. "I won't keep it if you don't want me to. I won't keep any of them. They aren't mine, and I should have asked. If you still don't think it's worthwhile, we can put it right back where you left it. But I like it. I think it's one of your best."

The drawing floated between Ms. Bixby and me, hovering beside the secret bottom drawer where Ms. Bixby kept a half dozen dreams. None of them were her dream, but she kept them safe anyways.

I took the picture, the one she'd rescued. Then I opened the folder again and put it on top.

I can see the hospital from the McDonald's—a dozen or so floors stretching skyward. It should have taken us three minutes to walk there, but we aren't moving as fast as when we started this morning, full of raisins and confidence and grand plans. I'm still limping and Steve seems woozy. I'm not sure if it's from George Nelson's left hook or from finally mustering the guts to stand up to Christina, but he staggers like a boxer after nine rounds.

I'm holding the bag of fries, which are already making grease spots through the paper. In my backpack sits a tattered paperback and a pair of now-useless speakers. They were supposed to be hooked up to Steve's phone to play music—Beethoven, and whatever else he loaded up. But the phone is dead. No music. No wine. At least we still have the cheesecake. Sort of. And the french fries.

And the picture.

The one tucked away in the second half of my now-torn sketchbook. The one that Brand discovered and went all Gollum-my-precious about. I had planned to give it to her when nobody was looking. Leave it on a table or tuck it under her pillow, somewhere she might find it later. Or maybe a nurse would pick it up and show it to her and say something, like "This is really good. Is this you?" She would know who did it, of course. And she would smile and say, "Yes, it's me. Where did that come from?" Then later, she could stick it in the green folder in the bottom drawer. Or maybe she would keep it some-where else. Somewhere closer.

The whole trip over, Brand stays behind us so that it's just Steve and me together. The two wounded warriors bumping into each other because neither of us can seem to walk straight.

"You might have said there was a chance of running into your sister downtown today," I say. "That might have been incor-porated into the plan somehow." Though I'm not sure what we would have done about it. Disguises maybe. Ski masks. Though three boys wearing ski masks into a McDonald's probably would have caused its own share of problems.

"The odds were against it," Steve replies. "A hundred to one. It shouldn't have happened."

"And yet it did. That's called destiny," I say. "She's your Voldemort."

Christina looked nothing like Voldemort. She needed to be balder and paler and a man. But throw a black robe on him, paint a scar on his forehead, and give him a stick to wave around, and Steve could probably pull off Harry Potter. At least the Japanese version.

Steve frowns. "She's not my Voldemort. She was just looking out for me."

"Tchya," I scoff. "Only because she was hoping to get you into trouble. She probably lied to us. She's probably calling your parents right now and telling them everything." I look behind me, half expecting to see Steve's father trailing us in his black Nissan, waiting for just the right moment to cut us off and shove us in the trunk to be delivered directly to Principal McNasty's clutches.

"She's not going to call," Steve says. "She promised she wouldn't tell."

"And you believe her?"

Steve shrugs. "She's my sister, Topher. Sure she's annoying. And bossy. And sometimes I can't stand how good she is at everything, but that doesn't mean I hate her or anything. You shouldn't give her such a hard time."

"Me?"

"Yes, you. You exacerbate the situation."

"I do *not* exacerbate," I say. "Wait . . . what's exacerbate mean?"

"You make it worse," Steve explains. "You egg her on."

I kick at the gravel on the sidewalk. Maybe he has a point—he usually does. Maybe I do exacerbate sometimes. But that didn't make his sister not-annoying. I glance over my shoulder. Brand is lagging farther and farther behind, like he's having second thoughts. Again. But we are way too close to give up now. "So what did she say to you back there, when you two were whispering?" Steve tells me everything. Anything anybody ever whispered to him, I would hear about eventually. Not that anyone but me whispered anything to him usually.

"She asked me if I was really okay," Steve tells me. "And if I really wanted her to take me home but was afraid to say it in front of you guys. Oh, and she told me I should probably stop listening to you all the time. She thinks you're trouble."

"She thinks *I'm* trouble," I sputter.

"She says you're no good for me. She thinks I could do better."

My mouth hangs. "Do better than me? Not likely. I'm

infinitely cooler than anyone else in your life, *especially* her."

Steve shrugs. "You asked me what she said, so I told you."

"Yeah, well, I hope one of her furry patients bites her and gives her rabies," I say. But then I think about it, what it would be like if Steve took her advice and ditched me for somebody else, found another best friend. I don't know if I could take it. "And what did you say to her? When she said that?"

Steve looks down at his feet shuffling along the sidewalk.

"I told her that nobody's perfect," he mumbles, then adds with a grin, "and that you were still infinitely cooler than anyone else in my life."

"Especially her?"

"Especially her," Steve repeats. Then he looks up and points. "We're there."

St. Mary's Hospital looms over us, two big buildings connected by over-street walkways. Steve told me once that there were about ten thousand different saints, that Catholicism is like the Hallmark of religions—a saint for every occasion. There's a saint for comedians and lepers. There are saints for alcoholics and reformed alcoholics and for people who are named Joshua (Saint Joshua). There is a saint for artists too: Saint Catherine of Bologna. The city, not the lunch meat. Steve says that's the one who probably watches over me. Her and Saint Christopher, who usually looks after sailors, motorists, and people with toothaches, though I get an automatic in because of my name. Of all ten thousand, though, I can only assume Mary is a first-round pick, if not the number one overall. Ms. Bixby is in good hands.

I can see the main entrance, and I stop for a moment and wait for the clouds to part, splitting to reveal a ray of sunshine, like a tractor beam, that will bathe St. Mary's in a sparkling pool of light. I see it in my head clear enough, I can even hear the choir, but it doesn't happen. It's just a hospital: steel and dark glass and sand-colored stone, though compared to the rest of the buildings around it, it looks brand-new and imposing, like some kind of impenetrable fortress.

"You think she will be happy to see us?" I ask.

"I don't know," Steve says.

"But we should definitely still go, right?"

"I think the fries are getting cold."

I take that as a yes. We stop at the automatic revolving doors and wait for Brand to catch up.

"We look like we should be going through the ER entrance instead," Steve says, prodding at his puffy lip. I'm limping. He's bloody. Our clothes are filthy from too much time sitting on curbs, rolling on sidewalks, getting knocked to the ground, or hiding behind Dumpsters. I reach over and do my best to tame Steve's hair. I don't even bother with mine. Lost cause.

"We made it," I say. Through fire and flipwads and stuffed

owls and sharks in toilets, we are finally here. So why am I even more nervous all of a sudden?

Brand steps up behind us, hands stuffed in his pockets.

"About time," Steve says, and we both turn and head toward the door.

Brand doesn't move.

"Dude, are you coming?" I hold up the bag of french fries like it's a ticking time bomb, wondering what could possibly be holding him back, now that we are right outside the door.

"Hang on," he says. "Before we go in there, there's something I've gotta tell you."

Brand

THERE'S A DIFFERENCE BETWEEN THE TRUTH and the *whole* truth. That's why they give that big spiel in court, when they make you place your hand on the Bible and promise to tell the truth, the whole truth, and nothing but the truth. Because they know if they don't, people will try and sneak around it. They will leave out the details, skip over the incriminating stuff. Keep the worst parts to themselves.

She told me I shouldn't tell anyone. She said it was against school policy. That the school board would have an issue with it. And my father would probably frown upon it. That maybe society at large would frown upon it. Who knows, maybe she could even get fired, though she didn't think so.

But the truth is this.

I saw Ms. Bixby every Friday for two and a half months straight. I don't mean every Friday during school. I mean afterward.

She would pick me up at my house. Except not at my house, because I didn't want my father to know, so instead I waited for her at the corner. And she would pull up in her little white hatchback, the one with the bumper sticker that reads *I ♥ Brains*, which she insisted was both a zombie reference and a warning to most of the men out there. She would pick me up and toss her satchel in the back and offer me a stick of gum, which I always took because I was worried my breath smelled like school lunch. And she would drive us to the same place as the Friday before. We would spend the hour together, like always, and then she would drop me off at the corner again and wait till I got in the door with my bags and waved good-bye.

Every Friday. Ten Fridays in a row. Starting with the day she found me nearly collapsed in the snow. All the way up until the last one, when we found my father collapsed on the porch.

The whole truth is this: I waited for each Friday like it was Christmas Eve. Or better yet, like it was March 31st.

I would stand at the corner with my arms crossed, unconsciously holding my breath, trying to look cool by trying *not* to try to look cool. My list was usually stuffed in my back pocket, along with the money I had taken from the bread box—a hundred bucks. I would see her Ford come around the corner and she would flash her lights or roll down the window and ask me if I needed a ride, even though she knew the answer, even though that was the whole point. And I would smile and nod and buckle in and look down at my shoes as she drove, or maybe just stare out the window. She would give me permission to change the radio station, to find something I liked, but I never touched it, no matter what it was. It was never the same kind of music. Sometimes it was classical. Sometimes it was talk radio. Once it was metal—she said she'd gotten in a little tiff with another teacher that day and needed Iron Maiden to help her unwind. She liked just about everything, but she had her favorites. She always turned it way up when the Stones came on. Her car always smelled like coffee.

We would park at the end of the row for no other reason than she said it never hurt anyone to walk, and we would pause outside to admire the shoots of green brave enough to sprout in early March, improbably breaking through the frost. Then she would pull out her list and I would pull out mine and we would each grab a cart. And I'm pretty sure I didn't stop smiling the whole time I was with her.

"Wait a minute. She took you shopping?" Steve stares at me, mouth like a Cheerio. "*Grocery* shopping?"

"The Kroger up on Sixty-First. By the Pizza Hut and what used to be a video store."

"Every Friday?"

"It's a long walk," I explain. "Groceries are heavy, and my dad can't drive."

That's not the whole truth. He *could* drive—the car is fixed so that he could use his hands to stop and go—he just chose not to. He also chose not to leave the house. But he couldn't choose not to eat, or at least he hadn't yet, so I walked to the grocery store. It was only two miles. But two miles is an eternity when you are carrying a gallon of milk, a bag of potatoes, and six family-size boxes of mac and cheese. Two miles feels like torture when you walk it in the freezing cold rain.

The revolving door of the hospital spins, and an old couple comes out holding hands. Steve is shaking his head. Topher is silent.

"I should have told you guys earlier, but she said it was better if it stayed between us. Something about the school and legal issues with driving me and everything. Plus, you know, the water fountain thing. If you let one person get a drink of water, then you have to let everyone get a drink of water."

"Ms. Bixby was afraid we'd *all* want to go grocery shopping with her?" Steve asks.

"Something like that," I say.

"I hate grocery shopping," he says.

Yes, well, when you have to start cooking all your dinners or else you won't eat, you suddenly take an interest, I think, but I don't say it.

"So that's it?" Topher finally says. "That's your big secret? You and Ms. Bixby went Krogering together? For a minute there I thought . . ." But he doesn't finish that thought.

"That's it," I say.

But it wasn't quite.

The whole truth is this: Ms. Bixby saved me. From the snow that first day and from other things other days. From the fog I woke up in. From the dark cloud that sometimes followed me. From having to carry so much weight around all the time.

There were days I thought about leaving town. Taking off for somewhere. I don't know where. Just away. I would stand in the door to my room, staring out across the hall at my father sitting in his recliner, legs covered with a blanket whether he was cold or not, just so he wouldn't have to look at them, staring at some show that he couldn't possibly care a thing about, about the world's cutest puppies or someone trying to eat too many hamburgers. Thinking, no doubt, about how life wasn't fair. To lose my mom and then his legs. To have to raise a kid when he can barely get out of his chair to take a shower. I would watch him and think that neither of us was doing the other any favors. If I left, he'd have no choice but to start taking care of himself. He'd have to do his own laundry. Wash his own dishes.

If I left, he'd be forced to go buy his own groceries. Then I wouldn't have to make that long walk anymore. The walk was the worst, every step reminding me what I could do that he couldn't, what I had to do that he didn't. I resented every moment I spent in the store, knowing this was food I would end up making and cleaning up after. If I left, he'd be forced to go himself or just sit in his chair and starve.

Some days—the worst days—I thought maybe that was what he deserved. He was my father. He was supposed to be taking care of me.

Then Ms. Bixby came and pulled up beside me. By accident the first time, but after that, right on schedule. Friday afternoons, with the sun blushing and Ms. Bixby holding her sunglasses in her teeth as we stopped at the bins by the entrance to look over the strawberries. And she would ask me questions—not about school necessarily, but about me. What I was interested in. If I'd ever seen the ocean. What my favorite flavor of ice cream was. If I liked dogs or cats better. She didn't ask about my parents—I'm sure it was all in my file at school. It was as if she knew that this one hour was all I had, and she didn't want to waste it.

She told me about her. Not that much, but more than Ms.

Bixby the teacher ever would. She told me that she was married once, for six years, till she came to the conclusion that her husband was a jerk (which she always kind of knew but hoped otherwise) and that he wasn't going to change anytime soon (a conclusion that she took longer to come to). She told me about her trip to Australia when she was in high school and the time she broke her arm falling off a trampoline. She told me about her brother, who was in the army but was coming home on leave soon, and her own dad—an English professor who lived out east and who used to pack her scraps of paper with quotes from his favorite books in her lunch box, which explained one thing, at least. The Bixbyisms were an inheritance.

She also told me that she spent a lot of time alone as a kid. That it was hard for her to make friends, sometimes, and that she used to spend whole afternoons just walking along the train tracks that ran parallel to her neighborhood, thinking that one day she wouldn't turn around and go back, she would just keep on walking as far as the tracks would take her. But she never did, she said, because your troubles are like your shadow: you can't always see them, but you can't run from them either.

Some days she was serious. Other days she would tell jokes or stories about former students—names excluded—and crazy things they had done. She explained how sampling one grape or one cherry wasn't stealing so much as "ensuring customer satisfaction." She turned coupon time into a math lesson (she apologized right after—it was instinct, couldn't be helped) and made me stop to admire the carnations at the florist's. Carnations get a bad rap, she said, because they are cheaper than roses, but she liked them better because they fight harder. Roses are quitters—they give up and die before you can even get used to them being around.

It's amazing how fast an hour at the grocery store can go, how fast your cart fills up, how soon you find yourself paying, and marveling at how much it costs just to survive. She would tell me how half the stuff I bought was likely to kill me if I kept eating it, especially the hot dogs. "Too much processed meat is bad for your health," she said.

"In that case, I have nothing to worry about," I told her, holding up the package. "There's no actual meat in these things." I sometimes tried too hard to make her laugh.

When we were finished and had our bags packed in her trunk—hers on the right, mine to the left—she would drive me back to my corner and say see-you-Monday and tell me to find some time for reading over the weekend. She usually said she had had a good time, though I always thought she was just saying it to be nice. She always told me to take care of myself.

Except for the night we spent in the emergency room. She didn't say any of those things then.

St. Mary's Community Hospital invites us through the automatic revolving doors with a rush of cool air. I've spent a lot of time in hospitals, more than I think is fair for someone my age. I know what to expect. First the lobby, so unhospital-like, set up like the entrance to a grand hotel, down to the fancy chairs and the grand piano that mostly just sits there unplayed. A vast space complete with carpet and a Starbucks and a Hallmark gift shop and a map that shows that *You are here.* The sun pours through the glass walls, reaches halfway down the halls, and the only sign that you're in a building where people often come to die is the empty wheelchair sitting by the elevators.

We walk in and Topher whispers for us to be cool and act normal, though he's the one limping and glancing nervously around. There is a security guard standing by the elevators and another behind the information desk. The only spot in the lobby that's at all crowded is a little window that says *Billing and Payment Support*, where there's a line of adults shuffling papers, waiting for their turn. I've been in that line before.

This would be easier if we had an adult to latch onto, I think, just someone to follow behind. We must stick out: three sixth graders walking way too close together, hissing at and jostling each other. Of course, the last time we enlisted an adult's help, he stole our money and used it to buy a bottle of hooch.

"Just keep walking," I tell Topher, "straight for the elevators." The guy at the desk doesn't even look up from his computer as we circle around. I look at the giant clock hanging above the desk. It's 1:22 on a Friday afternoon.

I used to look forward to Friday afternoons.

"Can I help you boys find something?"

We freeze right outside the hall leading to the elevators. The security guard who stopped us puts a thumb through his belt, settling it right by his gun. I'm sure it's just a habit, but it's unnerving. I suddenly start to wonder what the protocol is for hospital security. Like, if our packs will be searched. That would be bad. According to his badge, the security guard's name is Pete.

"No, sir," Topher says. "We're here visiting our grandmother. She had a heart attack and is recovering from surgery."

"Sorry to hear that," the guard says, and you know from his tone that he probably says that a hundred times a day. I don't add anything to that story. I hope Topher doesn't either, but his overactive imagination has a pipeline directly to his always open mouth.

"Oh, it's all right," he says brightly. "Maybe now she'll stop smoking three packs a day."

The guard cocks his head to the side, but before he can ask anything else, the closest elevator chimes and the doors slide open. We huddle in, still pressed close together even though we have the whole elevator to ourselves. Steve hits the button for the fourth floor. He has the room number memorized. I do too, actually.

"Three packs a day?" I say.

"The details are what make it believable," Topher retorts.

The doors close, and for a second, the whole world drops out from under me.

That's how it felt. Five weeks ago. Like the earth had split and I had been standing right on the crack. It was the last Friday in March, four days before April Fool's. It was the last Friday I spent with Ms. Bixby.

There was nothing remarkable about that afternoon. I think Pepsi was on sale instead of Coke, and there was a promotion to celebrate the start of baseball season—buy one get one free on hot dog buns, which I was told not to fall prey to and did anyway. We spent some time looking over the flowers that were set up outside, and Ms. Bixby taught me the difference between annuals and perennials. Then she quoted something about the flame that burns twice as bright burning half as long, which she insisted was from a Chinese philosopher but I was pretty sure came from a movie.

I splurged and bought Popsicles that day. They don't have

time to melt when your teacher drives you home and drops you off, and your father never asks how you managed to get them home. He only wants to know if you are making something for dinner and what it is. Ms. Bixby bought five quarts of blueberries that day, I remember. I counted them as she loaded them on the conveyor belt. I said she was going to be berry busy. She said, thank you berry much. As we left, we were stopped by a group of teenagers dressed in pink, collecting money to fight breast cancer. Ms. Bixby dug through her purse and gave them a five. I chipped in a dollar.

I didn't know, of course. She hadn't told us yet.

We loaded the car and she drove slowly back to my neighborhood, tapping gently on the wheel to some golden oldie on the radio. I said something about summer not being far away and asked her if she had any plans, any vacations or grand adventures. I was building to something. A bigger question. A question that concerned both of us. She might be around, she said, hard to tell at this point. I was about to ask her what she meant by that when she turned the corner onto my street and stopped the car.

There, in the amber glow of the afternoon sun, I saw him, sprawled out across the front porch. His walker tipped over at the bottom of the steps leading to the walkway, one arm hanging off the step. He wasn't moving.

"Is that . . . ?" she asked. I just sat there and nodded dumbly. I couldn't move or speak.

Ms. Bixby took out her cell phone and called 911 as the Popsicles in the trunk began to melt.

The head nurse, who is sitting at the station directly facing the elevators, watches us spill out, her hands poised above her keyboard, head twisted around, like Alexander's owl. She is dressed in mint-green scrubs. A collection of badges hangs around her neck.

"The gatekeeper," Topher whispers. I really can't imagine what goes on in his head.

"Maybe you should let me do the talking," I say. After all, I'm not sure how many fake grandmothers Topher can nearly kill off in a day. To my surprise, he nods.

The name on the front tag says she is Georgia Bonner, RN. I'm sure she's friendly. She's a nurse. You don't go into nursing if you hate people. But then I think about teachers, and not all of them are what you'd expect. They can't all be Good Ones.

"Can I help you boys?" she says curtly as we approach.

"We are here to see Maggie Bixby," I respond coolly. When all else fails, tell the truth. Just not the whole truth.

"I'm sorry, but Ms. Bixby is not seeing visitors right now. Only family."

"Oh, we're family," Topher chirps up from behind me.

I turn to glare at him. He shuts his mouth, but it's too late. I look back at Georgia and smile. "We're her nephews," I say, running with it.

"I'm adopted," Steve adds helpfully. "From Japan."

Nurse Georgia's eyes are powder blue and narrow, inspecting us with a frown. "Are you here with your parents?" She's clearly not buying it. Maybe she knows more about Ms. Bixby's family than we do. After all, I only know that she got divorced before she had kids and that she has an older brother in the army; I'm not even sure he's married. Maybe she has no nephews.

"They're down in the gift shop," I say. "They couldn't agree on a card. Dad likes the ones that sing when you open them, but Mom thinks they're annoying. They said we could go ahead and come up. Aunt Maggie's in 428, right?" It really is all in the details.

The nurse consults her computer, then looks back at us. I think she knows I'm BS-ing her.

"What happened to your lip?" she asks, noticing Steve, who is sort of hiding behind Topher and me.

"I got punched," he says, then points at me. "His fault."

"You punched him?" she asks.

"I ducked," I say.

Nurse Georgia nods slowly. "Right. And what's in the bags? Homework?"

"Homework," I confirm quickly, before Topher can think of something outlandish to say—in this case, the truth. This isn't going well either. I glance down the hall, looking at the numbers printed on the doors. There's no way she's going to let us pass. I'm about to just let loose, tell her everything like I did back at Michelle's, when Nurse Georgia sighs and sort of deflates like a popped tire.

"All right," she says at last. "You boys have ten minutes. No more. Your a*unt*," she adds, with way too much emphasis, "needs her rest." We all nod, no doubt looking like a pack of eager puppies waiting to go for a walk. "And be quiet, please. There are some very sick patients on this floor and they need their rest too."

"Yes, ma'am," we all chirp in unison.

Nurse Georgia smiles—finally—and points around the corner. I tell her thanks and give Steve a nudge, hoping that we get out of here before she changes her mind. We are almost to the turn when she calls out to us. "And boys . . . ?"

We stop and turn. She points to the grease-spotted sack of fries in Topher's hand.

"Ms. Bixby's on a strict diet, just so you know."

"Yes, ma'am," I say again. "We understand." No fries.

Can't imagine what she'd say about whiskey and cheesecake.

✦ ✦ ✦

I didn't eat that night, the night she drove us to the emergency room, doing sixty miles an hour to keep up with the ambulance. We were there all night, but I wasn't at all hungry. Ms. Bixby bought me a muffin from the cafeteria—apple cinnamon. Most of it ended up in the trash, the parts she didn't end up eating herself.

She stayed with me until the end. While the ER physicians and the neurologist on call ran their tests and performed their procedures, X-rays and blood tests and brain scans and more tests I couldn't even pronounce. They said my father probably slipped trying to navigate through the door with the walker. That was their word: navigate. Like he was a ship's captain lost at sea. He knocked himself unconscious when he fell and suffered a concussion—that much was clear, but they wanted to make sure he hadn't done any more damage to his spine, which meant more tests. And hours of waiting.

The nurses asked me a lot of questions, and I told them the truth. (Maybe not the whole truth, but pretty close.) I told them that it was just him and me at home. That I wasn't sure what he did while I was at school all day, but that he mostly stayed in his chair and watched TV when I was home. I told them that we didn't get much help and mostly made do on our own. One of the nurses asked if Ms. Bixby was Dad's girlfriend. I felt like hitting the guy for some reason, but Ms. Bixby just laughed it off and said she was a family friend.

They brought us both coffees from the lobby, and Ms. Bixby doctored mine, loading it with enough milk and sugar to make it sippable. She did everything she could to distract me while we waited for updates. We played tic-tac-toe on the back of a pamphlet for diabetes. We paced laps around the waiting room. Mostly we just sat and talked, or I talked. I told her things I never had before, things that would have ruined our Friday afternoons. Like about how much I wish I had a mother. And the hard time my dad had when I was growing up. And what it had been like for the past year and a half, watching him just fading away, sort of blending in to the background of the living room, taking less and less interest in the world around him. She listened, like she always did, patiently, intently, nodding until I finished.

And I waited for it: the Bixbyism. The one quote from Lao Tzu or Benjamin Franklin or Mick Jagger that would put it all into perspective and make it all better. But it never came. Maybe she didn't have one. Maybe she'd run out of inspirational sayings. Instead she just told me she was sorry. That life just sucked sometimes. Then she put her arm around me the way I imagined my mother probably would have.

That's how the doctor found me, sitting on one of the waiting room couches with Ms. Bixby holding me. He smiled when he delivered the good news: no further damage to my father's spine. Only the concussion and a sprained wrist, probably from trying to catch himself. He was also dehydrated, apparently, and his blood report showed that he was taking more of some medications and not enough of others, which they would need to talk about. Then the doctor said Dad was awake and was asking for me.

Ms. Bixby lifted her arm. We both stood up and I started walking toward the hall, but she didn't follow. She stood by the couch.

"Aren't you coming?"

Ms. Bixby shook her head. "He's your dad," she said. "He needs you. *Just* you."

I didn't move. "No," I told her. "I'm not going in there by myself. I can't." The doctor standing next to me put a hand on my arm, but I sloughed it right back off. Ms. Bixby took a few steps so that she was standing in front of me.

"I can't keep doing it all by myself," I said, my voice catching.

When she spoke, her voice was almost a whisper, as if she didn't want the doctor or anyone else to hear. "Do you remember when you said to me that you didn't know what you were good at? You told me it seemed like everyone else around you had some special gift and you didn't have anything."

I nodded. Took deep, shuddering breaths.

"Do you know why I would always show up at that corner every Friday afternoon?"

I shook my head.

"Because I knew you'd be there waiting for me. Not because you were counting on me, but because your dad was counting on you. Because even if I didn't show up, you'd still go, don't you see? You would go whether I was there to help you or not."

She bent down so that our foreheads were almost touching. "You don't give up, Brand Walker. That's what makes you special. You need to show him that. Show him what it means to be strong. *Teach* him how to not give up."

Then she gave it to me. The Bixbyism. The one she'd been saving. Whispered it in my ear. It was from one of her favorite books, she said. She whispered it to me and then she made me repeat it back to her. And even though I'm not Steve, I memorized it on the first try.

Then she gave me a quick hug and turned and left without saying another word.

And even though I tried not to, choking and pushing and biting it back as hard as I could, I cried. Not for Dad, who was waiting for me in yet another hospital bed. Or for Ms. Bixby, who, I later found out, would be right back in this same hospital the next day suffering through her own series of tests. But for me. Hot, selfish tears, smeared across my cheeks. Because this was it, and I knew it.

I'm not sure how, but I knew that it was the last day I would have her all to myself.

I know what I'm going to say. The moment we walk into the room. I've had it planned for a while now. Ever since I came up with the idea to visit her in the first place, the idea of the one perfect day. And even though just about everything has gone wrong and it won't even be close to perfect, as long as I say what I came to say, it will be all right.

I recite it over and over again in my head as we shuffle through the automatic doors and down the hall.

The place is graveyard quiet. The rooms are almost all dark. A few have televisions on, but the volumes are turned way down. In room 408 a nurse or an orderly is staring at an empty bed, slowly unfolding a crisp white sheet, getting things ready for a new patient or cleaning up after an old one. We move slowly down the hall, careful not to touch anything. The door to room 417 is open, but the old lady inside is fast asleep. There is a big bouquet of flowers on the table by her bed. Carnations. Letting Topher and Steve walk ahead, I slip in and out in a matter of seconds, then hurry to catch up. They don't seem to notice. The woman in 417 won't either, I'm guessing. She had enough to share.

The door to room 428 is shut, but the lights shine through the curtained window. Hopefully that means she's awake. This is already going to be enough of a surprise without waking her up in the process. I stand in front of the door for a minute, at least it feels like a minute, then turn and look at Steve and Topher. "Thanks for coming with," I say.

Steve nods. Topher says, "The fries are getting cold," which I take as *you're welcome* and *hurry up* all in one.

I take a deep breath and knock three times, reciting the line one more time in my head.

A voice says we can come in. The voice doesn't sound familiar. I give the door a little push and it swings in casually.

From her bed, Ms. Bixby turns and looks at the three of us crowded in her doorway.

And I'm suddenly speechless.

Topher

YOU HAVE TO SLAY THE DRAGON TO BE THE hero. Not easy to do, but at least you know what you're dealing with. Dragons are easy to spot. They live in caves and have large, leathery wings and smoke seeping out of their nostrils. They cool their hot bellies on rolling waves of hoarded gold. They might as well have a sign that says *Slay me* dangling from their necks.

But there are no such things as dragons. It's never that clear-cut. Sometimes, the thing you're fighting against is hiding from you. It's tucked away, buried deep where you can't see it. In fact, for a long time, you might not even know it's there. Maybe when it starts, it's just this tiny thing you don't even notice. Maybe you mistake it for something else or you ignore it. But then it starts

261

to grow, and before you know it, it's stalking you. Before you know it, it has you cornered.

Maybe it's a secret that you're afraid to share because you don't know what other people will think of you, especially your friends. Or maybe it's a sister that you're constantly compared to, who seems better than you in every way, even though she has pretty much the same problems you do.

Or maybe it's just a feeling. A nagging hole. A sense that nobody really understands or appreciates you. A sense that you don't really matter. That is, until you find your teacher digging through the bin one day and see the treasures buried in her bottom drawer.

Of course, sometimes it really is a dragon, or at least it's a monster, determined to destroy you or someone you care about from the inside out. And you know it's there. You just have no idea how to stop it.

I know what I'm going to say when we open the door. I figured it out on the walk over. I mean, there were a lot of options, but what I've got is killer.

We stand outside room 428 and Brand knocks softly. I think about the sketch still stashed in my backpack. I should have folded it up and put in my pocket, made it easier to get to. But today's one of those *shoulda* kind of days. There will still be time to give it to her.

A voice tells us to come in, and Brand opens the door. Someone looks over at me from the bed.

It's not Ms. Bixby.

Ms. Bixby has light-brown hair with a stripe of pink in her bangs like strawberry syrup. Ms. Bixby has bright-green eyes that make you think she is half cat. Ms. Bixby wears bright sweaters and boots that reach up to her knees and dangly earrings that look like she made them herself. The woman in the bed has no hair. The woman in the bed, just staring at us with her mouth hanging open, sallow cheeked and pale, is not Ms. Bixby. And for a moment, I think we've got the wrong room. That for the first time in his life, Steve actually remembered something wrong. But then the woman props herself up on her elbows and gives me an inquisitive smile, a don't-I-know-you-from-somewhere smile.

I take a step into the room, clear my throat, and deliver my line.

"I'm Luke Skywalker," I say. "I'm here to rescue you." Beside me, Brand's mouth opens and closes silently.

And the woman in the bed answers, "Aren't you a little short for a stormtrooper?"

That's when I know it's her.

"I brought some friends," I say, stepping aside so Brand and Steve can squeeze by. Steve waves sheepishly. Brand doesn't say anything, but he and Ms. B. exchange a look. It doesn't last long, half a second maybe. Ms. B. scoots up even farther in her bed.

"Wow," she says, which is what she says both when she's impressed with your work and when you've done something all wrong. I guess this could go either way. Her voice is raspy, faltering. "What are you three *doing* here?" She looks up at the clock by the television. "It's one thirty in the afternoon. On a *school* day."

She punctuates the *school*, but she's not really mad. You can see it in her dark-rimmed eyes. It's not an accusation. More of a curiosity. But I can tell she *really* didn't see this coming. We have the element of surprise.

"We heard you were leaving," Brand says finally. "Like, skipping town. And we didn't get a chance to say good-bye."

"Today's your last day," Steve adds.

Ms. Bixby makes a little sound, like she's got something caught in her throat.

"At school, he means," I add, giving Steve a kick in the shin.

"Right," Ms. Bixby whispers. "The party. So sorry about that." She looks past us down the hall. "You didn't *all* come, did you?" she asks nervously, leaning up on her elbows, looking for her other twenty or so students.

"Just the three of us," I say. "We got you these." I hand her the bag of french fries that I was forbidden by Nurse Georgia to share. But on the list of things I've already done today, feeding greasy french fries to a cancer patient seems like a mild offense.

Ms. Bixby questions us with her eyes, then reaches for the bag and opens it cautiously, as if she expects a trick, a dead mouse or a springing-coil snake. I've fallen for those same tricks before—when Brand first became friends with us, before I learned his tricks. She looks confused at first. Then she puts a trembling hand to her mouth. There are bandages all over her arms.

"Oh my God," she says. "Because of what I said that time? About . . ." She doesn't finish the thought.

"Are they all right?" Steve asks. "They're McDonald's."

Ms. Bixby grins. "Are you kidding? I haven't had these in *months*." She presses her face into the bag and takes three giant whiffs, like she's hyperventilating. Maybe she is. French fries are truly one of mankind's greatest inventions.

"There's more," I say. "We got everything. Or almost everything. Or some version of everything. But we can't do it here."

"Everything?" Ms. Bixby closes the bag and stares at me. I try to look straight at her, but it's hard. She looks so different, especially without the hair. I expected her to look different; at least I knew there was the possibility. But I wasn't prepared for how *fragile* she would be. She barely moves. At school, she can't keep still. I'm not used to seeing her just lie there. "Can't do *what* here? What are you talking about?"

"You just have to trust us," I tell her. "There's a place we can go. It's just outside. Maybe a block away. But we have to get you out of here."

I look over to Brand for confirmation, but he is busy staring out Ms. Bixby's window, as if he can't look at her either. Steve nods at least, backing me up. "There's not enough square feet to even lay out the blanket in here," he says. Steve's idea of an explanation.

From her bed, Ms. Bixby starts shaking her head; her eyes are swollen like Steve's bottom lip. I'm not sure if she totally gets it or not, but I can tell she is catching on. "Oh my . . . boys . . . this is so . . . it's really very sweet," she says. "But I can't just leave. I'm sorry. They won't . . . I'm not . . . see, I'm scheduled for a treatment, and just look at how I'm dressed." She points to the blue hospital gown that peeks out from the covers. "I'm really supposed to stay here. . . ."

She looks at us pleadingly, but I'm not about to give up. I'm about to tell her all about the cheesecake when Brand turns from the window.

"Atticus Finch," he says.

"What?" I say, looking at him strangely. The words are completely meaningless to me, but they seem to spark something in

Ms. Bixby. Brand is looking right at her now. He looks almost a little angry, as if he's challenging her.

"You read it?" she asks.

Brand nods. Ms. Bixby turns to Steve and me. "And you three skipped school and came out all this way just to tell me good-bye?"

"It was Brand's idea," Steve says, almost defensively, probably thinking he's about to get in trouble.

"That's not even the half of it," I tell her. "But we can't do it here. Not the way we're supposed to. At least let us get this part right."

Ms. Bixby looks down at her bag of fries. Then she cranes her neck to see past the three of us and out the door again. I can see the sparkle come back into her eyes, just for a moment.

"All right," she says. "Meet me by the elevators in five."

We stand outside the elevators, backs pressed against our packs, packs pressed against the wall. Steve is probably crushing what's left of white-chocolate raspberry heaven, but I'm guessing it really can't look any worse at this point. I'm staring at a poster urging me to eat healthy with a stupid picture of a kid smiling over a plate of broccoli like it's a bowl of Lucky Charms. Behind the desk, Nurse Georgia is occupied with her phone and computer, frantically switching from one to the other, which is good, because it means she's ignoring us. She doesn't look like a Georgia. She looks more like a Helga or a Svetlana, like something out of Norse mythology, broad shouldered and brick chinned with plaited blond hair, like she should be guarding the bridge to Valhalla. Thor would completely dig her.

"Atticus Finch. Is that some kind of bird?" Steve whispers. He doesn't want to draw any of Nurse Georgia's attention.

"It's a character," Brand whispers back. "From a book written, like, fifty years ago."

"Is he a superhero or something?" I ask. It sounds like the name of a superhero. Or his secret identity, anyways. Mild-mannered reporter, Atticus Finch. Obviously it's a decent book or Ms. Bixby wouldn't have told Brand to read it, but having superheroes would be a bonus.

"He's a lawyer," Brand says. "But the book's not really about him."

"Then what is it about?"

"It's about standing up for what's right, I guess."

"Oh," I say. "Is there any sword fighting in it?"

Brand shakes his head. He's not doing a great job selling it, but I'll make it a point to read it someday anyways, even without the sword fighting. Behind the desk Nurse Georgia groans and taps frantically on her mouse. I wonder how many books Ms. Bixby has recommended to Brand. Wonder if they talked about what they read as they steered their carts up and down the aisles of the Kroger, shopping for salsa and shredded wheat. Did he know what brand of shampoo she used? Or what she fed her cat? If she drank 2 percent or skim or some of that nasty organic almond stuff? Did he know if Ms. Bixby ate frosted or unfrosted Pop-Tarts? These are things I kind of wish I knew. Things I suddenly wish I had time to find out like he did.

Brand hisses and points down the hall.

Here she comes, out of her gown but still in her slippers. Wearing a pair of navy blue sweatpants, a sweatshirt that says *Hofstra* on it, and a sly smile that stretches near to her eyeballs. She's sliding across the tiles, much more ninja-like than me, even in her condition. In one hand is the bag of fries. The other holds a giant purse. Brand presses the elevator button. Normally we'd place bets on which one would come up first, but sneaking a cancer patient out of a hospital calls for our full attention. I look over to make sure Nurse Georgia is still staring at her computer screen and jabbering on the phone. The elevator tings and the doors slide open. Ms. Bixby starts pushing us inside, telling us to hurry.

"I can't believe I'm doing this," she says.

"Believe it, toots," I say, which is a line from a movie, though I'm not sure what the movie is and I have no idea what *toots* means. Judging by the severe look on Ms. Bixby's face, it's probably not a word I will use again. Brand presses the *L* button at least ten times.

"Come on, come on," he says.

Behind the desk, Nurse Georgia hears his coaxing and frantic pressing and glances up from her computer. She pulls the phone from her ear and cups it, speaking through a frown. "Ms. Bixby? Is that you?"

Ms. Bixby steps behind Steve, even though he is the shortest of us and can't possibly conceal her. Brand jams his thumb into the close door button this time, just holding it there. I think about the scene from *Aliens* where they wait for an eternity for the elevator doors to close and the one guy gets sprayed with acid. Elevators are the worst.

"Ms. Bixby, where are you going?"

Ms. Bixby shrugs.

Nurse Georgia stands up, looks like maybe she is going to leap right over that desk and come after us. A Valkyrie charge. I suddenly wonder if she has the power to call down lightning from the sky. The elevator doors start to close.

"Ms. Bixby," she calls again, voice growing steadily louder, "you have a treatment scheduled—"

And then Nurse Georgia is gone. The elevator drops. The numbers start flashing down. Four to three to two. I start whispering to myself, holding one hand to my ear.

"Special Agent Renn reporting in. The egg is in the basket. I repeat, the egg is in the basket."

"You're talking to yourself again," Brand warns me.

Behind us, Ms. Bixby is studying her reflection in the shiny smooth wall of the elevator. She runs a bandaged hand along her smooth head.

"It looks good," Steve tells her.

You can tell he's lying. You can always tell when Steve's lying because his eyes wander. Still, I offer him a proud smile. I was the one who taught him that if a girl gets a haircut you're not crazy about, you tell her it looks good anyways. At least I know he listens to me.

"Preemptive strike," Ms. Bixby says. "I shaved it before it could fall out on its own. I was getting tired of the pink anyway."

"I liked the pink," Steve says.

I liked it too. But it doesn't feel right saying it. Not now, anyway.

The doors open again with a ding and we are back in the lobby. I pop my head out and continue whispering: "No sign of the first guard. Second guard still in position. Proceed with caution." I look toward the information desk. "Anybody have a tranquilizer pistol?" It would be so easy. Just stick him right behind the ear and watch him face-plant on that desk.

Ms. Bixby rolls her eyes and then squeezes past us, reaching

271

behind and pulling me along by the front of my shirt as she heads for the front door. "Come on, boys," she says, "Let's blow this Popsicle stand."

We fall in line like ducklings, eyes straight, like we are filing through the halls at Fox Ridge Elementary. I try not to limp; I don't want to call any unnecessary attention to us. A few of the hospital's visitors look in our direction but just as quickly look away. I assume it's Ms. Bixby's new hairdo that does it. It's impolite to stare.

We walk past the front desk and the one man standing between us and the exit. I'm positive we are home free when I hear a voice call out.

"Hey," the guard says. He is holding a phone in one hand. I know who is on the other end of the line. It's Nurse Georgia, ratting us out. I'm sure of it.

Ms. Bixby freezes and we all nearly tumble into her, and I'm reminded of that one day on the playground when she told us there was no such thing as cooties, the day Rebecca Roudabush almost caught me. Behind me, Steve is dancing in place. *Whatever happens, don't search the backpacks,* I think.

The guard makes a gun with his free fingers and shoots Ms. Bixby in the chest.

"Go Pride," he says.

Ms. B. looks down at her Hofstra sweatshirt and the two

fierce lions charging across it. Apparently that's what people who go to Hofstra are called. The Pride.

"Go Pride," she echoes, pumping the fist holding the french fries. I turn and give two thumbs-up, then grab the tail of Ms. B.'s sweatshirt as she leads us out the door.

You know how, in movies, everything comes around full circle and you're back where you started? Like in *The Lion King*, where it kicks off with a monkey on a giant rock holding a baby lion and ends with the same monkey on the same giant rock holding another baby lion, and they sing a song that is literally about circles, in case you're a total idiot and missed the point? Or in *The Wizard of Oz*, where Dorothy wakes up right back on the farm and realizes it's all been a dream. Or in *High School Cheer Team Massacre 7*, when the killer passes on his evil ways to his daughter by entrusting her with the family machete after she's cut from the team?

Turns out real life isn't like the movies. Life doesn't come all the way back around again. It's not a straight line either. It angles and curves, shoots off a little, twists and turns, but it never gets right back to the place it started. Not that you would want it to. Then you wouldn't feel like you had gotten anywhere.

There are spots I'd like to come back to, though. Moments I wish I could capture, like in a snow globe, and when I'm feeling down I could shake it or even smash it open and there I am, in that time and place. Not a do-over, exactly. Just a do-again, like in the movies.

Where everything usually turns out okay.

It's a real park this time, not the little Band-Aid-sized patch of grass that we crowded into after snatching the whiskey from George Hazel Flopsucker Nelson. A real park with a swath of trees and a three-tiered fountain and at least one decent-sized hill. Not sled-worthy, but certainly big enough to spread a blanket on.

Ms. Bixby is standing at the foot of the hill, bathed in sunlight, looking a little like a mermaid who's just bargained for a pair of legs and is seeing the surface for the first time, and I wonder how many days she's been in the hospital. She has the empty McDonald's bag scrunched in one hand, having scarfed down the fries on the walk over. She tried to share them, offering them to us through potato-stuffed cheeks, but we insisted they were all for her. "My lucky day," she said finally, then licked the salt from the tips of her fingers. I remarked that I'd never seen anyone eat a large fries so fast. "Some things have a short shelf life," Ms. Bixby said, and that made us all quiet for a while.

When we get to the park, we ask her to give us a moment, just so we can get everything set up. We beg her not to look. She says she needs to catch her breath anyway, that the two blocks from the hospital are the most she's walked in three days. She puts a hand on my shoulder to steady herself, and I puff out my chest like that guy in Greek mythology who's got to hold up the whole world. I don't know why. Having her lean against me just made me feel stronger.

Halfway up the hill Brand unzips his pack and sets the bottle of Jack Daniel's in the grass. He pulls the blanket free and starts to unfold it. Then he shakes his head.

"Figures," he says.

I look at what he's frowning at. There in the center of the blanket looks to be a fistful of diamonds. Somehow or another Brand has managed to shatter the wineglass that he had folded inside, probably when he whopped George Nelson over the head with his pack. The glass stem is intact, but the cup part is smashed to pieces.

"I broke it," he says in disbelief. "I can't believe I broke it."

"The flopsucker's face broke it," I tell him. "It was a good swing. Besides, I'm not sure that's the kind of glass you use for that kind of drink."

We gingerly pick out what pieces we can, sticking them back in Brand's pack. Then we shake out the blanket just to make sure none of us slices open a butt cheek when we sit. It doesn't take long to get the rest set up. There is no music to cue—Steve's cell phone battery hasn't spontaneously recharged itself on the walk over, and a full symphony orchestra hasn't miraculously appeared by the fountain below us. I fish in my bag for the stack of bent paper plates. Steve slides the dilapidated cardboard box from his backpack and sets it in the center of the blanket. We don't bother to open it. I think we're all a little afraid of what we might find inside. When we are finished arranging (Steve adjusting and readjusting the placement of everything so that it looks "symmetrical"), Brand whistles and waves, and Ms. Bixby shakes her head as she starts up the hill toward us, moving slowly, hands on her legs, clearly straining with each step.

"Sorry about the music," Steve mumbles.

"It's all right," I say. "I don't really like Beethoven anyways." But as Ms. Bixby slowly trudges up the hill, Steve does the strangest thing, something I don't think I've ever heard him do once in his life.

He starts to sing. Soft at first, as if he's just finding his voice, but then louder with each of Ms. Bixby's steps.

"'And as we wind on down the road, our shadows taller than our soul.'"

I can't place the tune, maybe because Steve doesn't have it exactly right, but the lyrics sound familiar. I couldn't tell you the name of the song or the band, but Ms. B. obviously recognizes it, because she laughs as soon as she hears him. Normally that would be the end of it. Normally Steve would assume the laughter was directed at him and he would clam up, but if anything he just starts to sing louder, and I realize that he's actually got a pretty good voice, and that there are still things about him that surprise me. Brand and I look at each other and shrug, but Steve keeps serenading Ms. Bixby as she makes her way up the hill.

"'There walks a lady we all know, who shines white light and wants to show how everything still turns to gold.'"

Ms. Bixby reaches the edge of the blanket and Steve suddenly stops. She gives him a round of applause.

"Not quite the song *I* would have chosen," she says. "But a magnificent performance all the same. Thank you."

"It was supposed to be classical," Steve says.

"Instead it was classic," she says. She scans the blanket, still smiling, when her jaw drops. "Is that *whiskey*?" Her voice goes up an octave, one finger pointing at the Jack Daniel's now propped against the bakery box. Steve takes a step behind me.

Brand picks up the bottle and hands it to her. "Um . . . so . . . yeah . . . it was supposed to be wine," he starts to explain.

"Moscato," Steve says over my shoulder. "Or Brachetto."

"Bruschetta," Brand corrects.

"That's a kind of cheese," I whisper to him.

"It's toasted bread, not cheese," Ms. Bixby corrects me, taking the bottle of whiskey from Brand and holding it up to the sunlight. "And this is definitely not wine."

"It's better than wine," Steve says, repeating what he heard, and then instantly glances down at his feet when Ms. Bixby stares at him in disbelief. "Or so I'm told."

Ms. Bixby shakes her head. "*Please* tell me you didn't steal this from your parents."

I'm starting to think it would probably be best to just avoid this line of questioning entirely—no sense spoiling the mood—but Steve throws up his hands in protest. "No! Of course not! We got it off some stranger Topher picked up off the street." Ms. Bixby looks even more horrified.

"No. It's all right," I say. "Nobody stole anything. It's fine. We paid for it. *Trust me.* Just please, don't worry about it. This is your day."

She gives me a look, the same look she gave me when I told her that I couldn't do a math worksheet on the grounds that long division was a personal insult to calculators everywhere; then she points to the misshapen white cardboard mess that's no longer even square anymore. "That better not be a bottle of rum," she says. We all look at each other uncertainly, then Steve clears his throat and warily opens the lid.

"Ta-da," I say, pointing to the lump of dessert smashed nine ways to Sunday, almost unrecognizable as anything edible. I was wrong. Somehow it had actually gotten even uglier. "It's—"

"I know what it is," she says.

"It's from—" Steve starts to say.

"I know where it's from."

Ms. Bixby reaches to the corner of her eye with a taped-up hand.

"It looked a whole lot better when we bought it," I say.

Ms. Bixby sniffs. "It's still beautiful," she says. She clasps the bottle of Jack Daniel's to her Hofstra sweatshirt, staring at the remains of Michelle's white-chocolate raspberry supreme cheesecake, and shakes her head. And I'm not sure what to do. What to say. Probably something deep and wise. Like a Bixbyism. I *want* to say something, but this time Brand beats me to it. He stands beside Ms. Bixby and lifts himself to his toes and whispers something in her ear. More than just a word. She drops the bottle into the grass and reaches for Brand's hand, clutching it fiercely in both of hers, nodding over and over and saying, "I know."

And then she gathers Steve and me with both arms, drawing all three of us in. Huddled together. Ms. Bixby and us. And I know in that moment that this is as close as we will all ever be again.

✦ ✦ ✦

When she finally lets go, we suck the snot back up and wipe our noses on our sleeves, and I'm reminded of the time Brand tried to pick Steve's nose and how, for a while, Steve couldn't really stand him. But you get used to things. Or you learn to get past them, I guess.

We sit in a circle on the blanket, surrounding the sorry excuse for a cheesecake. Brand hands out plates and we use plastic forks and our snotty hands to shovel heaps of soft, raspberry-colored goo onto them. It doesn't look appetizing at all, but when I take my first bite, I realize it doesn't matter. It doesn't matter what it looks like or what kind of plate you put it on or how you eat it. It doesn't matter whether it was sold by some fancy French pastry chef named Michelle or some hulking Mexican guy named Eduardo. Doesn't matter that it cost a month's allowance or what you said or did to get it or that you never found the right bottle of wine to go with it. Because the man didn't lie: it really is heaven.

We eat in groans and grunts, long, drawn-out "mmmmms," with crumbs tumbling from our mouths and raspberry topping on our lips. I finish third, savoring mine a little more than the others, I think, though I don't lick my plate like Brand does.

Only Ms. Bixby doesn't eat all of hers, saying that maybe the french fries were overkill and that her appetite's not quite what it used to be. I ask her if she wants a drink, nodding to

Mr. Daniel's, but she takes the unopened bottle and tucks it behind her, saying she's going to save it for later. Later, she says, she will probably need it. It's obvious from her look that we're not getting any either. Not that I wanted it.

I gather everyone's pink-smeared plates and take them to the trash bin at the very top of the hill, and when I get back I can see that Steve has already fished the book I got at Alexander's out of my bag, and Ms. Bixby is trying to find the place where we left off. She keeps brushing the sleeve of her sweatshirt against her cheek. I take the spot on the other side of her, Steve next to me, the four of us scrunched close, even though there are no pictures to look at. "Chapter nineteen," Steve reminds her. "Page two hundred sixty-two. At least in the other copy."

Ms. Bixby thumbs to her place and coughs once, getting into character. "The Last Stage," she says.

And as she reads, I lean up against her, Steve beside me, and look to see Brand leaning on the other side. And I close my eyes and listen to the sound of Gandalf the Gray admonishing his favorite Halfling, of cars passing on the street behind us, and the sound of my own heartbeat keeping time to the rhythm of her words. And I totally forget what day it is.

When she's finished—and it takes a nice long while and her voice almost gives out more than once—I keep my eyes closed and we just sit there, the four of us, afraid to break the spell, afraid to say the word that will bring us back from Middle-earth or wherever it is we've gone to. Until, finally, we hear someone calling Ms. Bixby's name, and I open my eyes to see Nurse Georgia, the Viking, standing at the bottom of the hill.

Telling us it's time to come down.

STEVE

THIS IS HOW THE STORY ENDS: BILBO HANDS Gandalf the jar of tobacco, and Ms. Bixby closes the book, and we sit there in silence, which isn't unusual for me but is strange for Topher, who usually has to say *something*.

It seems a little anticlimactic, the ending. Everyone seems content just sitting there, so I keep my mouth shut and study the grass and think about what it must be like to come home after such a grand adventure, like Bilbo's, and not have to listen to your parents yell at you for it.

There is no escaping it. They will find out somehow, but not from Christina. She told me she wouldn't and I know she won't, despite what Topher thinks—even us Sakatas get tired of following the rules *all* the time, and I think she was, secretly, maybe even a little proud of me today, though she would never say it. More likely somebody from school will tell them, Mr. Mack or the sub. Or maybe they won't find out until they get my report card and cross-reference the number of absences against the calendars on their iPads. At the very least they will ask about my lip. I will tell them the truth. It just doesn't seem like a secret worth keeping, and I'm not that good a liar. Topher's tried to teach me, but he says I just don't have the gift. So they will ask and I will tell them and then suffer the consequences. I try not to think about what those might be. No sense spoiling the moment.

When the nurse from the fourth floor mysteriously appears at the bottom of the hill, Ms. B. hurriedly stashes her bottle of whiskey in her giant purse. "I'm not sharing with the nurses," she jokes. Then she hands the book to Topher and puts her slippers back on, looking at them for a good while.

"'If you want me again, look for me under your boot soles,'" she says. I don't know what that means, but it sounds a little morbid. I look down at my own shoes. I must look concerned, because Ms. Bixby reaches over and touches my knee. "It's from a poem," she says. She knows how I feel about poetry, but I don't say anything. Probably some poems are all right.

She stands and we stand, facing her, like we're back in the

classroom. Then she gives Topher a giant hug. And me too, though she doesn't smell at all like she usually does and she squeezes harder than usual and makes it difficult to breathe. She doesn't hug Brand, which I think is strange, but the two of them stand face-to-face, Ms. Bixby standing just below him on the hill so he can look at her level.

"I almost forgot." Brand bends down and opens the front pocket of his backpack and produces a pink-and-white flower. It's a little smooshed and bent at the stem, but he hands it to her anyway. It's a carnation. I know because my sister wears them all the time at her piano recitals. I have no idea where he got it from. I don't remember it being part of the plan. "Roses are quitters," Brand says, which strikes me as an odd way to describe a flower, but Ms. Bixby laughs and cries all at once.

"Thanks, boys," she says. "Today was so much better than I could have imagined it." Then she turns and starts down the hill.

We stand at the top and watch her go, her purse under one arm and Brand's broken flower hanging down at her side, Nurse Georgia lecturing her all the way through the park and out to the street, the way Ms. Bixby sometimes lectured the lot of us. Just as she's about to turn the corner out of sight, she looks back at us up on the hill and waves, even though she wasn't supposed to. There weren't supposed to be any good-byes.

When she's gone, I pick up the extra plates and shove them in my bag while Topher carefully folds the blanket and holds it close to his chest.

"This place is nice," Brand says, looking down the rolling slope of grass, hands in his pockets.

"It's perfect, actually," Topher says.

I tug on Topher's shirt sleeve. "Time to go home?"

Topher nods but he doesn't move, so I just stand between him and Brand, all of us staring at the empty space where Ms. Bixby used to be.

We have to hurry to catch the two forty-five at the corner of Fourteenth and State, the bus that will take us back to the school in time for dismissal. The plan is to just sneak back onto our own school bus, number 17, and go home, just like if we had been at school the whole day. At least that's the plan for Topher and me. Brand will walk. He says it's okay; he's used to it.

The city bus deposits us a block and a half from school, not far from the apartment complex where Topher wanted to strangle Mr. Mackelroy with a shoelace. We will still have to deal with his wrath on Monday, but Topher says Monday is a long ways away and that a lot can happen between now and then. We walk back to the school grounds in silence and stand behind the bushes. Topher says we should wait for the bell, for the surge of students to come erupting from the doors. Then we'll just merge with the crowd.

"Do you think we missed anything important?" I ask. I can't help it. Just looking at the school makes my stomach ache. Maybe I shouldn't have had cheesecake for lunch.

"Not today," Brand says.

The buses start to file in, making a parade. I can almost hear the sound of a thousand kids packing up, primed for the weekend, ready for adventure of one sort or another. Brand sighs and adjusts his pack like he's ready to take off.

"Hang on," Topher says. He unzips his backpack and roots around. I can hear the sound of torn paper, and his hand emerges with a thick sheet, edges frayed. "Here," he says, holding it out to Brand.

"What? Are you serious?" Brand says. He seems afraid to take it, which is strange given how hard it was for him to let go of earlier.

Topher shrugs. "I can always draw another one. I'll make it the first picture in the new sketchbook you buy me."

Brand takes the drawing of Ms. Bixby hesitantly. "Thanks, man," he says.

In the parking lot the buses are idling, waiting for us. The parents who come to pick up their kids every afternoon pull into the circle. Thank God mine don't do that. I want to put that part off as long as possible. The chimes of Fox Ridge Elementary's dismissal ring out, making me jump. Almost immediately the doors burst open and a crowd of kids spills out, jostling their way across the sidewalk.

"That's our cue," Topher says. He gives Brand a fist bump. "All right. So. See ya?"

"Yeah. See ya." Brand turns to me, points to my chin. "That lip is pretty frad, you know."

I reach up and touch my busted lip tentatively. I'm not sure what frad is—freaking radical, maybe—but it sounds like a compliment. "It hurts when I smile," I tell him. Then we bump fists too. Brand takes a few steps backward, like he's afraid to take his eyes off us, then gives a salute before disappearing down the street. I'm actually a little sorry to see him go.

"C'mon."

Topher pulls me along by my backpack loop and we merge with the crowd, just like he planned. Mrs. Thornburg, the assistant principal, glares at us. "You two," she snaps. Beside me, Topher tenses up. "Hurry up and get on your bus. It's Friday, for heaven's sake! Don't you want to go home?"

I shake my head, but Mrs. Thornburg doesn't notice.

We run to our bus—the sixth one I've been on today—climb aboard, and shuffle toward the back, ignoring the looks from the other sixth graders, who probably wonder where we've been all day, because they know where we weren't. Sarah Tolsen actually has the nerve to ask, and Topher just tells her we were on a field trip and that it's none of her business and that if she gets any nosier, she'll be able to pick her boogers with a shovel. Sarah huffs and whispers about us to the girl sitting next to her. I don't really care, though. Sarah Tolsen is the least of my worries. I look over at Topher and point out that he has a little raspberry topping still in the corner of his mouth. He scrapes it off with his thumb. "No evidence," he says.

"No evidence," I say, then suck gingerly on my lower lip.

As the bus rumbles down the street, Topher points out the window to Brand walking half in the middle of the road. Topher pounds and calls his name, but he obviously can't hear. He still has Topher's sketch in his hand, though, and he's looking at it as he walks. Behind him you can see the cherry trees that the third and fourth graders planted outside the school last year are just starting to blossom. Topher keeps staring out the window.

"Hey, Topher?" I say.

"What?"

"I want you to know . . ."

I think about all the things I'd like to say, but there are still so many I'm uncertain of, so I say the one thing I'm sure about.

"I had a pretty good day, today."

"Yeah," Topher sighs. I glance behind us and look out the bus's back window at the redbrick building of our school and wave good-bye. Then I lean in and put my head on Topher's shoulder.

He doesn't shrug it off.

Brand

MARGARET ELEANOR BIXBY DIED IN BOSTON AT
the age of thirty-five. She never told the class her full name
because she said it sounded too much like the Beatles song and
she didn't want to give kids any more ammunition for bathroom
stall graffiti. But she told me once, while we were waiting in line
to check out.

She died of complications from surgery resulting in trau-
matic blood loss during an attempt to remove one of the tumors
that had laid siege to her pancreas. The doctors at Massachusetts
General did everything they could and she fought to the very
last moment, but the odds were against her. Steve could tell me
what they were if I really wanted to know, but I really don't. Her
"soul made its return trip" sometime on a Friday afternoon in

the middle of June. That's what the obituary said, at least.

The day she died, Principal McNair called all the families of all her former students for the last five years, something like a hundred thirty kids, to deliver the news personally. I have no idea where I was on the list. I only know that my father answered the phone, and that instead of calling me out of my room, like he normally would, he actually stood up with his walker and came and knocked on my door. It was a scorching summer day, midnineties and humid, and Steve, Topher, and I had pledged to spend the majority of it inside, hands permanently attached to our Xbox controllers. Dad knocked softly three times and waited to whisper the news in my ear.

I turned to face the other two, but they already knew without my saying a word. They could see it. Steve closed his eyes and whispered something. Topher just looked at his shoelaces. I thought about saying something, but sometimes silence is best. Instead I just sat down at the edge of my bed and stared at the wall, at this one perfectly blank white spot, and thought about Mr. Alexander's riddle, the one that never got its answer. Then Topher bumped me with his shoulder. "Atticus Finch," he said, and pointed to the quote on my wall, the one I'd painted above my bed the day after my dad got out of the hospital, the second time around. I nodded. This wasn't good-bye. We had already said our good-byes.

That night my dad ordered in pizza for the four of us and then agreed to our request to go out for dessert, "in honor of Ms. Bixby," though I'm sure he thought that was a strange way to honor her. He said we could choose the place, provided he didn't have to drive too far—he still wasn't completely comfortable behind the wheel. Using his hands to accelerate and brake felt like he was piloting a spaceship, he said. "So where to?"

Topher, Steve, and I just looked at each other. I told him he should bring a little extra cash from the bread box, because the place we were going wasn't cheap, but it was totally worth it.

And afterward there was something at the bookstore down the street that I wanted him to see.

Live every day as if it were your last. That's a Bixbyism for sure, though even she would tell you that it's impossible. It's just way too much to ask most of the time. I've experienced one last day in my life, and it was enough to hold me for a while.

The truth is—the whole truth is—that it's not the last day that matters most. It's the ones in between, the ones you get the chance to look back on. They're the carnation days. They may not stand out the most at first, but they stay with you the longest.

Like the first April day you wake up to find a pile of rubber dog poop on your pillow.

Or the day you finally get permission to have your two best friends over to your house.

Or the day Mindy Winkler slips you a note in class for real this time asking if you will sit by her at lunch.

Or the day your sixth-grade teacher rescues you from the snow on your way to the grocery store.

Or the day your father knocks on your bedroom door and, for the first time in two years, asks you if you'd like to take a walk.

Topher

REBECCA ROUDABUSH HAS WRITER'S BLOCK.

You can tell because she's stuck her pencil in the corner of her mouth. She pouts when she's thinking hard, and her forehead matches the lines on the paper. It's kind of cute. I can't blame her for being stuck. Ms. Bixby hit us with a tough one this morning.

Imagine you had only one day left on the earth. What would you do with it?

Today's writing prompt is on the chalkboard. Not on the smartboard, but actually etched across the green wall behind it. Ms. Bixby likes chalk more. Not that she's antitechnology or anything; she says she just likes the powdery feel of it on her fingers. I can appreciate that. An oil pastel feels different from a charcoal pencil when it hits the page. Sometimes it's the feel of a thing that matters.

The prompt sits just below the date, January 7, and the quote of the day. "Courage is not a man with a gun in his hand. It's knowing you're licked before you begin but you begin anyway and you see it through no matter what."

It must be one of her favorites, because I've seen it there before. I don't memorize them all the same way Steve does, but this one at least sounds familiar. It's pretty heavy stuff for a Friday, though.

I take out my journal and open to a blank page and copy the prompt onto the top line. Beside me Steve has already got a couple of paragraphs.

"Last day on earth," Trevor Cowly says, leaning over between Steve and me. "Does that mean the mothership finally came back for you two?"

"Shut up, butt zit," Brand hisses from my other side. Sitting at her desk, Ms. Bixby says Brand's name, quiet but firm, and he immediately buries his face back in his journal. Outside, the snow still blankets the ground, pushed by the plows into mountains on the sides of the parking lot. During recess, I'm hoping Ms. Bixby will let us climb them. I've named the biggest one Everest.

We all write in sort-of silence for another ten minutes, "sort-of" because there's still plenty of whispering going on. I make a couple of doodles in the margins of my journal—killer robots, a crashing meteor—the prime ingredients for an apocalypse. I know the prompt said *my* last day, but I figure if you're going to go, go out with a bang. Steve glances at my notebook. "Is that the Terminator?" he asks.

"If I'm going, I'm taking the rest of you with me," I whisper. After another minute, Ms. Bixby tells us time is up. She circles around to the front of her desk. The dress she's wearing has strange swirly figures embroidered on it. They are mesmerizing if you stare at them too long.

"All right," she says. "Let's have a few volunteers share what they've written."

Immediately a couple of hands go up. Melissa Trotter goes first and talks about how she would spend her last day with her family back in Hawaii, which is where they spend every summer, lucky her. Ms. Bixby listens with rapt attention, unlike the rest of us—who are completely sick of hearing how fantastic Hawaii is, especially when it's twenty degrees outside. A couple more students volunteer. Missy McKinney says she would beat the snot out of her older brother without fear of punishment from her parents. I figure Steve could appreciate that, though to be honest, I don't think there's much chance of him beating Christina at anything. Kyle says he would just play video games all day. Sad but true.

I'm hoping Ms. B. won't call on me. I don't have much written. A few lines about going on some grand adventure with my friends. Mostly, though, my page is full of drawings. She doesn't collect our journals, so it's okay, she won't see it. She says they're mostly to inspire us.

She's about to call on somebody, you can tell, but Rebecca saves us.

"What about you, Ms. Bixby?" she asks. "What would you do?"

"With my last day? You really want to know?" Ms. Bixby asks, and I nod along with the rest of the class. If we get Ms. Bixby talking long enough, it will cut in on our math time and we won't have to take a quiz. Steve will be mad, but he'll get over it. "Okay, then. I guess my last day would have cheesecake."

In the back of the class, somebody makes barfing sounds. Ms. Bixby silences it with a look.

"Cheesecake?" Steve says. "Why cheesecake?"

"Well," Ms. Bixby continues, "if it were *really* my last day, I would want to appreciate all the things I've come to love about life. And honestly, one of those is cheesecake."

"Seriously? You wouldn't, like, spend it with family or friends?" Jamie Davies asks.

"Oh, absolutely I would. Of course. But there would also be cheesecake. And not just any cheesecake: the white-chocolate raspberry supreme cheesecake from Michelle's Bakery up by the mall. Have any of you ever been there?" Only two kids raise their hands. "You should go sometime. Completely worth the trip. And I probably shouldn't say this . . . but if I'm being honest, there would be wine. Something to complement the cheesecake. Oh, and french fries."

"French fries?" I just want to make sure I heard her right.

"*McDonald's* french fries," she amends. "And since it is the end of the world, go ahead and make it a large. With lots of salt. And there would be music. Tchaikovsky. Or Beethoven. Something grand and sweeping and maybe just a little bit sad. Played by a full symphony orchestra, just for my family and friends and me. And we would sit on a grassy hill, surrounded by trees, stuffing our faces on cheesecake and fries. Eating and drinking and laughing. There would be so much laughing. And remembering. But *not*"—she holds up a finger—"saying good-bye."

"Lame," Trevor says, coughing the word into his fist.

Brand twists around and mouths something, a word I don't quite get but starts with an *F*—probably something he just made up. I'll have to ask him about it later. One of these days Brand is just going to skip the comebacks and pop Trevor Cowly right in the nose.

"What about us, though? Would you at least say good-bye to us?" Mindy Winkler asks.

Ms. Bixby leans against her desk and smiles. "Not good-bye, but maybe au revoir."

"Isn't that pretty much the same thing?" I'm not exactly fluent in French or anything. I'm just guessing.

"Actually, good-bye is good-bye. Au revoir is 'till we see each other again.' But believe me, even when I'm gone, you're still going to remember me. You will all be talking about me when you are grown and have kids of your own. 'Remember Ms. Bixby,' you'll say, 'with the pink hair and the thing about the chalk, who was always spouting quotes at us and making us write in our journals all the time? She was the best.'"

The class groans, some kids shake their heads, but they are just giving her a hard time because they know she's probably right. No doubt I'll remember her when I grow up, though I plan to put *that* off as long as humanly possible. I figure we'll all remember her in our own way.

After all—you never forget the Good Ones.

ACKNOWLEDGEMENTS

I've come unplugged. There are no explosions in this novel. No fireballs. No ogres. No armies clashing in the night. This is a much quieter book than I'm used to writing. Quiet books are much harder to write than loud ones. At least for me.

In other words, I couldn't have done it alone.

Ms. Bixby would not have happened it weren't for the combined efforts of the outstanding team at Walden Pond Press, most notably my tireless editor, Jordan Brown, who saw my embryo of a story and coached me through its many evolutions. Without him, this multifaceted novel would have been short several facets, making it infinitely less frawesome. And to his partner in crime, Debbie Kovacs: many thanks for creating a space for me at Walden where I can stretch my narrative muscles.

Your constant encouragement makes me believe I will grow up to be a writer someday (I'm putting it off as long as possible too).

Thanks to Emma Yarlett, who brilliantly captured the inquisitive, potentially troublemaking nature of my three protagonists in her cover art, and to Katie and Amy for making the rest of it look pretty, and to David and the rest of the production team for making it a real book with pages and everything. To Renée and Valerie for their razor-sharp efforts to make my stumbling prose readable. And big thanks to Danielle, Jenna, Patty, Caroline, and the rest of the marketing and promotion team at Walden Pond who have the gargantuan task of selling a novel about three kids skipping school to visit their teacher who is dying of cancer. Not exactly a beach read. Props to Viana Siniscalchi for her behind-the-scenes efforts and for having such a delicious-sounding name. And much appreciation from this humble writer to Donna Bray, Kate Jackson, and Suzanne Murphy for running the show and letting me be a part of it.

Thanks to Quinlan Lee for being the first to cry over the manuscript, letting me know I was on to something, and to Adams Literary Agency for continuing to find a home for my work, regardless of its volume.

Finally, I would like to thank the mentors in my life: My father, who taught me the value of beginning even though you think you are licked and seeing it through, no matter what. My mother, who taught me the power of books and beauty and imagination. Nick and Isabella, who inspire me to try to inspire them. And my wife, a public school teacher of nearly fifteen years, who continues to bless me with her kindness and patience and selflessness. In the words of Topher—she's one of the Good Ones.

I am fortunate to be able to do what I do for a living. I am more fortunate to have wonderful people around me who support me in moments of doubt and confusion and hardship. To those who struggle, and to those standing behind them propping them up and cheering them on—best wishes.

A sneak peek at
JOHN DAVID ANDERSON'S

I PUSH MY WAY THROUGH THE BUZZING MOB AND FREEZE, heart-struck, dizzy. It takes me a minute to really get what I'm looking at.

Notes. At least a hundred of them. Pressed all over the freshly painted locker.

Some clump together, overlapping like roof shingles. Others orbit like satellites, reaching up toward the wall. They vary in color—pale blue, fluorescent pink, lime green—but most of them are yellow, like dandelions before they fluff white and wither away.

I stand motionless and read a few of them, softly enough so only I can hear. They are just words and they are not just words. I think about everything that's happened. About Bench

1

and Deedee and Rose. And Wolf. About all the terrible things that were said. About the things that should have been said and weren't.

There was a war. This was where it ended.

I can't tell you exactly when it changed, when it spiraled out of control like a kite twisting in the wind. When it stopped being something funny and clever and became something else. Maybe there was no single moment. Maybe underneath all the squares plastered on the walls and the notebooks and the windows there was the same message over and over—we just ignored it because it was easier to stomach. And now I'm standing here, dumbstruck, wondering if this changes everything.

I know what you are going to say: sticks, stones, and broken bones, but words can kick you in the gut. They wriggle underneath your skin and start to itch. They set their hooks into you and pull. Words accumulate like a cancer, and then they eat away at you until there is nothing left. And once they are let loose there really is no taking them back.

Truth is, I can't tell you exactly when it changed. I can tell you how it started, though. And I can tell you how it ended. I will do my best to line up the dots in between.

I'll leave it to you to draw the line.

THE CATALYST

IT STARTED WITH RUBY SANDELS.

That's her name, swear to God. Ruby freaking Sandels. Yes, sandals aren't slippers, which would have been worse, and it's not even spelled the same, but it still counts as a form of child abuse, IMO. Might as well just fix her black hair into a permanent ponytail, buy her a shaggy terrier to stuff in a wicker basket, and teach her to sing about rainbows. I'm sure her parents thought they were being cute with that name, but a thing like that could mess a kid up for life.

It didn't, though. Mess her up for life, that is. But only because Ruby looked nothing like a lost farm girl from Kansas. With her dark brown skin and tight jeans, Ruby was no Dorothy, and she was hard-nosed enough to stare down anyone who even *thought* about teasing her, which was always somebody. This was middle school. Everyone got teased by somebody sometime about something. At the very least Ruby would give back double what she got. You had to admire that.

Don't get the wrong idea. Ruby and I weren't friends. I will just say that up front. In fact, you can just assume that anyone I talk about isn't a friend of mine unless explicitly stated otherwise. Ruby was just a girl who sat in front of me in math class and ignored me out of habit. She had a backpack covered in faux sapphires. You didn't have to look close to tell the dark blue stones weren't real. This is Branton, not Beverly Hills. Anything flashy around here is fake.

That's Branton, Michigan, by the way. Don't try to find it on a map—you'd need a microscope. It's one of a dozen dinky towns north of Lansing, one of the few that doesn't sound like it was named by a French explorer. Branton, Michigan. Population: Not a Lot and Yet Still Too Many I Don't Particularly Care For. We have a shopping mall with a J. C. Penney and an Asian fusion place that everyone says they are dying to try even though it's been there for three years now. Most of our other restaurants are attached to gas stations, the kind that serve rubbery purple hot dogs and sodas in buckets. There's a statue of Francis B. Stockbridge in the center of town. He's a Michigan state senator from prehistoric times with a beard that belongs on Rapunzel's twin brother. He wasn't *born* in Branton, of course—nobody important was ever born in Branton—but we needed a statue for the front of the courthouse and the name *Stockbridge* looks good on a copper plate.

It's all for show. Branton's the kind of place that tries to pretend it's better than it really is. It's really the kind of place with more bars than bookstores and more churches than either, not that that's necessarily a bad thing. It's a place where teenagers still sometimes take baseball bats to mailboxes and wearing the wrong brand of shoes gets you at least a dirty look.

It snows a lot in Branton. Like avalanches dumped from the sky. Like heaps to hills to mountains, the plows carving their paths through our neighborhood, creating alpine ranges nearly tall enough to ski down. Some of the snow mounds are so big you can build houses inside them, complete with entryways and coat closets. *Restrooms are down the hall on your right. Just look for the steaming yellow hole.* There's nothing like that first Branton snow, though. Soft as cat scruff and bleach white, so bright you can almost see your reflection in it. Then the plows come and churn up the earth underneath. The dirt and the boot tracks and the car exhaust mix together to make it all ash gray, almost black, and it sickens your stomach just to look at it. It happens everywhere, not just Branton, but here it's something you can count on.

But I was telling you about how it started. The ban and the notes and then the war that followed. I was telling you about Ruby Sandels getting into trouble, getting us all into trouble.

Also, just so you know, this isn't Ruby's story. She's what my chemistry teacher calls a catalyst. Something that jump-starts a reaction. The thing about Ruby, like pretty much every other kid in Branton Middle School (me being one exception), is that she was never without her phone, despite the rule against having them out in class. Nobody followed that rule. If the teacher's back was turned, texts, tweets, and ticked-off birds were flying, videos were being downloaded, villages were being raided, and walls were being posted on. Everyone did it. And if I was lucky enough to have a phone (if it ever fit into "the budget"), I would have done it too.

Which is why it wasn't unusual to see Ruby taking furtive glances at her lap during class. The problem was, on this day, she decided to do it in math. With Ms. Sheers.

Unlike Ruby "Don't *Ever* Call Me Dorothy" Sandels, Ms. Sheers lived up to her name. Sharp as a scalpel, with thin lips and dagger eyes—nothing escaped her. She wasn't like Mr. Hostler—near-sighted and three years from retirement, only really concerned with getting home and finding out who won *Dancing with the Stars*. You could come to class newborn naked and Mr.

Hostler would probably just sigh and check you off the attendance sheet. Ms. Sheers, on the other hand, was a bloodhound. That didn't make her a bad teacher, necessarily. But she wasn't the sort to look the other way when she saw the flash of light glinting off Ruby's phone, or heard the nearly imperceptible click of Ruby's painted nails on the screen. She zeroed in on the desk like a sniper, then snapped her fingers and opened her hand. "Let's have it."

"Have what?"

"The phone, Ruby."

"I don't have a phone," Ruby said, sounding suddenly Dorothy-like, all innocent as she attempted to slide the phone she didn't have into her glitzy bag. It caught the edge of the pocket and clattered, much too loudly, to the ground.

Naturally, this was hilarious. At least to everyone but Ms. Sheers, who shot down the aisle and reached for it, hawklike, snatching it out from underneath Ruby's fingertips.

"Give me my phone back," Ruby said, her face suddenly flushed, lunging upward as Ms. Sheers held it out of her reach.

"You don't have a phone," Ms. Sheers reminded her. She looked at Ruby's screen and her expression changed, Jekyll to Hyde. If it was possible for a teacher to be pretty, Ms. Sheers *might* qualify, but when she looked at that screen her face transformed into something pinched and contorted, like she had just taken a swallow of rancid milk. She looked from the phone to Ruby, then back to the phone. Ruby's eyes fell to her desk, head dropping so fast you would have thought someone had tied an anchor to her chin.

"Is this . . . ?" Ms. Sheers stammered. "Did you . . . ?"

Judging by the lack of response, the rest of us could only assume *it was* and *she did*. About a half dozen students, me included, telescoped our necks to get a look at the screen, but Ms. Sheets pressed the phone close to her chest.

We all turned and looked expectantly at Ruby, waiting for her comeback. Sarcastic or apologetic, it could go either way. I've found that kids will apologize instantly if they think that it will keep them out of trouble. I know I will. But there are some times you just know an apology—even one you actually mean—won't be enough. Then it's best to just keep your mouth shut.

I'm guessing that's what Ruby Sandels was thinking, because she didn't say a word at first. Just blushed and refused to look up.

Ms. Sheers took a deep breath. "You understand we need to go see Mr. Wittingham."

Low murmurs among the class. The Big Ham. Principal Wittingham was even more hard core than Ms. Sheers. You

8

could sometimes feel the tremors when he shouted at a kid from behind his office door. Ruby's head snapped up.

"But Ms. Sheers, I didn't mean anything by it. It's just talk."

She knew she was in it deep. I suddenly felt bad for her. Ms. Sheers had her gorgon stare on—turn you straight to stone—the phone still pressed to her heart.

"This isn't a game, Ruby. It's one thing to violate school policy and use your phone in class, but this . . ." Ms. Sheers looked at the phone again, as if to confirm that what she'd seen the first time wasn't a trick of her imagination. Her face knotted up again and she shook her head. "This is *inexcusable*."

Which meant that whatever it was, it must have been good.

Ruby Sandels groaned and angrily stuffed her notebook into her pack. Then we watched her be escorted to the front door. "I will be back in two minutes," Ms. Sheers warned. "Take this opportunity to complete the problems on your sheet. Silently."

We all nodded meekly. Ms. Sheers closed the door and at least twenty other phones flew out of pockets and backpacks as we all tried to figure out just what it was that Ruby had done, the wonderfully terrible things that she'd said.

Behind me Jasmine Jones squealed and clasped her hand over her mouth. She showed her phone to Samantha Bowles.

(Not Bowels. I made that mistake once. Only once.) "Oh no she didn't," Samantha said, eyes wide.

Apparently, yes, she did.

And we were all about to pay for it.

I said Ruby wasn't my friend, and she wasn't. But that doesn't mean I didn't have any.

In fact, for a while there, I thought I had just enough.

Nobody is friendless. I honestly believe this. We all have *somebody*. Even the crazy lady who lives down the block from us has her pet schnauzer, though the thing is uglier than she is, with its snaggletooth and gimp leg. Even my father—an editor for an online magazine who works out of his lonely one-bedroom apartment near the beach and thinks humans generally suck—even he has real-life people who he talks to. My mother's just not one of them.

Point is, none of us is alone. We might *feel* alone sometimes, but more often than not we are just lonely. There's a difference. We aren't alone because it's basic human nature to band together. Herd mentality. We are programmed to find our people.

That's how my mother put it. Right before my first day at Branton Middle School, a little over two years ago.

We were back-to-school shopping—gathering the instruments of torture that my teachers would use to slowly bore me to death over the next nine months. I was nervous and irritable. A better word might be "snappish" (I'm a sucker for a good word). I was headed to a new school. A *middle* school. It wasn't that the classes would get harder, or that I would get lost in the labyrinth of halls, or that I might forget my combination and look derpy just standing there, aimlessly spinning the lock, though these thoughts crossed my mind more than twice.

No. What scared me most was lunch.

People talk about nightmares where they are falling or where they are trapped in a burning building or buried alive. But ask any incoming sixth grader with at least two forehead zits and a Great Clips haircut and he will tell you the prevailing image from his nightmares is standing in the middle of a buzzing cafeteria, tray in hand, desperately looking for somewhere to sit. That was what made me sweat through my sheets at night.

Forget the boogeyman; the lunch lady haunted *my* dreams.

Standing in the back-to-school section with a half dozen other kids and their parents, trying to decide between college- and wide-ruled, Mom could tell there was something bothering me. Mother's intuition. Some people might call that a good thing. I'm not one of them. It was spooky how she could read my mind.

"Don't be nervous," she said, the corners of her mouth drawn, somehow out-frowning me.

"Easy for you to say," I muttered. "You're not the one going to a new school where you know almost nobody."

It wasn't an exaggeration. I literally knew about four people who attended Branton Middle School, and I wasn't friends with any of them. My mom and I had recently moved to a new house, a smaller one, a grand total of twenty-three miles from the older, larger, more comfortable house I grew up in. It was all part of the separation, one of a thousand aftershocks that came with my parents' divorce. The old blue house with the white shutters was too much for either my mom or dad to handle financially, so she found a three-bedroom in Branton and he found that apartment in Sarasota.

That's Sarasota, *Florida*. You should be able to find Florida on the map all right. It's the turd-shaped one falling into the ocean.

"No. I get it," Mom said, dropping school supplies into our cart as I checked items off the printout. She bought store-brand everything: pencils, pens, markers. Even my backpack was the cheapest we could find, generic black with a little pocket for the phone I didn't own. Mom's salary as an administrative assistant at a dental office didn't cover name brands. Not that I needed Crayolas for middle school. What I needed was someone to trade sandwiches with.

Mom put a hand on my shoulder and leaned close so that

nobody around us could hear. "It's hard starting over. Trust me. I know. But it will be all right. You will find your people."

That's exactly how she said it. *Your people.* Like I was a prophet preparing to gather my flock. At least she didn't say "peeps." My mother never tried to be cool. It's one of the things that made her cool sometimes.

I grunted at her anyways.

"Give me that look all you want, Eric, but it will happen. It's instinctual. Inherited from our prehistoric days. We are wired to form groups. Otherwise we would have gone extinct eons ago. It will be hard, but you'll make it."

That's another thing about Mom. She doesn't sugarcoat it for you. She tells everything straight up. And her hugs are fierce and quick, like the one she gave me just then. "It will be awkward at first, but it gets better. You find your people and you make your tribe and you protect each other. From the wolves."

"That's middle school?" I asked her.

She gave me a sad kind of smile. "That's just life," she said. Then she threw three packs of off-brand sticky notes in the cart and pushed on to the next aisle.

I stood there by the Elmer's glue display, imagining my body being ripped apart by ravenous beasts. In the middle of the school cafeteria, no less, with everyone around me pointing and laughing. Mom was smart and I loved her. But she didn't always know the best thing to say to a guy.

You find your people. Sure. But it was those wolves I worried about.

Ruby Sandels wasn't one of the people I'd eventually found, but I still felt bad for her as Mrs. Sheers escorted her out of the room. The Big Ham was surely going to eat her alive.

I knew what she said. By the end of fourth period we all did. It's not difficult. I'm pretty sure that's the whole reason the internet was invented: to make it easier to spread gossip. I know what Stephen Curry eats for breakfast. I know what the president thought about the new Marvel movie. I know how many Ping-Pong balls a man can fit inside his mouth at one time. You don't even have to know where to look. Just be patient enough and eventually somebody will tell you whether you care or not.

Ruby's message was passed around, jumping from phone to phone like a skipping stone, each of us gawking at it in turn.

The kids all knew before the parents. We probably even knew before Ruby's mom did. There was no way to take it back. You can't erase what everyone else has seen, and you certainly can't stop the gossip train once it has gathered steam and rocketed out of Branton Middle School Station. The whispering was like static in the halls.

"She actually *said* that?" Bench said with a whistle.

We were walking together to lunch, the day Ruby's phone was taken from her. It was the four of us: Deedee with his *Lord of the Rings* lunch box that wasn't retro enough to be cool yet and Wolf with his brown paper sack that was. Me wearing Bench's last pair of Nikes and a T-shirt that said *SAVE THE WHALES— THEY MAKE GOOD LEFTOVERS*. My uncle sent it to me for my birthday. He's kind of demented, but he always remembers, which is nice.

Bench was leading the way. We always let him take point.

"Technically she typed it," I said. "I don't think you'd ever hear her say those words *out loud*." I tried to imagine Dorothy from *The Wizard of Oz* dropping the kinds of bombs that Ruby did in that text message. Some of the things she wrote would have made the Wicked Witch turn white.

"She's going to get suspended," Wolf said.

"Or worse," Deedee added.

"I still can't believe she said that about *him*."

Bench shook his head. The *him* was a big part of the problem and one of the reasons Ruby was sure to get sent home this time. It wasn't some guy she'd had a crush on or some other kid who

15

bad-mouthed Ruby behind her back. The *him* was Mr. Jackson. An adult. A *teacher*. He apparently gave Ruby an F on her last science test because he suspected her of cheating. In response she thumbed a long rant to her friends, calling him several choice names and saying that he could just go kiss a certain part of her backside. With three exclamation points. She only sent the text to two people, but it didn't matter. Friends have friends. The message made the rounds. Ruby was going to have a really hard time passing science this year.

"I saw Mr. Jackson in the hall. He looked bad. All sweaty and red," Deedee said.

"He always looks like that," I said.

"Yeah, but he looked like he was going to have a heart attack."

"He always looks like that, too." Mr. Jackson was not a small man, as many of the crude drawings in the boys' bathroom could attest to. He was a few hundred pounds, much of it pillowing around his center like a monster truck tire. *One* of the unfortunate F-words Ruby used in her text was "fat."

"Definitely expelled," Deedee said. "You just can't say those kinds of things. Not in school. Not about a teacher."

Actually, I wouldn't dare say some of things Ruby said about anyone. Not in any way that could be traced back to me, at least.

"Why not, though?" Bench asked. "I mean, she's entitled to her opinion, right? Like, Constitutionally?"

I gave Bench a look. He wasn't defending her. He wasn't friends with Ruby any more than I was; he was only playing devil's advocate. We learned about the Bill of Rights in social studies earlier this year—from a droning Mr. Hostler. I didn't pay too close attention. Most of the amendments only seemed to matter if you got arrested, which wasn't in my foreseeable future (Mom would *kill* me), though Bench's comment made me wonder if Mr. Jackson could have Ruby arrested for defamation of character or something. Verbal abuse. Assault with a deadly text.

"The first amendment says nothing about sending texts calling your science teacher a—" Deedee tried to muster the courage to repeat what he'd read, but it was too much for him to say out loud. He wasn't exactly a rule breaker. None of us were. We weren't total suck-ups either—we just tried to keep our noses clean. We flew under the radar. It was one of the many keys to survival. "I'm pretty sure it just keeps you from being arrested for saying what you think. Doesn't mean you can't get in trouble."

"I think she was better off keeping her opinion to herself," Wolf said from behind me.

Wolf. The voice of reason. We counted on him for that. Just like we counted on Deedee to find drama in everything and Bench to keep us from getting beat up. And counted on me . . . I'm not sure what we counted on me for.

"Mark my words—this isn't over," Deedee divined. "Somehow or another it's going to come back and bite us all in the you-know-what."

"Are you going to roll for it?" I asked. "Or are you suddenly psychic?"

"I'm telling you," Deedee said. "Stuff like this doesn't go unnoticed."

"Nothing's going to happen," Wolf countered. "Nothing ever changes around here."

I nodded, sure he was right. I'd never seen Wolf get flustered over much of anything, even the little shoves and digs that come with being in middle school, the needling comments and sidelong sneers. Wolf took them in stride, and he certainly took enough of them. Bench called him "composed," which made a lot of sense when you thought about it. Sometimes that meant that you didn't know exactly what Wolf was thinking, not if he was being quiet, which was kind of a default for him. Unlike Deedee, who might as well have billboards above his head spelling out his feelings for anyone who cared to know, which was usually just the three of us, and not always that many.

"I'm serious," Deedee said. "You wait and see. We're all going to pay for this."

Wolf gave him a playful shove as we pushed into the cafeteria, Bench and I waiting in line, Deedee and Wolf headed toward our usual seats. The same seats we'd sat in for a couple of years now. Just the four of us.

My people. The ones I found.

The ones I counted on for everything.

DON'T MISS THESE BOOKS BY
JOHN DAVID ANDERSON!

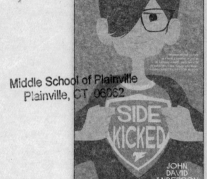

Middle School of Plainville
Plainville, CT 06062

WALDEN POND PRESS™
An Imprint of HarperCollinsPublishers

WWW.WALDEN.COM/BOOKS · WWW.HARPERCOLLINSCHILDRENS.COM